Electric Shadows of Shanghai

Electric Shadows of Shanghai

Clare Kane

First published 2015
by Watchword eBooks, an imprint of Impress Books Ltd

Print edition published 2017
by Impress Books Ltd

Innovation Centre, Rennes Drive, University of Exeter Campus,
Exeter EX4 4RN

British Library Cataloguing in Publication Data

A catalogue record for this book is available from the British Library

ISBN 13: 978–1–911293–03–3 (pbk)
ISBN 13: 978–1–907605–75–8 (ebk)

Typeset in Sabon
by Swales & Willis Ltd, Exeter, Devon

Printed and bound in England
by imprintdigital.net

Contents

OCTOBER 1931

怨情　李白

美人捲珠簾，

深坐蹙蛾眉。

但見淚痕濕，

不知心恨誰。

A Bitter Love by Li Bai

The beautiful woman rolls up her pearl blind,
In deep stillness she sits, her brow furrowed.
One sees only the damp traces of tears,
But one knows not who provokes her bitterness.

I

Over a million women in Shanghai and one in thirteen a prostitute. Another myth of the Orient, Will thought, when Rollo told him a couple of hours earlier. But he recalled it now on the threshold of the Paradise, its neon promise reflected on the cobbles of the alleyway darkening in milky dusk. They were right on the edge of the International Settlement now, where the sombre sobriety of the Bund gave way to the sweet tang of the night that made the two syllables of Shanghai so thrilling to the foreign ear. Outside the moon had yet to take her full shape, but inside the Paradise was dark, with flickering red and green lanterns casting pale shadows over sheer stockings and full mouths of blood red. Will started at the sight, his skin prickling. But as the Filipino band called an end to one song, they started another he knew from parties in London, and taking a large inhale of the Paradise, he knew he would be staying a little while longer.

'I'd say it was about time you saw the other side of Shanghai.' Rollo's voice vibrated in his ear over the lyrics of a lonely heart.

'Quite,' Will said, stealing a glance at a line-up of girls in front of the band, their faces rendered both beautiful and sinister by the long shadows stretching across the dancefloor.

'Take a seat. I'll try to flag down a waiter.' Rollo, the proud old China hand, waved self-importantly towards the bar, where a young Chinese boy laboured over hundreds of bottles, knocking into one another on makeshift shelves, their labels – Old Pensioner gin, Haig whisky, Moet champagne – curling and peeled.

Will took in his surroundings warily, not hungrily like the other men, already roaring with the effects of drink and charged with the potential of sex. Will kept a quiet eye on the girls, rouged and pouting, standing around in faded sequins, faces betraying centuries of weariness but young eyes still glinting for a dollar. Rollo almost bumped his head on a low-hanging chandelier as he wound his way back to the table, balancing two glasses sweating droplets of gin.

'Is this a regular haunt of yours?' Will asked his colleague, taking a tentative sip.

'Every so often I do like to plan a little escape, out to the Rialto, Eldorado or this place.'

Will had been pleased when Rollo chose him, the new arrival slotted between stacks of files in the most overlooked department in the consulate, to join him for a night of genuine entertainment, away from the sometimes stuffy air of the clubs that could choke a young man looking for a good time. Until tonight, Will had seen only the Shanghai of oak panelling and village green politics rewritten in a foreign hand. But out here, in the Shanghai of the imagination, he wasn't sure where to look – his eyes darted from conversations of a sinister air between foreign and Chinese patrons and the whisperings of the petulant line of ladies at the front of the room. One in thirteen out there and ten out of ten in here, he thought, made it fairly dangerous for a man alone in Shanghai. Although he wasn't strictly alone.

'Drink up – the ladies are waiting,' Rollo said. Some of the dancers tapped their heels impatiently, while others, fresher looking ones, giggled behind hands soft and blushing as rose petals. 'Most of this lot are Russians. They're not much better than the Asiatics, but by God, they're lookers.' Rollo threw back the last of his gin with all the brimming confidence of an Englishman a long away from home and pointed to the front of the cabaret, where a pretty Chinese singer had taken centre stage. Wearing a high-necked Chinese dress with a slit halfway up her thigh, the young woman had a low, husky voice, its deep tone matching the dim light of the Paradise.

Will watched this apparition with the swaying hips of America and the painted face of Peking. Her lilting songs and the hard gin softened his thoughts and a dull realisation formed that although Shanghai left him spinning with its unending energy, its shallow breaths and vertiginous buildings, he might actually quite like the city. It had been foolish to assume he knew China, just because he could recite each last character in Confucius' *Analects* and name every emperor going back to the Qin dynasty. The Shanghai he had discovered was more than dead characters on a memorised page, it was alive, a cloying, heavy scent that clung to him long after the sun dipped into the languor of the Shanghai night. The city promised the world, with its glittering neon signs down Bubbling Well Road, vast department stores, boastful ships and proud colonial buildings. It was a record that never stopped playing, from the time the first market trader arrived with his wares in the morning 'til the last good-time girl slipped between silk sheets at night. The city's unfamiliarity had scared him at first, but here in the Paradise he felt an electric attraction towards it – not the Shanghai he had imagined on blustery days in Oxford, but the Shanghai of now.

Will was pulled out of his thoughts by a murmur of excitement. The singer carried on, but her heavy-lidded eyes swivelled towards the entrance. Will turned his head to see the crowd by the door part, pushed aside by two burly Russians. He watched as she came into sight, tall heels encasing tiny feet, then the soft stretch of silk over slim legs. His gaze travelled slowly up to her face and Will felt his mouth go dry as the woman's features came together, a vision of perfect proportions, a painted calendar girl brought to life, her skin a dewy canvas for the harmonious arrangement of her face. The cabaret seemed to melt away, the music fading to nothing as the woman picked her way past the people fighting to speak to her, her carriage strong and confident as she led an elegant Chinese man to a table not far from Will's, stealing a quick wave at the singer. Will watched the way she sat down, with a careful poise unmatched to the backdrop of a tawdry cabaret. She was Chinese, with the permanent curl in her hair the fashionable ladies favoured. One curl was plastered to her forehead and her eyes, open and alert, were dramatically outlined in black. When she leant in and parted her lips to whisper something to her companion, Will wished suddenly that he could hear what she had said.

'You not seen Wu Feifei before, then?' Rollo laughed.

'Wu Feifei?'

'The girl you can't stop staring at. Star of the silver screen. God only knows what she's doing in a place like this.' Rollo tugged on the shirt sleeve of a passing waiter. 'Hey! Two more of these, if you would be so kind.' The waiter dipped slightly and wordlessly cleared their glasses.

'She's a film star?' Will said, trying to pull his eyes away from the woman, whose mouth moved in circles of smiles and laughs.

'Perhaps the most famous in China. Married. That chap's not her husband though – he usually can't stand up by this time of night.' Rollo sat back in his chair, a playfulness dancing on his lips.

'She's certainly glamorous,' Will said quietly. Feifei gracefully arched her neck towards her companion, the stiff collar of her dress creasing. Will wondered how it felt to attract so many ardent gazes, if the attention felt hot on her skin. The atmosphere had shifted since her arrival. The jazz sounded more sensual, the drinks tasted sweeter and conversations had risen in pitch.

'That's Shanghai for you.' Rollo slapped him on the back

as the next round of drinks materialised on their table, the waiter once again disappearing silently. 'Hookers, gangsters, *taipans* and film stars. Just a shame such beauty is wasted on a Chinese woman.'

The girl on stage launched into the frenzy of an upbeat number and Will let Rollo lead him to the glittering line of jittery taxi dancers.

'Pick whichever one you like! I'll pay. Welcome you into the fold and all that,' Rollo said warmly. Feeling shy, Will went immediately to a slim, dark European girl, who reminded him with a momentary pang of Amelia. She stood up without feeling, mechanically placed her hands on his shoulder and waist and let him guide her round the room. Will had never been a dancer and he led her badly, tripping over both of their feet.

'Do you want me to teach you?' she said, surprising him by speaking in French.

'You're French?'

'Russian,' she said, correcting the position of his feet and steering him around the other couples. Of course. Thousands of White Russians had poured into Shanghai after the Bolsheviks drove them out and they now peopled the lowliest jobs, with many girls supporting whole families through taxi-dancing or prostitution. Their indignity was made worse by the fact that the majority had been privileged and wealthy in their homeland. This girl, however, seemed more bored by her fate than tormented by it.

'What's your name?' Will asked, suddenly feeling an almost fatherly concern for her. He noticed now how thin she was, the way her bones almost pierced the skin, her limbs at sharp angles resembling a broken doll.

'Lilya.' She nodded to the band. 'New song. You pay or you go.'

Will sat down, throwing back gin until his head buzzed.

'Time for the floor show,' Rollo said, catching his breath and taking the seat next to Will. He raised a glass to Will and both men turned to face the stage. A young girl appeared.

Her hair fell to her waist and curled at the bottom, framing a face as fresh and round as new-born's. Will calculated that she could not have seen in more than fifteen new years. She paraded up and down the stage, twisting her body this way and that, a mockery of sexuality. Suddenly a man appeared on stage, bearing a whip. He struck the girl and she fell to the ground, eyes wide and fingers outstretched, squealing and wriggling on the floor. Will's eyes were fixed on her. He felt he should do something but the other spectators watched the violent spectacle in agreeable silence. This was the show. The man hit her again and the girl moaned loudly, twisting her body and biting a virginal lip. Will leant over to Rollo, who shushed him with a wave of his hand. In the silent anticipation of the next strike, a heavy thud broke the stillness of the room. The spectators turned, and there was the actress, Feifei, who had jumped out of her seat. She had dropped her handbag in her haste and now stooped to pick it up. 'Disgusting,' she hissed to the man next to her, loudly enough for Will to capture her ungraceful vowels, the inelegant inflection of poverty in her voice. The whip-bearing man was frozen, staring warily at Wu Feifei, unsure of whether to continue with the show. 'We're leaving, we're leaving,' she said, her voice rising as she beckoned the man next to her, but her acquaintance shook his head. Will strained to hear what he was saying. Feifei sighed, pushed away her chair and stalked out of the cabaret with strident haughtiness.

'There goes the most modern woman in Shanghai.' Rollo gave a low whistle and turned back to the show, which had restarted with gusto.

Will had no time for the torture show at the front of the cabaret. Instead, his mind was on Feifei. He tried to picture her delicate steps down Shanghai's gutters. Was there a chauffeur waiting outside? Where did she live? With the show over, the dancing took up again and as Rollo went to find a new girl to hold close over a round of seamy jazz, Will took the opportunity to excuse himself. 'I wouldn't like to worry Amelia. It's almost midnight,' he explained.

Rollo shrugged and offered a half-hearted wave, one eye already trained on a slip of a girl in a white dress, twirling seductively at the front of the room.

Amelia was curled up in a stiff armchair, reading by the light of the one lamp left on in the house. The staff had gone to bed around an hour ago, after serving her what she felt to be a slightly mocking dinner for one.

'Master Will not home, eh Missy?' the cook Qi had said, a line he had repeated the past ten evenings while Will set the world to rights at the Shanghai Club's Long Bar, or whatever it was he did with the other men in suits, the King's envoys in the Far East. Amelia had eaten the simple meal of chicken and rice in silence, every swallow echoing round the room. She thought of how she had often shared those quiet dinners in London with her mother, neither of them speaking, more cowed by her father's absence than his presence.

Now she was reading one of Will's books, a poetry compilation from his days of teaching Chinese. She tried to focus on the ancient verses, willing the embossed envelope she had tucked between the book's pages to disappear. She saw the poem Will had recited to her the day they had met at his uncle's Christmas party, and tracing the indistinguishable characters with her fingers while skimming the English translation, she remembered that sure rush of adventure and decision, when she had decided to hold Will's hand and leap blindly into a new existence in Shanghai.

'*White dew gathers on the jade steps,*
'*And soaks my stockings on this long night,*
'*But I lower the crystal curtain,*
'*And gaze at the autumn moon.*'

He had spoken those lines to her by the bookcase in Roger's Belgravia house, where she had retired to avoid watching her parents painfully attempt to penetrate a strata of society far above their own, instead inspecting the spines of unread titles. When Will had eased one book off the shelf and read those lines to her she saw in him all the shining potential her life lacked.

Amelia heard the door swing open and Will's steps down the hall, a little less steady than usual.

'Amelia, darling! You're awake.' Will came into the room and glanced briefly at the book in her hand. 'And you're reading.'

'Oh, yes,' she said softly, thinking of the things her mother had told her before she came to Shanghai. *Men need their own time.* 'Where have you been this evening?' She kept her voice steady.

'Out. With some of the chaps from the consulate. You know how it is, having to meet everyone and get my feet under the table.' Will took off his jacket. 'It's warm in here tonight.'

'There's food left if you want some. It's just chicken.'

'I'm all right.' Will eased himself down into a chair next to her. 'Why did you wait for me? You should have gone to bed. I wouldn't have minded.' He stroked her arm, which suddenly looked a ghostly white to him. 'I'm going up to bed. Are you coming?'

'Not now,' Amelia said. 'I would like to read a little longer.'

'Don't be upset, darling.' Will leant over and nuzzled her neck. 'This is just the way it is at the consulate. I don't have as much time on my hands as I did at Oxford.'

Amelia said nothing, shifting her gaze to the floor. When they had first arrived in Shanghai, the consulate had organised a welcoming committee, a blur of people to meet them off the ship, show them around town and warn them of the many dangers lurking in Shanghai's dark corners. But after the large official party for Will's arrival ten days after they had set up home in the International Settlement, attended by the best gold-buttoned and rosy-cheeked Shanghailanders, Amelia had been left to fend for herself, resulting in two weeks of wistfulness while Will continued to enjoy the city's hospitality, sampling new pleasures every night. She felt all the glittering prizes of the Orient lying beyond her front door and craved a like-minded soul to guide her through its offerings. Now that invitation lay hidden between the pages of poetry, taunting Amelia with its dual promise of social interaction and the crushing realisation that in the most cosmopolitan city in the world she was destined to spend her days listening to the whines of starched, disapproving English wives, when she got out at all.

'Let's go,' Will said gently, pulling her out of the armchair and leading her to her bedroom. He closed the door gently as she turned to undress, stealing to his room, where as he settled beneath his light blanket the secret dark space under his eyelids filled with Feifei, the star of Shanghai, sashaying out of the Paradise.

Will and Rollo met again in the searing sunlight of lunchtime on the Bund, cutlery poised over seafood at the Palace Hotel.

'Thank you for your report this morning,' Rollo said. 'Very thorough. You're a fast worker. I think we can probably find something more interesting than translation to occupy your time.'

One of Will's jobs as the new head of the translation department was to read the Chinese press, picking up anything that could be of importance and translating it. The Japanese had invaded the northern province of Manchuria not long before Will's ship sailed into Shanghai, so the press rang with alarmist rhetoric about China's 'dwarf bandit' neighbours. That morning two things had caught his attention, one article in a youth publication called *Struggle* that had called for a city-wide protest against the Japanese occupation in the north and another, dealing with a far more light-hearted subject. *Things got a little bit too heated for Wu Feifei last night,* one of the tabloids had written. *Out with Tang Jin, her bachelor du jour, little Feifei, very upset by a risqué performance at the Paradise, stormed out. Tang let her go. Is Feifei getting a little too 'modern' these days? And where is that husband of hers? Better ask beautiful dancer Rong Meili.* Will smiled to himself when he first saw Feifei's name but frowned with each new word. Having seen the soft contours of Feifei's heart-shaped face and the sharp lines filling her silk dress, he felt it improper for her to be spoken of in such a casual and disparaging tone. He folded the paper in half and returned to the students' call to arms. When he dropped off his report in the political department, the head of the section, Saunders, was at a meeting and Rollo took it instead.

'From now on, all of your reports should come to me,' he said. 'I'll take care of you here, Will.'

Rollo buttered a bit of bread and looked at Will thoughtfully.

'So, how worried should we be about this protest against the Japanese?' he asked. 'I can't read much of the original hieroglyphics, so I need you to tell me.' Will knew this was a test and cleared his throat.

'Not that worried. It's a radical youth publication. How many people actually read something like *Struggle*?' Will spoke steadily, but was unsure of his words. The job at the consulate had been sold to him as a role not unlike that he had held at the University. But together with his team – an ex-policeman so scarred by the front line he had been given a safe sinecure in the consulate by the force, and Harry Mac-Donald, a Eurasian who disappeared regularly with the air of having better things to do – Will had been forced to pull his head out of the past and into the present, trying to make sense of the shifting Shanghai landscape.

'We don't want a repeat of 1925. Thousands of the Chinese protested then, some got shot and then we had a right bloody mess on our hands. So, in this town, don't underestimate anything, even the slightest rumblings of protest,' Rollo said, smacking his lips. 'We don't want the Japanese getting any ideas about Shanghai. But we also don't want the natives running amok over some trouble up north. I have to say, I hope the Japs give the Chinese the bloody nose they deserve. They kicked off all this trouble just in time. Over the summer we were about to cede ground to the Chinese on trading terms. That's all been forgotten now, but still, the empire isn't what it was.' Will nodded, though Shanghai's international role still mystified him. The port wasn't a British colony but it was treated as such by most of the residents. The pair were sitting in a dining room that could easily have been in London, save for the deafening clash of languages surrounding them.

'I saw something else in the press today. About Feifei, the actress we saw last night.'

Rollo laughed. 'Well, that may be of great interest to you, Will, but I'm not sure it's a priority for the consul-general.'

'I'm just saying, because, well, we saw her and it seems she has a difficult life ...' Rollo waved Will's concern away.

'Yes, a very difficult life being a film star. Going to rescue her from her hardship, are you? Oh, that's just fantastic!' He laughed louder, then lowered his voice. 'See, over there? That group of men? Japanese businessmen. For short men, they've got very big plans. Focus on what we need you for, Will, and you'll go far here. Forget the film stars.'

Will, slightly annoyed that Rollo had so swiftly changed the subject, protested that he was happy as a translator.

'Of course you are,' Rollo said, his smile insincere. 'Oh, the consul's wife is hosting a tea for the ladies tomorrow. Apparently your wife hasn't responded to the invitation yet. All the wives will be there, no doubt ruining hard-won reputations with domestic tittle-tattle.'

'That's odd. Amelia hasn't mentioned it. I'll ask her this evening.'

II

'Oh, Amelia! How lovely that you could join us. Please let me introduce you to the other ladies,' said Cordelia, the consul's wife, wearing an all-enveloping mauve dress and with an impressive display of jewels splashed across her neck. Amelia surveyed the grounds of the villa which, despite being full of lush and tropical plants, were as ordered as any garden in the Home Counties. The Anglo-Saxon layout gave Amelia a sharp and unexpected stab of longing for the trimmed lawn her parents kept in London. She was escorted to a table where a few women were already perched on white garden chairs, heads together as they sedately sipped Chinese tea in the weak autumn sun. Cordelia introduced Amelia to the group, most of whom were plain-faced English ladies she had already met. Amelia had forgotten their names from the flutter of social events she had attended by Will's side, a wifely smile on her face amid the uncomfortable familiarity of English tones and cemented social hierarchies. She steeled herself for an afternoon of conversations rotating around problems with servants, the unbearable heat and the declining standard of British boarding schools, Will's junior position at the consulate meaning her opinions would be hastily overlooked in favour of women further up the pecking order. The wives sent soft and unconvincing smiles in Amelia's direction before continuing their conversation unperturbed.

'Have some tea, dear,' Cordelia said, bustling by Amelia's side and motioning for a young servant girl to pour. 'Now, tell us how you are settling in. Your husband is doing rather well in the translation department, I hear.'

'He can't speak Shanghainese,' Amelia found herself saying. 'He has to learn it. But it's all written the same, isn't it, Chinese? So he can translate documents easily.' What a stupid thing to say! What would her mother have told her? *Always praise your husband's strengths and ignore his weaknesses.*

'He seems to be a very talented man. And are you happy here?' Cordelia said smoothly, before her head snapped round behind her. 'Oh, *Julia!*'

Amelia watched as a blonde woman in a dress cut tighter and lower than any of the other women's made her way across the garden. She felt relief at the new arrival. All she needed to do now was keep her mouth shut. These consulate parties were worse than the stiffest gatherings she had endured in London and she carried that same uncomfortable desire to belong to a social circle she internally regarded as tiresome that had haunted her socialising in England.

'Cordelia!' the blonde called out in decidedly American tones, which carried from under her broad-brimmed hat on a soft breeze. 'Wonderful to see you!' The woman settled herself into a chair with a sigh, ignoring a servant fussing over seating arrangements.

'Oh, it's just far too hot for the beginning of October!' She pulled off her hat. 'Well, ladies, what's the news? Oh gosh, who is this lovely young thing? Look at you … gorgeous!' Julia reached across the table and brushed Amelia's cheek.

'Hello. I'm Amelia.' Amelia kept her eyes lowered, hoping she wasn't blushing under the strident American's gaze.

'Lovely to meet you. I'm Julia Hart. What brings you to Shanghai, Amelia?'

'My husband works at the consulate.'

'Ah, and that's the only reason, is it?'

Amelia stuttered in response, trying to draw words from somewhere.

'Now, now, Julia. We can't all be independent like you, running from one end of the country to another. Some of us have domestic lives to tend to,' Cordelia said. 'Amelia is just recently married and arrived in Shanghai a few weeks ago. I'm sure she'll find plenty of interests soon, won't you, dear?'

Amelia nodded thankfully, aware Julia was still watching her closely.

'I'm sure these ladies could get you involved in the Volunteer Corps or something similar. That is, of course, if you're interested in saving the poor of Shanghai and promoting morality throughout the empire,' Julia said. Cordelia nodded enthusiastically and Julia winked briefly at Amelia. Or had she imagined it? 'I wanted to go to Manchuria this week but the paper sent someone else. Someone without breasts, you won't be surprised to hear.' The other women looked away at the mention of this shared physical characteristic.

More guests arrived in dribs and drabs, with most of the ladies already seeming to know each other. After two cups of tea, they stood up and moved around Cordelia's garden in little groups, the boundaries of which were laid out in private jokes and low-volume gossip under fashionable hats. Amelia did her best and moved from group to group with as much ease as she could muster from her tired body. But socialising, especially in humidity, was exhausting. Moving away from one group of ladies, who Amelia had noticed were all wearing dresses in a new cut that made hers look frumpy, she spotted a slim woman of around forty standing by herself. The solitary figure smoked a long cigarette, her body angled away from the party. She had a severe face and was dressed entirely in black, in stark contrast to others at the party, flowers competing for sunlight in stretched silks. Amelia moved towards her.

'Hello. I'm Amelia.' She proffered an uneasy hand.

'Tamara,' the woman said in a heavy, unfamiliar accent, not moving to greet Amelia.

'Pleasure to meet you,' Amelia said, though her voice strained from an afternoon of stilted conversations.

'You're the only one here who has spoken to me today, apart from Julia,' the woman said. 'Why do you think that is?'

'I've no idea,' Amelia said with genuine innocence. The woman snorted at her response.

'No idea? It's because I'm Russian.' Amelia had heard there were some wretched Russians in Shanghai, in fact a man on the ship that brought them here had told her the Russians of Shanghai were thieves and temptresses, to be avoided at all costs. 'These Englishwomen don't want me here. I am a disgrace to our race. An embarrassment to the whites of Shanghai.' She spat out the last words, her voice wobbling. 'Julia told me to come because they have money. Well, not them, but their husbands. They hold the purse strings to this city.'

'Oh, do you need money?' *This is just like me,* Amelia thought. *Come to a party and end up trapped talking to a Russian undesirable.*

'No, I don't need money for myself,' she said, a little viciously. 'I work for my money. I need money and more crucially, I suppose, *interest,* for a project of mine. I won't bore you with the details. As you have deigned to talk to me, I can conclude you are probably of no use to me or the project.' Tamara took a long drag on her cigarette.

'Oh, I see. What do you work as?' Amelia was already backing away a little, wondering how to extricate herself.

'I teach dance. I was a ballet dancer in St Petersburg.'

'Really?' Amelia immediately softened. She knew now why Tamara had such a thin, hard form, why her face was pulled so taught. 'I adore ballet. I danced when I was a girl. My grandmother taught me, she used to be a *prima ballerina* in fact ... but I wish ... It's always been something I've regretted, giving it up. My mother ...' She trailed off as she saw Tamara smirking at her. Amelia was thinking of how her mother had reacted when she found out her young daughter was learning ballet from her grandmother, whose joints had long locked and muscles turned to rope, but who could still relive moments of stage glory through clipped instructions to her granddaughter. The family's foreign element had long been a source of embarrassment, something her mother had sought to cover up with the dull, heavy Englishness of Amelia's father. Her mother had tolerated Amelia's learning with steadily growing disapproval before she introduced an outright ban on *pliés* and *tendus* when Amelia was a teenager. Her grandmother had died soon afterwards.

'English women don't dance ballet,' Tamara said, matter-of-fact and sceptical.

'My grandmother wasn't from England,' Amelia explained quickly. 'I have missed ballet so much. I would like to–'

'Of course, but there is little interest in the fine arts in Shanghai,' Tamara said, cutting Amelia off. 'Everyone is addicted to empty hedonism here, don't you think?' Amelia ignored the question, her brain already leaping from one possibility to the next as she looked at the hard frame of the woman in front of her.

'You said you teach ... Perhaps I could ... come to a class?'

'No. Out of the question. I do teach some adults, but they are very different to you.' Amelia frowned. For the first time since arriving in Shanghai she had felt a thrill of excitement, of possibility, of the liberation she had longed for before leaving London behind. 'It was a pleasure to meet you,' Tamara said, moving swiftly away across the lawn, cigarette still burning in her left hand.

Amelia felt a hand on her shoulder.

'She can be a bearcat, that one. Hope she wasn't too hard on you.' It was Julia. 'I suppose if you had lost all your possessions, your place in society, your family ... you might be a little bitter too.'

17

'I asked her for dance lessons.'

'Mmm, bad idea. She doesn't like teaching. She wants to be a real dancer. She needs to drum up interest in ballet in Shanghai, that's why I invited her, to see if she can persuade everyone away from the foxtrot. Anyway, I'm leaving. Do you want a ride?'

'You've arranged a driver?' Amelia asked.

'No, in my car, of course. Where do you live? I'll drop you off.'

Julia tied a silk scarf around her blonde curls as she sat at the wheel while Amelia instructed Su, the maid who had accompanied her to the house, to walk home.

'Don't be silly, Amelia. The more the merrier,' she yelled. 'Servants come for free.' To Amelia's surprise, worldly Julia delighted in Su's company. The servant said she had never ridden in a car before. Amelia shifted in her seat, trying to make herself comfortable.

'So, what are you doing in Shanghai?' she asked Julia.

'I'm a journalist. I write for the *North China Daily News,* on the Bund just over there. But I dabble in other things too. I helped to set up a women's magazine. It's in English and Chinese and it contains pretty much everything you need to know to survive as a woman in this city. Make-up, clothes, work.'

'So you speak Chinese?'

'Passable Shanghainese. After all, my lover is Chinese and you can't help but pick up a little that way, can you?' Amelia felt a frisson of excitement. Not only did this American woman have a job, no, several jobs and her own car, she had a Chinese lover.

'Unusual,' was all she said, prompting Julia to make a coded joke to Su that made the maid dissolve into sniggers. Amelia wondered what Will would think if he knew she had spoken to a Russian ballerina at the party and was now going home with an American who had a Chinese lover. Will had told her that men at the consulate who married Chinese women were shunned and sacrificed any chance of promotion. She probably wasn't behaving as a diplomatic wife should, but something about Julia's mischievous smile made Amelia relax into the seat of the car.

'Chinese men are wonderful lovers. Or mine is at least,' Julia said with a broad grin, ready to eat up whatever Shanghai laid out for her. 'Say, you ever been to Hall & Holtz? To buy clothes I mean?'

'Not yet.'

'I'll take you next week,' Julia said as they pulled up in front of Amelia's house. 'There are some new fashions from Europe arriving this weekend, I'm told. How's Monday at ten? I'd like to be on the frontlines of war, but I'll make do with the fashion battles for now. Shanghai can be tough when you're new in town.'

And so Amelia found herself committed to a social engagement with an American female journalist who had a Chinese lover. As she entered the house, she looked down at the sad blue dress hanging on her exhausted limbs and thought that she had actually quite enjoyed the tea.

Will was late home again that night. Qi had bought some tender beef at the market and Amelia invited him to sit and eat at the table. The cook shook his head furiously.

'No, no, I happy in kitchen. Missy eat here!'

Amelia found herself a little disappointed not to have the cook's company. Things were getting desperate, she thought, if she was craving conversation in a half-language with a foreign man she had nothing in common with. She wondered about the other women at the party and what they did with their time. At midnight she decided to go to bed, watching herself closely in the mirror as she put on her silk nightdress. She was still lovely, she could see that, but getting a little bony. The food Qi cooked didn't entirely agree with her. She slipped under the covers, listening to the sounds of the street outside, sure she wouldn't sleep, her head spinning with Julia's candid conversation and the dim but thrilling prospect of ballet classes taking place somewhere under the same sky. She tossed her body from side to side, the trundling of rickshaws and the

19

low confessions of drunks walking together a gentle accompaniment to her thoughts until they lulled her into sleep.

She woke with a jolt when Will slammed the front door behind him. She called out to him and after a delay of a few minutes he opened the door to her room a crack, the pale moonlight outlining his suit, slightly rumpled from a long day's wear.

'Hello, darling. I didn't mean to wake you,' he moved towards her and kissed her forehead. 'Go back to sleep.'

'Oh, I was waiting for you. I must have fallen asleep.'

'How was the party?' he asked and she inhaled the sticky gin on his breath.

'Fine. I met some interesting ladies. One was from–' She stopped. That evening she had planned how she would tell him all about the outrageous Julia and her Chinese lover but now she cradled the story to herself.

'Good. It's very important that you make friends here, Amelia.' She smiled at him and then shifted forward, placing her lips on his and touching the side of his face. 'I'm tired,' he said softly, turning his back towards her. 'Oh, we've been invited to the Cathay tomorrow. Wear something nice.' Amelia blinked back furious tears as he slipped out the doorway without a backward glance and silently vowed not to sleep all night, as though that would punish him.

Feifei was just stepping into the new high-heels she had first bought for the disastrous night with Tang Jin at the Paradise when she heard the violent slamming of the door that habitually announced the arrival of her husband. She fastened the buckle on the left shoe and walked as quietly as she could towards the bedroom door, straining to hear Longwei and gauge his mood. Her husband hadn't been home for four days.

'Feifei!' His voice was soft and round. Maybe he was in an amorous mood. Feifei could fix that quickly and then leave him at home to sleep off the alcohol ingested and the financial losses incurred during his absence.

'Yes?' She tottered out onto the landing, feeling unsteady on the new heels. Longwei was standing in the hall, gazing up at her, his Western suit slightly ruffled but his hair as smoothly slicked back as it had been the morning he left.

'I missed you, Feifei. Come here, my darling.' He flashed a set of brilliant white teeth and Feifei felt the hard core of her heart melt a little. She walked down the stairs, his unwavering eyes leaving her more self-conscious than the bright smiles and clunky cameras that followed her steps every day at the studio. When she reached the last step he grabbed her by the waist and spun her around in imitation of the western dances he watched but refused to participate in at the clubs.

'Where is my beautiful wife going tonight, looking so stunning? I hope I'm invited.'

'There's a dinner at the Cathay. It's to celebrate the tenth anniversary of Green's, the department store.'

'Englishmen?' Longwei stiffened. He had planned to study at Cambridge but after Feifei fell pregnant those plans quickly evaporated. Luckily for her, instead of channelling his disappointment into Feifei, Longwei had instead developed a deep, irrational hatred of the English born out of the inferiority of a playboy who felt his zeal pale amongst intellectuals.

'Yes, they're English. Now, my darling, I'm sorry, but I must go.' Feifei rested a hand on Longwei's chest and kissed him gently.

'Don't be late,' he said sternly. Then softly, he added: 'I'll wait for you.' That might have been a veiled threat, but at least she was getting away.

Feifei pulled her fur stole around her shoulders as she settled into the car. Ling was already sitting stiffly in the back, resplendent in a lilac *qipao*.

'I'm sorry I'm late. Longwei came home,' Feifei said, sighing.

'Oh, Feifei, what are you going to do about him? This situation can't go on,' Ling said. 'I heard he was out with Rong Meili last week. She's a little whore, you know. Eighteen years old, she thinks it will last forever –'

21

'I can't just leave,' Feifei said, cutting the conversation off. 'There needs to be a plan.'

Amelia felt a jolt of excitement when she saw the Cathay, its twenty storeys stretching up to a sharp green pyramid. She linked her arm with Will's, her head tipped up as she took in the lustre of the hotel, all the pomp of Shanghai promised in its arches, its winking windows looking out over the river. The day had been better than she might have expected. She woke late to find Will sitting by her side in bed. He had greeted her with a kiss and they spent a lazy hour making love and talking under the sheets. Then he insisted Amelia buy a new dress for the evening. Nothing was said about his late return the night before and Amelia was happy to match Will's new-found contentment. She chose the most beautiful dress she had ever owned. Midnight blue, it fell to the floor in graceful sweeps. It was backless, a feature she had accentuated with a long draping of pearls that fell down her bare spine. As they went through the revolving doors and swept into the pink and grey speckled marble of the cavernous lobby, Amelia felt she was drawing closer to the magic of a new life.

They swept past the low rumble of conversation from the hotel bar, taking the wide stairs up to the dining room, with its tall ceilings, exotic plants dotted around and a neatly-suited band at the far end of the room. Guests arrived in handsome pairs, the ladies in long dresses that skirted the floor as they circled the room, the men in carefully tailored suits topped with shiny hair. Will and Amelia sat at their table, where Rollo and his date for the night, a robust girl called Augusta, were already waiting. Augusta fiddled with her napkin, not looking in Rollo's direction, but watching the band through the long curls of painted eyelashes, one elbow resting by the edge of a gold-rimmed plate.

'Augusta went to school with my sister,' Rollo said to Will, standing up to shake his hand. He dropped his voice: 'Your wife will be delighted to meet her, I trust.'

'Yes, yes, of course.' Will looked at Augusta, a woman

with all the grace of a carthorse. Definitely not Rollo's kind of woman. In the grey shadows under Rollo's eyes, Will saw traces of the night before, when the pair of them had ventured to a new cabaret that made the Paradise look upmarket, its floor show a parade of near-naked girls with dull smiles and lively hips. Will had drunk too much gin to quiet his nerves. In London, dubious entertainment could be come by and flesh could be bought in Oxford too, but none of it was ever with the easy exuberance and immoral immodesty of the Shanghai night. Will had departed half an hour after Rollo disappeared upstairs, trailed by an adolescent Chinese prostitute. With only a drink for company, Will had attracted hot, uncomfortable attention from the other girls on offer and decided to abandon his friend to the night.

Once the guests were settled around tables, Alfred Green, the owner of Green's and a plump man well-fed on Oriental success and Western food, stood to make a speech.

'Ten years in the most wonderful city on earth,' he started, his voice booming. 'Ladies and gentlemen, I thank you all for being here tonight to celebrate with me.' Will looked around the room, his eye catching on a lone table populated only by Chinese guests. He looked at the women, with their slim, elegant necks in their *qipao* dresses. Suddenly his chest caved into his stomach. One of them had raised a glass of golden bubbles to her mouth and was watching Alfred Green with a half-smile, her lips grazing the rim of the glass. There was no doubt as to who she was. She was sitting next to the singer from the Paradise. Will's heart started to beat crazily. He tried to drag his eyes away from her.

'... being a merchant is not easy anywhere, but Shanghai's leisure activities more than make up for ...' Alfred continued. Will's gaze was still fixed on the corner table. He felt Amelia stir next to him but didn't shift his vision. Then he got what he had been hoping for and dreading in equal measure. Feifei swivelled her long neck in his direction and locked her eyes into his. To his utter bewilderment, she sent him a sweet, short smile and then turned away. His heartbeat returned to normal and he turned in his seat to give Alfred his full attention.

'What's the matter?' Amelia whispered and he shook his head. He saw Rollo turn to look at him, flirting with a playful grin. Green finished his speech and the guests began to eat. Will had lost his appetite and moved his food helplessly around his plate in traces of gravy, drinking one, two and three glasses of champagne 'til the very room seemed alive, the chords of conversation deafening and the scrape of cutlery searing across his brain. He tried to tell himself to calm down, that this was an actress, a *Chinese* actress. He was married. If he wanted a Chinese girl, the streets were crawling with bodies for sale. But this Feifei, she was a glistening jewel in the gutter of Shanghai, a fine woman who would invite desirous glances even in the dining rooms of London. She was a celebrity, he told himself, trying to squeeze away his perilous thoughts, perhaps it was normal, a passing admiration of a decorous woman, not unlike the passions that had populated his celibate youth.

Once the waiters had cleared away the last of the plates the dancing began. Rollo invited Amelia to dance, leaving Will to talk to Augusta. Will watched his wife with a stranger's eyes, noticing the dramatic sweep of her dress, the large expanse of exposed back, the loose tendrils slipping out of her hair. The pair came back and Will took his wife's hand. He spun her round the floor, the jazz band lifting his spirits higher than the gilt-edged ceiling. Amelia was a natural dancer, leading Will gently as he tried to make his feet obey the instructions of his wife's steps. As she pulled him past one couple, he brushed against the silk dress of a Chinese woman.

'I'm so sorry,' he said in hasty Shanghainese. Turning around to see whose foot he had trodden on, he found his face just inches from that of Wu Feifei. Close up, it was just as luminous as from a distance, as though the actress was lit from inside.

'It's no problem. Please don't worry,' she replied, the Chinese man leading her in the dance nodding respectfully in

Will's direction before setting his hand back on Feifei's waist and beginning another round of careful steps.

'That woman is an actress,' Will said to Amelia. 'Wu Feifei. Perhaps the most famous actress in China.'

'Oh. We could have picked someone else to bump into!' Amelia said, her cheeks pink and girlish.

When the pair rejoined Rollo and Augusta, Rollo cleared his throat and rose from the table. 'Ladies, if you don't mind, there's someone I need to introduce Will to.' He stood up and Will followed him, feeling a little sorry for Amelia stuck with Augusta.

'I really do want to introduce you to Green,' Rollo said confidentially. 'But Augusta is trying my nerves too. Luckily she's leaving next week.' Rollo led Will towards the circle of men crowding around Green. As they approached the edges of the group, Will saw Feifei, her arms folded across her chest, squeezed in between two of the guests. She smiled archly at Will as she presented her hand for Alfred Green to press to his spittle-licked lips. Pulling away from the group, she fixed her eyes on Will.

'How do you speak such good Shanghainese?' she asked. Rollo moved aside to penetrate the self-congratulatory group of merchants orbiting around Green.

'I don't really. I speak Mandarin but I'm learning *Shanghaihua*,' Will replied.

'Oh, Mandarin? My *guoyu* is terrible! I lived in Canton as a child. Thankfully the movies are silent!' She broke into an easy laugh. Diamonds in her ears twinkled, reflecting the lights of the room. He needed to keep this conversation going, he felt that every moment in his life had been a faded rehearsal for this moment, all the words he had spoken wasted because they weren't received by the ears of Wu Feifei.

'Are you an actress?' he asked.

'Yes, yes, I'm in the *electric shadows*. It's very refreshing to meet someone who doesn't know that already.' She placed a hand on his shoulder and he felt guilty at his lie. She probably knew there wasn't a man left in Shanghai who didn't recognise her face. 'And what brought you to Shanghai? It must be lucrative for a European out here who speaks the local language so well.'

'I work for the British Consulate.'

'Really? How fascinating!'

Feifei asked where he had learnt his Chinese. Will found himself telling China's most famous film star about classical poetry. Those words, bundled in centuries of hidden meanings and new connotations, rose from a well he couldn't cover, and he found them newly brilliant as they tumbled from his lips and directed themselves towards Feifei.

'Tang dynasty poems are my favourite,' he found himself telling her. 'So much meaning contained in so few words.'

'And your favourite poem?' she asked, brushing her neck with elegantly painted fingernails.

'White dew gathers on the jade steps,

'And soaks my stockings on this long night,

'But I lower the crystal curtain,

'And gaze at the autumn moon.'

As he said it he was flustered by the thought of Feifei sitting on stairs, dew seeping through her stockings. Her painted lips gave way to peals of laughter.

'So beautiful!' she said. 'How can you possibly be an Englishman? Your Chinese accent is better than mine!' Then she started telling him about her films. 'They are very modern. We try to reflect society and encourage the younger generations to change things. But then I hear you recite a poem like that,' she said thoughtfully, 'and I wonder if being modern is always a good thing.' Will coughed. He looked round guiltily and saw Rollo had returned to their table and was chatting half-heartedly with Augusta and Amelia.

'Miss Wu,' he said. 'It's been a pleasure. I must get back to my table now. Enjoy the rest of your evening.'

'I hope to see you again,' she said softly. Will made his way towards the table, bracing himself for the cold front blowing in from Amelia's direction.

'Who was that man?' Ling asked, laughing and jostling Feifei. 'The blond one. You were talking to him forever!'

26

'I told you I had a plan, didn't I?' Feifei said. 'He works for the consulate. I didn't know that before, but it seems things have turned out even better than expected.'

'Oh, Feifei, what are you up to now? You want to take a boat all the way to his rainy country where nobody knows your name?'

'No, of course not.' Feifei batted Ling away. 'He was reciting poetry to me. Old classics, can you believe it?'

Ling covered her mouth and giggled through her fingers.

'I think he's fallen in love, Feifei. Be careful!'

Feifei shrugged and looked towards Will's table. He was with two women, one plain and one pretty. She wondered if one of them was his wife.

'This Rollo is your best friend at the consulate?' Amelia asked when the couple took their car.

'Well, I wouldn't say that. One of my friends,' Will corrected her, thinking that he really must make more of an effort with Ralph and Harry over the coming week. Rollo was his *only* friend at the consulate.

'He was very impolite to Augusta,' Amelia said.

'He's gregarious, that's all.' Amelia shrugged at Will's response and turned to look at the street, her eyes following the trundling rickshaws in hostile silence.

When the couple arrived home, Will told Amelia he was going to read for a while.

'You go up to bed, darling,' he said. She went with reluctant steps and Will cracked open one of his poetry anthologies.

'People are separated, brought together,
'Lost and found in sadness and delight.
'The moon waxes and wanes,
'Turns dim and then bright.
'Things have been this way since ancient times,' he read quietly to himself, his tongue settling into a familiar rhythm. He kept reading until he was sure Amelia would be asleep and then crept upstairs to his bedroom, slipping under the

covers, his heart still flying from his conversation with Feifei.

Julia Hart pulled up outside Amelia's villa on Monday morning as promised. She honked the horn and waved, her long blonde hair wrapped in a bright orange scarf. Su chuckled when she saw her.

'Tell Miss Julia hello, Missy,' she said, patting Amelia's back as she left the house. 'Very nice lady.' Amelia had made an effort to dress fashionably, wearing the long string of pearls that had hung down her back at the Cathay, but next to Julia's lipsticked glamour, she instantly felt plain again.

'Hey kid, jump in,' Julia said, patting the seat beside her. Amelia couldn't stop peering out at the street as they drove through the International Settlement, passing the big villas with windows like gap-toothed smiles and the crowded apartment blocks splattered with Chinese washing lines.

She didn't like to tell Julia how much Shanghai still fascinated her, mostly because she felt that way because she was locked away from the city and its potential remained distant and hazy.

Once they had passed the stern Sikh policemen by the entrance and the Union Jack over the doorway to Hall & Holtz's, Julia took command. She led Amelia between the display cases and hanging rails, one arm bundled with clothes and materials while she gesticulated with the other.

'It's always important to have clothes tailored,' she said knowledgeably. 'Clothes made to fit mannequins will only fit one lucky woman – the one who was the model! They have a wonderful tailoring service here.' She imparted advice to Amelia as they walked through the store, sales assistants trailing Julia and her heaps of fabric. 'Of course, if you want to know what the next fashion is going to be, you need to watch the courtesans. That's where we get all our tips from, though we'd never admit it. They've got patrons and access to all the new styles.' Amelia said nothing to this. Taking style advice from courtesans surprised her, but seeing the glamorous ease with which Julia addressed the shop girls by their first names and rejected last season's models, she was willing to listen to whatever she had to say. 'Oh, and never wear lipstick and kohl. It's too much. Let one feature speak at a time,' Julia continued as she made her way towards the till, a mountain of fabric in the crook of her arm. On the way, she lifted a scarf off a display case. 'Oh, Amelia. This would look fabulous with your eyes. You just have to take it.'

'You know a lot about fashion,' Amelia said, as Julia handed the bags to a young boy in a serious uniform, shouting instructions in Shanghainese about where her car was parked.

'Just enough. You know I told you I run a magazine? I need to know a little for that. What they're wearing in Paris and New York. And London, they say, but the English ladies I've met here are all hideously dressed. Except you, my dear.'

'What's the magazine called?' Amelia asked, brushing off the national insult.

'*New Woman*. It's got everything a Shanghai girl could need,' Julia said, filling with pride. 'I like to think that I'm helping women, that I'm demystifying certain things. Even somewhere as worldly as Shanghai, a lot of women have lived very sheltered lives.'

When they reached the car Julia suggested they go for a cup of tea. 'I know a wonderful place,' she said and so it was decided. They drove to a teahouse in the style of a pagoda, sticking majestically out of swirling pools of lotus flowers. Only Chinese faces looked back through the windows at them.

'Are we allowed in?' Amelia asked Julia, who guffawed in response.

'We may ban Chinese from our parks and clubs but they are far too sensible to do such a thing to us. Of course we're allowed, the Chinese aren't such terrible snobs as you British. Come on.' Julia swung open the door and doled out a smattering of hellos to the people sitting in the teahouse, most of whom were young, intense-looking men. She ordered a pot of Chinese tea and started chattering away in her usual unstoppable style. Amelia felt uncomfortable and boring. She didn't like standing out as much as she did in this teahouse. Julia at least was vivacious, giving the people something to watch over their steaming tea. Amelia, on the other hand, felt frozen, a wax figure of a foreigner.

'Relax,' Julia said, lowering her voice. 'I know lots of these people. They're good guys, trust me. It's just a teahouse, for Christ's sake! No one's going to hurt you. Most of these men are May 4th intellectuals.'

'What do you mean?' Amelia envied the way Julia had the world so ordered. It was as though she just walked out the house in the morning and found everything in its proper arrangement, just the way she understood it. Amelia wanted to feel the same, to see the alien faces around her and respond only with a casual greeting.

'May 4th. It was a democratic movement to modernise China. Move away from all those old Confucian values, like the rigid social hierarchy and women always having to obey men. I like to think *New Woman* embodies some of those values.'

Amelia needed to talk to someone. She looked at Julia, with her sparkling eyes and glistening teeth. No doubt she saw marriage as a mouldy tradition that had to be toppled rather than a revered institution deserving of repair. But as the only other hope she had was in the form of domestic staff, Amelia decided to take the risk.

'Julia, I went to a party at the Cathay on Saturday.'

'Oh, for Green? He's a real flat tyre. Love the store, can't stand the man.'

'Yes, but anyway. There was a woman there, an actress.'

'Ooh, this sounds interesting.' Julia grinned.

'She seemed, uh, very taken with my husband. I don't really understand what happened. They spoke for a very long time, just the two of them.'

'What did they talk about?' Amelia shook her head. 'Well, if I were you, I wouldn't worry about what your husband is doing in front of you …' Amelia bit her lip, trying to quash the terrible possibilities Julia's comment brought up. 'I'm sorry, I'm sure it's nothing. Who was the actress?'

'She's Chinese. Woo … Faye? Faye something?'

'Wu Feifei?' Julia slammed her cup down. 'Wu Feifei?'

'Uh, yes, I think so.'

'She's incredible! Have you seen any of her films? She is the ultimate modern woman. We would absolutely love her for the cover of the magazine. You know, her mother was forced to become a maid after Feifei's father died. Then the son of the employer's family got Feifei pregnant and – you won't believe this – he married her! He was a May 4th type too, didn't believe class distinctions mattered. Gone a bit off the rails now. But he had to move out of the family home after the scandal and he decided to look after Feifei and her mother. Then he got Feifei into one of the studios. I mean, with a face like that … She's uneducated but she's risen to the top.' Amelia felt a little sicker with every word that fell from Julia's slick red lips. She did not want Feifei to be a legend, to be famous, to be someone worth knowing. At least she was from a poor background. Will wouldn't like that, she thought, trying to comfort herself. At least the Will she had met at that distant Christmas party in London wouldn't have liked it.

'But what would she want with my husband?' Amelia asked.

'I haven't seen him.' Julia took a sip of her tea. 'How long have you two been married?'

'Only a few months. When Will found out he was being sent to Shanghai he proposed immediately.' Julia nodded sagely, as though she understood a deeper meaning in Amelia's words. But Amelia didn't tell Julia what she had heard at that party not even a year ago, when Will's uncle had said in low tones to his parents that there was a chance of a job in Shanghai. 'But the boy needs to settle, take a wife,' he had said. She had shrugged off that sentence, thinking that marriage was what everyone wanted for the next generation.

Besides, marrying Will offered her a new chance at life away from her parents in their melancholy house. But now sometimes she turned those words over in her head at night when she waited for Will to come home.

'Oh! Talking of the movies, you know Richard Cable is coming to Shanghai?' Julia continued.

'Richard Cable, the actor?' Amelia quite liked Cable, a good-looking man from the south-west of England who had made it to Hollywood.

'Yes, he's coming here for his honeymoon. Your consulate's throwing a big party. The Americans are upset, of course, because we consider him ours. But as he is actually British, you get him. He must be the biggest star ever to pass through Shanghai.' She took a contemplative sip of tea. Amelia wanted to ask Julia about her Chinese lover, if those kind of things were different with foreigners. She knew Julia would welcome frank questions but Amelia couldn't work herself up to it. Maybe she was just too old-fashioned for this city and besides, she worried some of the men might understand English.

When Amelia got home she took the silk scarf out of its wrapping, twisting it this way and that in her hands. She decided to tie it around her head the way Julia had done with a similar model, but immediately felt that she looked like a child dressed up as a grown woman. She tugged it off and tied it round her neck instead, taking up her place in the armchair to wait for Will. Julia had given her a copy of *New Woman*, which lay in her lap, the cover model a young Chinese girl with plump lips and a blunt black fringe, tugging demurely on the neck of her dress, staring straight back out of the page at Amelia.

'Good evening, darling,' Will said, arriving just as Qi was resigning himself to preparing another dinner for one. 'Sorry I'm late. We actually had a department meeting for once.' Will had decided to discuss how best to share the team's workload with his colleagues Harry and Ralph but had found them both unwilling to change their working patterns. 'I do what

I do and that is not going to change,' Harry had said. He dealt mostly with consulate correspondence, only occasionally asking to deal with political affairs, and Will had no idea why someone would be so keen to hang onto such a boring job, but decided not to argue with him. Maybe Will wasn't meant to manage others. He was better slavishly copying Chinese characters and making them line up into neat English sentences.

'That's all right.' Amelia took her place at the table, wondering if Will would notice her new scarf. She tugged at it self-consciously. 'I heard today that Richard Cable is going to visit Shanghai.'

'Oh, really? First I've heard of it.'

'The consulate's having a party for him. I'd be interested in going.'

'Well, I really am the last to know! No one's mentioned it to me.'

'My new friend Julia told me,' Amelia said, trying to sound casual. Will squeezed her hand and smiled at her. That night they made love. It always made Amelia feel better to know that they could be close physically. If she could draw him into her body, maybe she could pull him into her mind too.

Longwei was gone again. When Feifei had arrived home from the Cathay, content with the night's events, she had expected him to be there, either violent or amorous. But he had already gone, probably with the dancer whose name Feifei refused to remember. Her mother came out from her bedroom, her spine curved and weary, and threw her hands up in the air.

'How you two expect me to bring up this girl normally when both of you are running around town all night, I don't know. If Lili didn't have me she would probably be for sale right now, out on the streets with no parents to care for her.'

'Ssh, Mama, please. I just want to go to bed.' Feifei pushed past her mother and made her way upstairs, high heels dangling from her left hand. Her feet ached from all that dancing. She was due to start shooting a new film on Monday and had decided she would sleep in tomorrow and spend the afternoon with Lili. That way she would be fresh for the start of *Shanghai Dreams*. She was enthusiastic about the script. It was the kind of film that people queued up to see. Flopping down onto the bed, Feifei undid the rivets of her dress and reached across to the bed stand. She eased out of the drawer the photograph she had ripped from a past issue of *New Woman*. There was Anna May Wong, star of Hollywood, resplendent in her Chinese silks, the foreignness of her face exaggerated for the Americans with big swooping lines around her eyes. Feifei once again read the caption under the picture: *Anna May Wong, Hollywood's first Chinese star. Wong has wowed audiences with her stunning performances. American cinema-goers have fallen in love with this exotic and dramatic beauty, who has made China come to life for Americans who know little about our country.* Anna May Wong, she thought, pressing the picture to her chest, if you can do it, I can do it too. She put the picture back in the drawer and fell fast asleep, her dress still clinging to her.

Feifei whiled away the following afternoon with Lili, playing games with a set of porcelain dolls. Lili was seven now and Feifei could see her face was shaping into that of a beauty. It pained her a little to know that Lili would one day make men's pulses quicken. Although a striking face had saved Feifei from a life of sure poverty, it had also been the cause of much of her trouble. Feifei's heart tugged when she watched Lili act out love stories with the dolls. She hoped her daughter would not find herself in such romantic tangles in the future.

'Lili, you're learning English in school, aren't you?'

'Only a little,' the girl said, placing her doll down on the floor.

'Do you want to teach your mama something?'

'*Hello! How do you do?*' Lili laughed. 'Now you say it!' But Feifei shook her head. All those sounds were so ugly to her, even worse than Mandarin. She couldn't tell where one word stopped and the next began.

'You're so clever,' Feifei said, wrapping her arms around Lili.

'No, Mama, you're the cleverest.' Feifei smiled to herself, hoping her daughter was right.

Will was in a fog of Feifei. On Monday morning Rollo came bounding into the office, overflowing with boyish energy.

'Am I going to see you in the gossip pages today?' he asked, lifting up a Chinese newspaper from Will's pile and shaking it towards him. 'Wu Feifei, Wu Feifei. New man in town doesn't mess around, does he?' He perched on Will's desk and addressed Harry.

'Do you know this man spoke to Shanghai's premier acting talent, the one and only Wu Feifei, for a whole thirty minutes on Saturday? I would say that's true love, wouldn't you?' He laughed loudly.

Harry MacDonald scowled. 'Do you like Chinese girls?' he asked Will.

'I'm married,' Will protested. 'Please, all of you, I'm married!' But he was laughing as he spoke.

'Yes,' Rollo said. 'I'm not sure how enamoured Amelia was with Wu Feifei.' His expression turned serious. 'Anyway, I wanted to say thank you for pointing out the anti-Japanese protest on Saturday in your report last week. It turned out to be bigger than the other ones over the past few months. Good work.' He rose and left, allowing Will to slip back into his thoughts of Feifei.

On the way home that night Will took a long route to soak up the pink dusk. He had a new lightness to his step every time he thought about Feifei. Of course, he knew the situation was hopeless. He had Amelia, a beautiful house and a comfortable job and there was no way he would risk it all for a Chinese actress who was nothing more than an attractive stranger to him. He only wished to see her again, to breathe the same air as her. When he passed the Phoenix Picture House, Will was immediately drawn to the sign outside that announced the film playing that evening – *Good Night, Shanghai!* Three characters stood out to him – 吴菲菲. *Wu Feifei*. He stood in front of the poster and before letting himself think about it too much, slipped into the dark womb of the cinema. He paid the entrance fee, aware that the gaggles of Chinese around him were watching him closely. He doubted many white men came in here to watch silent movies made in China. He dived into the anonymity of the screening room and settled down in his seat. Feifei's face popped up on the screen in the opening credits.

Will found himself totally engaged in the film, just like the young women around him, who cut their gossiping the moment the first scene began. Feifei played a talented artisan who fell into an all-engulfing relationship with a merchant later paralysed in an accident. Devoid of physical love, she began an affair with his brother. But overwhelmed with guilt at betraying the merchant, she jumped into the Huangpu, sinking to nothing at the bottom of the murky river. Will remained in his seat for a full five minutes after the film ended, feeling devastated. All the way home he couldn't rid himself of the image of her body sinking and disappearing into the Huangpu. Feifei's film really was an *electric shadow*, as the Chinese called them, tracing Will's steps closely down the twilight streets, flickering constantly in one corner of his brain.

When he arrived home Amelia was already having dinner alone. Will didn't like seeing her forlorn as she forked the meat and steamed vegetables into her mouth. He didn't mind arriving after she had eaten alone but the reality of her creased frown and downturned lips was too much. He preferred her tucked up in bed, eyes closed and face calm when he came back late.

'I'm sorry I'm late, darling,' he said and she simply nodded. Qi served him up a plate of slightly cold beef and the couple ate in silence, with only the scraping of cutlery and gentle chewing to interrupt their thoughts.

III

Feifei sat patiently in the chair while the make-up artists turned her into a film star. She always lost herself in the mirror when they painted her lips and exaggerated her eyelashes with their magical brushes, unable to pull herself away from the transformation. There was something about those heavy cosmetics that almost made her look grotesque, but she loved the dramatic changes to her features.

Ling was milling around the make-up room, looking for something to keep her busy. 'Eh, Feifei,' she called. 'Want to come and watch me sing again? The Paradise has made me a regular on Thursdays and Fridays.'

'So, beautiful ladies,' the young girl now circling colour on Feifei's cheeks said. 'What's this movie about?'

'It's really a nationalist spectacular!' Ling called from the other side of the room, dropping her magazine. 'Wait 'til the dwarf bandits see it.'

'The Japanese?' the girl said, her brow creasing as she smoothed out the paint around Feifei's cheekbones. Feifei nodded.

They were shooting one of the opening scenes, where Fei-fei, playing a brave and patriotic prostitute, mimed negotiations with customers in a brothel. She made flirtatious faces at the camera, turning the art of seduction into something closer to farce for the benefit of audiences denied sound.

'Fantastic, Feifei!' the director called out every so often, before being dragged into conversation with one of the assistants who swarmed around him, insects drawn to the sweetness of power. They finished the scene and Feifei pulled a silk gown around her.

'Director Xu,' she said, walking up to him. 'Was everything all right? You seemed a little distracted.'

'Hmm, of course. Your acting was as superb as ever, Feifei. Just some administrative nonsense.'

'Really?' She lowered her voice. They'd had a candid chat just two months before and some of his sentences were still etched into her brain – *You can't be in talking movies with an accent like that.* 'Are you sure there's no problem?' she asked.

'I'm sure.'

Will's breath quickened as he neared the block where the Paradise was located. He decided to take a quick detour in order to make a final decision about whether to go in. There was only one reason he was going and it wasn't to hear Ling's singing, he knew that. His daily task of reading the press served him with the distinct advantage of keeping up with all the goings-on of Shanghai's nocturnal world. Every day he scanned lines about the city's high class courtesans and the rich businessmen who kept them in champagne and *qipaos*, looking for the three brilliant characters that made up her name, Wu Feifei. He had almost missed the mention of Ling, so narrow was his vision. Now the singer was to be a regular fixture at the cabaret. That didn't mean Feifei would be there tonight, he told himself, skirting a murky puddle in the street. He looked around him at the low apartment blocks. They were coloured a sooty grey and spilled over with the indignities of life – people living and dying, all packed together in a way that was barely human. Will paused and looked around him.

He suddenly remembered with a jolt of embarrassment his conversation with Harry earlier that day. He hadn't been able to help himself asking if Harry ever watched Chinese films. It was as though Feifei lay poised on the end of his tongue, always threatening to fall out and expose him.

'I understand, Graves. You're not like the others, that's what you want me to think,' Harry said. Ralph coughed drily, his nerves shaken at any hint of aggression.

'No, it was just an innocent question. You have to stop being so sensitive, Harry.' Will tried once again to assert his management status but Harry's cold expression batted him down.

'It's fine, Graves. We all know you went to Oxford to study my glorious half-culture. You fit right in.' Harry gave an exaggerated sigh and shuffled some papers around. Will knew he had crossed a line but didn't understand exactly how he had managed to do so. 'Still got your eye on an actress, do you?' Harry continued. 'Let me tell you something, Will, the Chinese think actresses are no better than prostitutes. A woman who shows her body on screen for money is a prostitute. So save yourself the effort and go to a brothel like the rest of the consulate.' He cleared his throat indicating the conversation was finished and Will bowed his head, letting Harry claim a victory.

Now, as he stood in this filthy neighbourhood, where the drains ran with dirt and dreams of gold, he wondered if Harry had pinpointed something in him that was similar to the others, the arrogant, ignorant British he secretly considered himself better than because of his genuine interest in China. But he realised now that he didn't like this neighbourhood, wouldn't want to live here, couldn't understand how people did live here. But that discovery wasn't what worried him most. It was what Harry had said. Hearing the rise and fall of Shanghainese from behind flimsy walls, he wondered how much he really understood China. A film actress a prostitute? Did they also work … ? He couldn't bring himself to think it. Every time he saw Feifei she was with a different man. He started walking again. He wouldn't go to the Paradise. This was madness. Yes, he really should have stayed away, Will told himself, as the Russian doorman pushed open the door to the cabaret.

Will sank into the red-tinged darkness of the Paradise. It was filled with its habitual conspiratorial buzz, streaked with the seductive potential of danger. Being alone, he took a seat by the bar, loosening off his jacket and ordering a gin before allowing himself to take a stealthy look around the room. No Feifei. He felt a wave of relief swiftly followed by panic. What would he do here in this palace of darkness without her?

'*Only in dreams do I reach her, crossing the bridge, passing the flowers on the walk to her chamber,*' he found himself reciting under his breath.

The door burst open and Ling flung herself into the room. She was followed by a snaking line of people, their laughter gathering in cheery clouds above their heads. Midway down the line, he saw her. Feifei's head was thrown back in a casual joke, her slender arm linked with that of a paunchy man of around fifty. From the corner of an embarrassed eye, Will saw Feifei's group sit around a table, spreading a bubbling harmony he envied.

Ling took to the stage five minutes later.

'Oh, my baby's gone,' Ling sang, her voice creamy over the chords. 'They say he was dancing with another, well, let me go and find a lover!'

He felt a light tap on his shoulder and he turned quickly to find Feifei standing behind him. She looked more pronounced, more real than the last time he had seen her, her eyelashes dancing on the tops of her cheeks and her lips looking freshly kissed.

'Oh, hello,' he said. She had her arms crossed coquettishly behind her back.

'Well, if it's not the English Li Bai! I wanted to introduce

40

you to someone.' She gestured to the man standing behind her. How many men did she have? 'This is Director Xu.'

The man smiled, showing slightly crooked teeth, and offered his hand.

'This is the English poet I was telling you about,' Feifei said. 'I didn't expect to see him again so soon. He works for the consulate.'

'The consulate, eh? I hear they're hosting a party for Richard Cable,' Director Xu said.

Will gave a low whistle. 'It seems to be the talk of the town,' he said. Feifei's forehead crinkled and she paused, before catching her breath and continuing. She was so close, Will hoped she couldn't detect the stale alcohol on his breath or the circles of sweat around his armpits.

'Director Xu thinks it would be a very good idea for someone from the China Star studios to go and meet Cable, to tell him about Chinese film. We need all the international support we can get, you know,' Feifei said.

'I didn't even know about the party,' Will said. 'I'm afraid I don't have much influence at the consulate, but I'm sure someone from the studio could come. In fact, why don't you both come? The star and the director?' Will knew he was talking too fast.

'That would be wonderful,' Director Xu said.

'Just get in touch with the studio,' Feifei said, digging in her purse for a card. She handed it over to him and he read the characters. 'This address. If it's not too much trouble, of course. We really appreciate it.'

'Not at all. Also, I meant to say that I recently saw *Good Night, Shanghai!* Fantastic film.' Will regretted the words as soon as they were spoken. The pair looked at him with unconcealed shock.

'Perhaps we have more international support than we realised,' Director Xu said drily to Feifei. She gave a shy wave and they wended their way back to their table, Will's eyes locked on the soft sway of Feifei's hips encased in blue and white silk. He took a gulp of his drink.

41

'Yes, they saw my baby with another, but tonight it's my turn to find a lover!' Ling trilled.

Julia picked Amelia up early the next day. Will had left just fifteen minutes before with tired eyes and a hastily-knotted college tie. He had fallen over his feet going up to bed the night before and Amelia could smell the sickly sweet stench of alcohol throughout the whole house. She had put on a white starched dress, wanting to feel clean and fresh. Will was going to be late for work.

'Morning, kid,' Julia said as Amelia slid into the car beside her. 'Say, you look a little tired.'

'Will woke me up last night when he got in.' She straightened her hat. Julia had promised to take her to a Chinese haberdasher's to get a dress made for the Richard Cable party. It was only a week away and Shanghai's inner sanctum was already awash with speculation about the evening. Securing an invitation was a sure sign you were a Shanghai somebody, leaving the nobodies with nothing to say when the party was brought up. Julia, as a pillar of the Anglo-Saxon community and a magazine editor, had been one of the guests at the top of the list, even if her behaviour sometimes caused raised eyebrows in conservative circles.

'We need to be quick because I'm interviewing a poet later,' Julia said, turning towards Bubbling Well Road. 'He's written some beautiful patriotic poetry and I'd like to print some of it in the magazine. It's particularly poignant as the Japs rape and pillage their way across Manchuria. I'm certainly not cheering them on and the rest of the international community shouldn't be either.' Amelia wasn't listening, already imagining the frothy silk creations the haberdasher might be able to make for her. She thought about the way Will had looked at her the night of the dinner at the Cathay, how he had watched her while she danced with Rollo, recalling a Will she had long lost. She kept holding onto those moments, willing her marriage back into health.

'Hello? Amelia?'

'I want to look really, really nice at the party, Julia. So your tailor had better know what he's doing.'

The two women rifled through Mr Li's silks. Amelia fingered a rose pink fabric similar to the shade she had seen Feifei in. Julia frowned.

'Wear black. Dark colours suit you best.' She pulled a midnight streak out of the pile. 'This. You can take a look in the magazines he has over there for a style but I already know what would suit you best, a nice draped neckline ... low back ... yes.' Amelia was quick to agree with anything Julia suggested.

'I'm going to buy some for Tamara too,' Julia said, inspecting a long wrap of red silk. 'I'm taking her to the party as my guest.'

'The Russian?'

'Yes, the ballerina.' Julia smiled. 'The bearcat.'

Amelia hadn't thought about the Russian for a day or two, but the mention of Tamara's name brought back a suppressed longing for crushed toes and aching calves.

'Julia, do you think she would reconsider and let me take ballet lessons? See, I feel I really need something to do with my time. I used to dance in my youth.'

Julia sighed. 'I'm never going to turn you into a modern woman, am I, Amelia? If you need something to do with your time you could come and work at the magazine with me, or volunteer to help Chinese orphans. But ballet lessons?'

'I know, but it was such an important part of my life. I had to stop but–'

'Now you mention it, you do have lovely posture. I'm afraid Tamara's not that focused on teaching at the moment. But look, some advice, strictly *entre nous*. At the party, why don't you offer to help with this project of hers? She might warm up to the idea of lessons then.'

'What is this mysterious project?'

'I think it's best if Tamara explains it,' Julia said.

Will sat down in his chair, his bones heavy. He ran his fingers through his hair, willing the last drops of gin out of his brain. A stack of newspapers and correspondence looked up at him from the desk, accusing. He reached for the first one, a local Chinese paper.

'BOYCOTT!' yelled the headline. 'We'll show the Japanese who's boss with this latest boycott,' ran the subtitle. He flipped to the next paper, which featured a hive of angry workers waving placards outside a Japanese factory. That paper also announced a boycott. He was going to have a lot of translating to do.

'You're late, boss,' Harry MacDonald said, in mock servile tones.

'Everybody's late sometimes, Harry.'

'Have you seen the boycott? Are you doing a report on it?'

'I will.'

'Let me do it. You look like you've had a long night.' Harry moved round to Will's desk, bringing his cheek close to his boss' face. 'They say the sun never sets on the British Empire. It never sets on a Shanghai night either.' He chuckled and picked up half the stack of papers. 'I'll take care of this.'

Will looked at Harry. He hadn't been able to warm to him because the man seemed so distant and contained. But with his pulse echoing through his brain and Chinese characters blurring in front of his eyes, Will saw no reason to turn down Harry's unexpected kindness.

'I've some correspondence to deal with, so that would be very helpful, Harry.'

'No problem, boss.' Harry smiled, carrying the pile of papers to his desk. Will felt a twinge of nerves, a little pang reminding him that he was meant to be the one in charge. He hauled himself up to look for Rollo.

He knocked on the door. He could see Rollo hunched over his desk, eyes skimming over piles of notes.

'Come in,' Rollo said, without lifting his eyes. 'Oh, Will! Something major in the papers today?'

'Boycott of Japanese goods.'

44

'Big one?'

'We're just ironing out the details right now. I'm not actually here about that.'

'Oh, what can I help you with then?' Rollo shuffled the papers on his desk self-importantly and smiled broadly.

'The Richard Cable party. How do I get an invite?'

'Oh, you and Amelia will automatically be invited, you're a permanent member of staff.'

'I know. I mean, I thought so. What about, you know, other people?'

Rollo cocked his head to one side. 'Who?'

'People from a Chinese film studio. I need two tickets.'

'Wu Feifei?' Will nodded, his eyes on the floor. 'Are you joking? Don't tell me you've invited her.'

'She asked me, actually. I met Director Xu from China Star, he seems to be an interesting chap ...'

'Oh, Will. You really are too much. I will take care of it. Off you go and write up that report.' Will felt horribly exposed as he walked down the corridor towards his office. But he told himself all that mattered was securing an invitation for Feifei.

'Mail!' One of the studio administrators, a skinny, hungry-looking youth breezed through the set as the China Star actors wrapped the last scene of the day. Feifei accepted her envelope greedily, tearing it open to find what she had spent five days waiting for.

'Director Xu! We're going to meet Richard Cable!' she sang out. Director Xu nodded in her direction, but he was caught up in conversation with an actress who had recently been signed to the studio, a girl from Beijing who was just seventeen. Feifei had been doing her best to ignore this softly-spoken slender beauty from the north. Her plan was falling into place now anyway and soon she wouldn't need Director Xu or anyone else in China. Feifei took a fresh sheet of paper and in painstaking characters wrote:

Dear Wei'er,
Many thanks for the invitation. Would you be able to meet
sometime before the party as I need to ask you a few things? I
hope this is not an inconvenience for you. Please let me know
when and where to meet.
Best regards,
Your friend,
Wu Feifei
There was no way the Englishman would say no, and Feifei
knew it.

Will felt acutely alive waiting for Feifei to arrive, electric with
longing and suspense. The actress had suggested a French-
style coffee bar – she knew the owner, a Francophile Chinese
who already owned three restaurants. Will tapped nervous
fingers on the tabletop.

He had never been in love before, he realised now, waiting
for Feifei to appear, an unreal vision he sometimes swore he
had created in his mind. He loved Amelia in a way, but more
in the manner one might love a friend or a family member.
She had been so sweet and devoted and, most importantly,
easy to get along with, that when his parents pushed for marriage he thought of her affectionate letters and sweet cheer-
fulness and decided that they were right. She was the one who
should come with him to Shanghai. Where the other girls he
knew laughed at his obsession with China, Amelia indulged
his interests. Even here in Shanghai, he thought, she let him
do as he pleased. Other women had been interested in him,
girls of the same social standing, who wanted to control him,
to take over his life with demands and expectations. It was a
claustrophobic world and China, the land he had created in
his head, had been his escape. Only Amelia had respected that.
His uncle had encouraged marriage when he secured the job
for Will, saying a woman by his side would make life easier
for a young man in Shanghai. Now he was in Shanghai, Will
had a better understanding of why his uncle had endorsed
the pairing, convincing Will's parents that the girl was the

right candidate despite her distinctly lower social standing. The night-time pleasures of the Shanghai buffet were so rich a single man couldn't help but gorge himself.

The door to the private chamber slid back and Feifei walked in, head high. She wore a dark green *qipao* with a white trim and a pair of round sunglasses.

'Hello.' She slid down into the chair next to him. 'Thank you so much for agreeing to meet me. You must be very busy at the consulate at the moment.' She took the sunglasses off and placed them down on the table. The little thud they made reverberated around the small room. Will could see his expression, flustered, silent, in the mirrors that walled them in together.

'It's lovely to see you, Feifei,' he said, his voice uncharacteristically smooth. 'What did you want to ask me about?'

'It's embarrassing.' Feifei lowered her head and grazed her cheek with a sharp nail. 'You can say no if you want.' She fiddled with her the stems of her sunglasses while he willed her to keep talking. It was so obvious, he thought, the way she had walked in so proudly in her perfectly-matched outfit, the way she had coquettishly pulled off her sunglasses, those slim fingers brushing her skin.

'No, no, tell me.'

'Well, I'd like English lessons.'

'English lessons?' he repeated, willing her to correct him.

'Yes. I really must improve my English. You speak Mandarin and Shanghainese and English. You even know poetry. There are Russians peddling English lessons like they do everything else, and old English women who could teach me too, but I want to learn from someone who knows Chinese.' That wasn't what she really wanted, Will decided, judging by how fast she was speaking and the way she wouldn't meet his eye. There were thousands of Eurasians who would be happy to take on such a safe, respectable job, especially with the added glamour of teaching a film star.

'I'm far from the only Englishman in Shanghai with some knowledge of Chinese,' he said.

47

'Well, you're the only one I want as my teacher,' Feifei replied firmly.

'In that case, I'd be more than delighted to give you lessons,' he said. 'But why do you want to learn?'

'Do you promise you won't laugh?' He nodded. 'I want to go to Hollywood. There's all this talk of films with sound coming to China and I have a terrible peasant accent! Listen to me! My Mandarin is hopeless, I grew up speaking Cantonese. I'll be finished in this town. Do you know Anna May Wong?'

'Can't say I do,' Will said, choking back his surprise at her explanation.

'She's a famous Chinese actress in Hollywood. You see, if I play Chinese characters it doesn't matter what my accent is like! But I must learn English before anything. Could you spare some time now to help? Just twenty minutes or so. I would like to learn some introductions for the Richard Cable party.' He thrilled at the blush that coloured her cheeks.

'Where have you been, Will? The consul wants to see you.' Rollo was already waiting for him when he returned to the office. He was sitting on the side of Will's desk, one foot jerking against the floor. Will saw papers were ruffled, as though Rollo had been going through them.

'The consul?' Will had only spoken to the consul a few times, notably at his welcome party, when Terence White had enquired about his uncle's well-being. In the hierarchy of consulate mandarins, Will occupied a lowly rank.

'Yes, you made a right hash of your report about the Japanese boycott.'

'Japanese boycott?' Will's elation from his meeting with Feifei drained.

'Yes, the report that came through from the department was so flimsy, it was as though nothing had happened. Then the consul heard about huge trouble at the factories, protests verging on riots. These things matter, Will. It's not a case of jotting down a weak two-page report and then going for a gin sling.'

'Rollo, Harry MacDonald wrote the report,' Will said weakly.

'That is quite beside the point, Will. You're in charge of this department.'

The consul's office was of heavy mahogany, stacked with unread books and decorated with paintings of rural English scenes.

'William, please do come in.' Terence White was grand, full of pleased pomp at being one of the most important men in foreign Shanghai. Will settled uneasily into a stiff-backed chair.

'I had hoped we would have a chance to talk properly under more auspicious circumstances but I'm afraid I had no choice but to speak to you about this matter. A very weak report about the latest boycott of Japanese goods came through from your department last week.' He cleared his throat and leaned further over the large desk that separated them. 'Our contacts in the business community have now told us that the situation is extremely serious and that some Japanese in Shanghai genuinely fear for their lives. They want a guarantee there won't be mob rule if Chinese rage about the Manchuria situation boils over. You can well understand, I'm sure, although you are a man of letters rather than commerce, that some British businesses in Shanghai are concerned by these developments. We aren't always the most popular masters either, though we are fair.'

Will nodded, trying to match the severity of Terence White's expression.

'The issue here, William, is that we must keep abreast of developments, of the sentiment in the Chinese community. That is one of the most important roles of the translation department and unfortunately one you have failed in. I will personally be keeping an eye on reports from you for the foreseeable future to ensure standards are maintained. We can't rely on the policemen on the Municipal Council to keep track of unfolding issues alone.'

'I understand.' Will cursed Harry MacDonald, cursed

49

himself, cursed the bloody Paradise and its drinks. 'It won't happen again. I am terribly sorry.'

'Good. I trust you are enjoying yourself in Shanghai?'

'Yes.'

'Your wife is simply charming, Mrs White tells me.' Will left the office, resisting the urge to slam the door behind him. As he softly pulled it to, he saw Rollo turn around the corner.

'My turn now,' he said with a brotherly grimace. 'Still invited to the Cable party?'

'I assume so,' Will said, an unfamiliar coldness seeping into his vowels.

In the car on the way to the party Amelia and Will were silent. He had been in a sour mood for days, but Amelia didn't care. She was going to the Cathay again, she was going to see Richard Cable, and all she wanted was to bask in the neon carnival of Shanghai's night. She pointed out a cigarette advertisement to Will, commenting on the beauty of the girl reclining on a table, a pot of arching white flowers behind her, the slit in her *qipao* exposing an entire gleaming, slender thigh.

'She's lovely, isn't she?' Amelia said.

'Yes,' Will replied, disinterested. 'Listen, I have a lot of consulate business to take care of tonight so I'll have to make the rounds, I'm afraid. I hope you don't mind.'

'Of course, Will, I understand. I'll be by your side,' she said, placing a hand on his shoulder. He looked ahead, stony-faced. Amelia removed her hand, feeling glad that Julia was going to be there, and also that she had her own little challenge to complete – tracking down Tamara. The roof of the Cathay was already tinkling with champagne-fuelled conversation when they reached the terrace. Amelia took a moment to let the glittery dew of the party set on her skin, turning her head from side to side to sweep across the Bund and the grand buildings of the International Settlement. The Huangpu ran fast and dirty along the regal shore of the Bund, not stopping for the arrival of a superstar on its banks. Will made his way to Rollo and she followed, a little reluctantly. Rollo was with a young girl, whose dress swamped her skinny frame. Rollo reached over and patted Amelia's arm.

'You look lovely, Amelia,' he said, and she felt a rush of warmth. That was just what she had wanted Will to say to her before they left. As the pair made small talk with Rollo, Amelia noticed Will turning his head from one end of the roof terrace to the other, eyes always trained on the other party guests.

A woman's voice announced what sounded like a greeting in Chinese to Amelia's ears. She turned and saw Feifei with a short, older man. Feifei, in plain white silk, smiled softly and said something to Will. Rollo stiffly offered his hand to the man, choking out some rudimentary Chinese. Amelia felt embarrassed at not understanding the rise and fall of their tones. After a brief interaction with Will, Feifei set her starry eyes on Amelia, opened her mouth once or twice, steeling herself, and then blurted out: 'Hello, pleased to meet you, I Feifei.'

'I *am* Feifei,' Will corrected gently.

'Yes, I *am* Feifei.' She smiled. Amelia, surprised that the actress could speak English, nodded encouragingly.

'Your English is very good,' she said.

'Yes, your–' Will took Feifei's forearm, cutting the film star off mid-sentence.

'Feifei has requested to meet Richard Cable. So I shall see what I can do. She and Director Xu would like to promote Chinese film abroad.' He said something in Chinese to Feifei and she smiled and followed him, the stout man with glasses trailing them. Amelia followed the soft grace of Feifei's carriage across the room. Rollo and the girl he was with looked at the floor without a word. Amelia moved away from the pair of them, feeling suddenly naked.

Julia watched from the sidelines of the party, a drink in hand. This was how she always operated at these kind of events – staking out a corner, watching and deciding exactly when

51

to pounce. An American sang wistful jazz, her blonde bob swinging in time to the trumpeter. Richard Cable was toured around by the consul, who looked mightily pleased with himself. Secretly, Julia thought it was unseemly for the consulate to pay for parties for Hollywood stars, but she didn't like to say anything, especially as this party offered a big opportunity for *New Woman*. If she could get something from Cable, or even his pneumatic, adolescent fiancée Harper Dee, they would shift more copies of the magazine. She watched with curiosity as a foreign man led Feifei across the terrace, the actress radiant as the sky turned apricot over the party guests.

'Hello, Julia.' Amelia tapped Julia's shoulder. Her friend really did look lovely, Julia thought, in her new midnight silk and carefully painted face. 'That's my husband with the Faye actress.'

'You look wonderful.' Poor Amelia, Julia thought, maybe her husband really was carrying on with the actress. Will was better-looking than she had expected, in a creeping, low-key way where his looks first seemed safe and familiar and then suddenly hit you as remarkable. At least most men in the Settlement had the decency to take care of their extra-marital needs at the brothels. Only an Englishman would think he was entitled to sweep into Shanghai and romance her leading lady.

'I'm looking for Tamara,' Amelia said, her mouth drawing downwards. 'Have you seen her?'

'Oh, she'll be somewhere by herself scowling at the rest of us,' Julia said lightly. Amelia turned and Julia guiltily cut quickly across the roof to reach Will.

'You must be Will,' she said in her brashest, most American tones. 'I'm Julia. A very good friend of your wife's.' Shanghai had taught her that if you wanted the British to obey you, you were simply as forthright as possible and then interpreted their panic as permission. She thrust her hand out to meet his and he shook it limply, one eye on Feifei.

'And Wu Feifei, what a pleasure.' She turned to the actress, switching into Shanghainese. 'I'm from *New Woman* magazine.' Feifei smiled easily.

'I am a big fan of your magazine. You wrote about Anna May Wong a few months ago.' Julia decided to seize the divine moment she had been presented with.

'Would you be willing to be interviewed for the magazine?' she asked Feifei.

'I'm taking Feifei and Director Xu to meet Richard Cable,' Will broke in.

'Well, do you think there's space for one more in your welcoming party?' Julia smiled at Will, enjoying the way she unnerved him.

'I would be delighted to do an interview for the magazine,' Feifei said confidentially to Julia. 'You're an American. Do you know anyone in Hollywood?'

'Not yet. But I think we're about to meet one of its stars.'

Amelia circled the party unsuccessfully. She recognised some of the wives from the consulate tea in Cordelia's garden but instinctively avoided them. The way they crowded together, heads fused in gossip, made her feel unwanted and excluded. By coming to Shanghai she had hoped to escape that terrible English struggle for acceptance, but it only seemed to be worse here. Out of the corner of her eye she saw Julia talking to Will. Will wouldn't like Julia, Amelia knew that. She shrugged at the hopelessness of trying to control the colliding planets of her Shanghai galaxy. Then she saw her. Tamara was standing in a corner alone again, her long fingers wrapped around a champagne flute. Her hair was pulled back in the same severe bun that she had worn last time, and her fitted black dress grazed her ankles. Amelia noticed again how thin she was. She made her way over to the dancer, heart beating a little faster.

'Hello, Tamara,' she said, in a way she hoped sounded breezy.

'Hello,' Tamara said dourly, wafting a cigarette.

'I wanted to talk to you about dance lessons. Julia says you have a project I could help with.'

'I'm sure Julia meant it as a joke,' Tamara said, taking a leisurely sip of champagne.

'I'm serious. I really want to learn again.' Amelia looked across the roof at Will and Feifei and imagined pirouetting herself out of her life. 'Please. Tell me what I can do. My grandmother taught me for ten years in London.'

'Fine, Amelia. You don't have money and you don't have power. But you do have a pair of feet. So maybe I can find a use for you.'

Amelia nodded enthusiastically. 'Anything.'

'Why don't you come to a class next week?' Tamara suggested. 'I teach some women every day at ten a.m. I'm not sure you are right for the group, but you can come along and see. Then we can come to a decision.'

'Wonderful!' Amelia said. She clasped her hands together, feeling happiness bubble inside. 'Thank you so much, Tamara, I really appreciate it. I can't wait to dance again.'

Tamara smirked.

'You haven't been to the class yet,' she said.

Will was nervous about approaching the consul after the previous week's debacle. Since the ticking-off in White's office he had personally read all of Harry's reports, though he was increasingly relying on the Eurasian to write them for him. He was drinking with Rollo most nights now, and when he didn't go out with him, he would meet Feifei for English lessons. They often went to the same coffee house, where they could enjoy the mirrored seclusion of the private room. Feifei would sometimes get lost in chit-chat about her new film, but she always brought their talk back to learning English. She was determined and improving slightly. Will knew he was underqualified for the job, teaching someone who had never written with an alphabet (and only recently written at all) to cross t's and hook y's. But he did have some teaching experience from Oxford, and Feifei didn't seem to be complaining.

'Mr White,' Will said, boldly. 'I have someone here who

would like to meet Mr Cable, if it's not too much trouble.'
Cable smiled broadly, used to dealing with fans.

'No problem at all,' Cable said, though the consul looked
displeased. 'Who is this person that wants to meet me? I hope
I'm not too much of a disappointment.'

'I Feifei.' The actress stretched out her hand and the beaming star of Hollywood reached over and took it in his, gently
kissing it.

'Wu Feifei is the most famous actress in all of China,' Will
said. 'She was keen to meet someone with an equivalent
career in Hollywood.'

'I'm nervous,' Feifei whispered to Julia in Shanghainese.
'Will has been teaching me but maybe my English isn't good
enough to talk to Richard Cable.'

'Will's been teaching you English?' But Julia's question
went ignored, as just then Richard Cable said in loud, slow
English to Feifei: 'I am delighted to meet you, my dear. What
a beauty!'

'Thank you,' Feifei said shyly. 'Mr Cable, I want – want
– talk you.' He shook his head as though he didn't understand and Will cringed on Feifei's behalf. She had been learning quickly, but ten days of lessons wasn't enough for her to
speak to this man in any meaningful way. Cable was already
pulling away. 'I want go – H-Hollywood,' she stumbled, as
he kept avoiding her eye.

'Good luck with your career,' he said, and the consul pulled
him away, while Julia chased after them, hunting for a quote
from Cable. Feifei looked sadly after them. Will couldn't help
but grab her hand, squeezing her fingers in sympathy.

'I'm going home,' she said, pulling her hand away.

NOVEMBER 1931

列女操　孟郊

梧桐相待老，

鸳鸯会双死。

贞妇贵殉夫，

舍生亦如此。

波澜誓不起，

妾心井中水。

Song of a Pure Girl by Meng Jiao

Wutong trees mature in pairs,
Mandarin ducks die side by side.
If a chaste girl is devoted to her husband,
And lives in this faithful way,
What wave could possibly rise above an oath,
Made by a spirit deep as water in a well?

IV

Amelia arrived at Tamara's studio in Frenchtown at five to ten on Monday morning. The studio was up crumbling stairs inside an unloved residential block. Though the space was small, Tamara had fitted large mirrors and a ballet barre. Amelia was the only student there when she arrived to find Tamara in heated Russian conversation with an older woman who sat at a battered piano in the corner of the room.

'Hello, Tamara. I do have the right day, don't I?' Amelia walked to the centre of the room, taking in the faint smell of stale sweat.

'Yes, yes,' Tamara said. 'The other girls aren't quite as punctual as you. Oh, you even have dance shoes.' She nodded approvingly at Amelia's feet and told her to choose a place by the barre.

Amelia bent over, stretching her back, fingertips grazing her toes. She pulled her legs up and behind her, curving her feet towards her head. Her muscles responded happily, remembering some of their flexibility. Tamara looked up every so often, checking Amelia's posture and calling out praise. It reminded Amelia of the lessons with her grandmother and she stretched her arms and legs as long as she could manage, hoping to please her new teacher.

At five past, the first students arrived in a group of three. Two of the girls wore bright red lipstick and Amelia was horrified to see them kick off high heels and take up their places at the barre barefoot. The third girl, small and dark like Amelia, had none of the cosmetic embellishments of the other dancers. Her skin was yellowed and tired, her limbs sharp and hair limp. She stood beside Amelia at the barre, wearing thick men's socks on her feet, and did not turn to greet the new student. The other two talked in low voices and Amelia realised they were Russians. By quarter past, another three girls had arrived and Tamara clapped her hands, indicating the class was to begin. As they moved through the drills, Amelia saw that her classmates were settled into the routine, that they executed each move with precision, their necks extended and elegant, each movement fluid. Tamara barked instructions in Russian, and while the French terms were the same, Amelia was unsure, waiting to see what the other girls did before starting. She stumbled over some of the harder moves and was surprised at how easily her legs tired from *pliés* and *tendus*. All those weeks on the ship had rendered her muscles softer than she remembered. But she could do it, ballet was etched somewhere in her memory, and every time Tamara smiled in her direction, she felt her heart lift. She caught the other girls sending occasional sideways looks her way, their faces blank, not displaying any reaction. After an hour and a half, Tamara called an end to the lesson and said something to the other dancers, who turned to look at Amelia.

'Welcome to our class,' one said in halting English and the others nodded, moving away from the barre and decorating themselves once more in their street wear.

Tamara waited for the other girls to leave, a smirk on her face. No one paid her.

'Well, did you enjoy that?' Tamara asked.

'Yes, very much so. It's just fantastic to be dancing again,' Amelia said. 'Please may I come to the classes? Perhaps you could tell me about the project now.'

'Come for a week,' Tamara said. 'Show me you're serious and then we'll talk.'

Amelia passed Tamara's test. After a week of lessons, she waited expectantly at the end of the class.

'So, Tamara. Will I be allowed to continue?'

Tamara gestured for her to sit on the floor, shooing the old Russian pianist out of the room.

'I have to say I'm impressed,' Tamara started. 'You have a natural ability and some remarkable training for someone from England. Where did you learn?'

'I told you before,' Amelia said, a proud blush colouring her face. 'My grandmother. She was a dancer with a company in Budapest. My grandfather was a journalist and was sent to the Austro-Hungarian Empire for a year or two. Apparently he saw my grandmother and that was it. She was the woman for him.'

'An unusual story,' Tamara mused.

'Very. My grandmother passed her love for ballet onto me. But after my grandfather's death my mother was so desperate to be English she hid it all away, the ballet, the fact her mother was Hungarian.'

'Remarkable,' Tamara said. 'I am impressed. But now I need your help. You may have noticed the other students are not exactly like you.'

'They're Russian,' Amelia replied.

'Not just that. They're taxi-dancers or ... well, I don't need to explain, do I? These girls have extremely difficult lives. I want to help them. I've been going around all the cabarets, finding girls with a history of dance, girls who wish to better themselves. I plan on setting up a company eventually and making money, providing them with a new living. But what I am lacking right now is respectability. Julia does her best for me, but what is more respectable in Shanghai than a British woman? The wife of a man from the consulate? It can't be bettered.'

'I would really like to help, Tamara. All I want to do is dance.'

'It's ugly, the reality of these girls' lives,' Tamara said solemnly. 'Come with me tonight, I'm going to see a dancer at a nightclub. If you survive it, then I'm sure you'll be a great help to me.'

'Wonderful,' Amelia said, though she felt a little worried. She hadn't even told Will about the dance classes, as he was always gone long before she needed to leave the house. She knew Tamara was setting her another hurdle, after she had jumped cleanly over the first, believing that Amelia was too privileged and protected to operate in Shanghai's underworld and dance next to women who sold their bodies. But Amelia was ready to carve out her Shanghai, and if that meant going to nightclubs, she would do it.

Amelia wondered what to wear to the Harbin Club, so she decided to walk from the studio just off Avenue Joffre to the *North China Daily News* office on the Bund to ask Julia. The American could almost always be found there, unless she was working on *New Woman*. Amelia found Julia typing furiously at a desk. She looked up and smiled warmly when she saw Amelia.

'I'm really busy here, kitten, but tell me what you need.'

'What does one wear to the Harbin Club?'

'Nothing, if one is a dancer there,' Julia responded. 'What are you doing going to a place like that for?'

'To help Tamara with her project.'

Julia expressed surprise that Amelia had taken up the unorthodox offer. 'Be careful there, it's not pretty. I mean, it's more or less a brothel. Are you sure you want to go?'

'Of course I am,' Amelia said, feeling defensive. Why should she be denied the secrets of Shanghai, while people like Will and Julia explored the city in all its grit and glamour, encountering every kind of illicit pleasure? Chinese writers, Chinese actresses and only God knew what else.

'Hey, I didn't know Will was an English teacher these days,' Julia said, changing the subject.

'An English teacher?' Amelia frowned. 'No, no, he used to teach at Oxford. But he taught Chinese.'

'But he's giving classes to Wu Feifei. She's coming in for an interview at *New Woman* later– '

'What? What did you just say?'

'That Will's teaching Feifei English. You must be so relieved it's just English classes.' Amelia sat down clumsily in a chair next to Julia, her head suddenly heavy.

'My God, they're having an affair, aren't they? It's actually happening.'

'No, doll, they're speaking English together. You've got nothing to worry about. I thought you would already know. Now, I'm sorry, but I have to finish this article. I'll ask Feifei about it later. Stop worrying. Will probably just misses teaching.'

'Don't tell her I know anything. This is awful ... awful.' Amelia buried her head in her two sweaty palms, imagining the self-satisfied wives of Shanghai discussing her misfortune with glee.

'Oh, and to the Harbin, nothing too risqué,' Julia said. 'It doesn't attract the best class of man.'

Amelia left without another word.

Just a little further down the Bund, Will was panicking. He had come in that morning to find no Harry. Even ex-policeman Ralph, normally reserved, had expressed surprise at Harry's absence.

'He's always here before us,' he said. 'Very odd.' Will's head, blurred by alcohol, raced with reasons why Harry might not be there. He had become accustomed to Harry writing reports independently and now the workload facing him and Ralph was huge. There was more about the Japanese in the newspapers after a Chinese student group had said they would take 'any measures necessary' to combat Japanese colonisation of their land. Those words were open to interpretation, but most of the papers were convinced this meant violence, likely brutal and bloody if provoked.

'These Japs just don't give up, do they?' Ralph said, flicking through one of the local Shanghai papers. He normally dealt with day-to-day correspondence at the consulate and kept his head of out politics, well aware he had been shunted off to the consulate for a quiet life. Will was sometimes frustrated by the uselessness of the staff he had under him but despite their faults, they always arrived on time. He had arranged to meet Feifei for an English lesson near the China Star studio at lunchtime and unless Harry turned up soon, Will would never get away.

'Do you think the Japanese really believe it when they say that Asians should join together as a super race, that they see the Chinese as brothers? I've heard about what's been going on up in Manchuria–'

'For God's sake, Ralph, we don't need your amateur commentary on this. Head down and translate, please. We'll piece together a report.' Ralph dipped his chin closer to his papers and Will took a breath to steady himself. Feifei had seemed down for the last week or so, ever since the Cable party, which he knew hadn't gone as well as she wanted. But she was determined to persevere with her English lessons and her Hollywood dreams, even if Cable had dismissed her. Will desperately wanted to see her again. Could these chaste classes last forever, or would she one day give him a signal? His ambivalence about that possibility had turned into a gnawing desire, something like suppressed rage, a heavy feeling that he could never relieve. As the two men scrabbled together newspaper articles, Ralph's correspondence carefully set aside, the door swung open slowly.

Harry, with a sleek smile on his face, walked in brimming with confidence.

'Miss me, lads?'

Will jumped to his feet. 'Where have you been, MacDonald? It's eleven o'clock. If you're going to be late for work, you tell me.'

'Relax, I had a meeting. Promoting the interests of the consulate, and most especially the translation department. We have to let people know that what we're doing is important, don't we, boss?' There was a sprinkle of mocking in Harry's tone, but Will didn't let it put him off.

'Who did you meet? Any meetings must be approved by me!'

'Please, Will, calm down. What are you so angry about? Let me guess – this student group and their threat? It's nothing.' Harry eased himself into his seat, placing that morning's paper on the desk. 'The Japanese won't bat an eyelid. We shouldn't react hysterically to this kind of stuff, though obviously nobody told the newsmen that.'

'Well, we're still doing a report. You had better get started right now.' Will threw a pile of papers onto Harry's desk and went back to his work, his eyes drifting over a gossip piece amid rabid reports of Japanese wrongdoing. *Su Longwei doesn't seem to mind that his wife is always disappearing into a private room at one of our city's finest coffee shops. He's got other things on his mind – two identical things to be exact. The dancing Xu twins! What is Wu Feifei doing now? Who is she meeting for these secret rendezvous?*

Will's heart, calmed somewhat by Harry's arrival, now turned black. This was a terrible morning.

At twelve noon he left the office, hopping in a cab to the Chinese restaurant Feifei had recommended for the lesson. The owner, a rotund man with a moustache and a grinning leer, showed Will to a private room. The wallpaper was slightly peeling, the table was scratched and the tea set on the table was chipped. It was a place perhaps once seeped in grandeur that had mildewed in the Shanghai heat. The city was full of places like this – faded former glories. He drank the tepid jasmine tea and waited. He waited and waited, watching the hands of the rusted clock on the wall tick away, five minutes behind his own. But she didn't come. So he picked himself back up, leaving some coins for the tea and avoiding the fat man's smirk on the way out.

Feifei picked up her handbag, ready to leave the studio. She was still angered by the gossip piece in the morning paper. She might only have been learning English from Will, but she could never protest, knowing secretive meetings with a married man, especially a foreign one, would never be understood. She felt that people in the studio were looking at her differently. She certainly couldn't go to meet Will today, but she would go to the interview at the magazine. That would give her a chance to present a better face to the public and might even further her plan. After all, half the magazine was written in English. You never knew who was reading.

'Feifei.' Director Xu swept across the room towards her, the bland-faced new girl from Beijing behind him. 'I'm taking Lan for lunch. She would love some advice for her scenes this afternoon. Perhaps you could join us?' Feifei stopped cold. It was as if the old director knew she had planned to meet Will.

'I have an interview with *New Woman* at two,' she said, hoping he would be pleased with her publicity efforts. 'About the new film,' she added. 'But I could certainly join you for a while.'

'Good. Lan here tells me she's never had *xiaolongbao*. I thought we'd better put that right.'

So the three of them, the wrinkling, cynical director, the sweeping, elegant leading lady and the innocent, red-cheeked northerner, walked to a local restaurant where Shanghai's soupy dumplings were heaped on expensive platters. They sat together at a round table, Lan's eyes greedily taking in her surroundings, including Feifei, who she stole hidden glances at.

'Thank you, Miss Wu, for joining us,' Lan said shyly, her sweet voice playing like flutes in Feifei's ears. She did her best not to scowl. Once she too had been young and unsure, though by the time she joined the studio at seventeen she already had a baby of her own. In their new film, *Shanghai Dreams*, Lan played an optimistic student, enjoying the educational rights bestowed to women and indulging in talk of democracy and modernisation with serious, bespectacled boys. It was a small part, suitable for a young actress starting out. And she would never steal attention from Feifei's brave and sometimes hysterical prostitute.

'Do you have any advice for me?' Lan asked, her voice keen. Feifei touched the girl's shoulder tenderly.

'Just do the best you can. Become your character, that's the trick. There is no division between you and the person you play,' she said. Director Xu nodded approvingly.

'Yes, good advice, Feifei. I told her she should go to the teahouses and watch the students and intellectuals. That way she can become one of them.' He ordered another pot of tea and Feifei watched the young girl piercing her dumplings and sucking the soupy liquid out of them, trails of broth trickling down her chin. She had a while to go before she would become a real contender, Feifei thought, taking a bit of nasty pleasure from the realisation.

'I must leave now,' she said, folding her napkin and standing up. 'Thank you for lunch, Director Xu.'

'Stay out of trouble,' he said, with a forced laugh, patting her arm as she made her way out.

Julia, full from an American lunch at the new brasserie near the magazine's office, arranged her notes for the interview. *New Woman* only occupied a tiny room in Frenchtown so she had arranged to meet Feifei at the bar of the Metropole Hotel. The luxurious hotel, finished just the year before, would project a better image of *New Woman* than the tiny room the writers worked in. Julia liked the imposing building, the way its storeys crawled closer to the sky to reach a neat point, like the buildings in New York. A Chinese writer from the magazine, Suping, had come to assist with translation if Julia's Shanghainese faltered.

'I like Wu Feifei,' Suping said thoughtfully, biting her always loose hang nail. They were waiting for Feifei at the bar, Julia sipping a martini, Suping with a gleaming Coca-Cola. 'But did you see what it said in the newspaper this morning? That she is having private meetings in a coffee house? I think she's becoming vulgar.'

'No, she's having English lessons,' Julia said, shaking her head. 'I'm sure that's what it's about. She's just trying to improve herself.'

'Keep herself relevant, more like, and compete with her husband and all his scandals. He's out with someone different every week. Do you think she's a suitable cover girl for us, really?'

'There are a lot of people less prudish than you in Shanghai, thank God,' Julia said, wondering if it had been a good idea to bring Suping to the interview. But as a twenty-one year-old girl from Shanghai, Suping was the magazine's target market. She was a little serious though, preferring to write only about politics and failing to see that pretty faces sold magazines. They both looked up as Feifei crossed the bar towards them. Sheathed in a light pink *qipao* with a white fur stole tossed casually over her shoulder, she waved to them, seemingly unaware that the bar had stilled, patrons abandoning conversation to drink in the beauty and fame she trailed after her.

'Hello!' She sat down, a practised smile on her face. 'Sorry I'm late.' Even Suping was impressed by Feifei in person. There was something about her perfectly put together face that hushed every audience.

After Feifei had ordered a drink she started to tell them about her new film.

'We realise,' she said, eager and seemingly unrehearsed, 'that many Chinese people are suffering as a result of Japanese aggression in our country and we want to reflect that reality. We believe cinema should not only be a source of entertainment but also of information. And most importantly, hope. This film will break your heart,' she paused and her two interviewers nodded encouragingly, 'but we also want you to leave the cinema full of inspiration.'

'We should quote that on the cover,' Suping said.

'Am I on the cover?' Feifei clasped her hands together joyfully and flashed two neat rows of teeth. 'They'll be so pleased at the studio.'

'Of course you are. Now, tell me, right now ninety percent of films consumed in Shanghai come from Hollywood. Does Chinese film matter?' Julia wanted to push Feifei, to interview her in her trademark tough but fair American way, though she too was falling under the spell of Feifei in the flesh.

'Of course it does. We love Hollywood films. I watch them all the time too. We have a lot to learn from them and we can thank the wonderful Antonio Ramos for building all these cinemas and bringing these movies to us! But we are not here just to imitate but also to build an art form. I believe we Chinese are the best storytellers in the world.' Feifei smiled readily.

'There's a new actress in town now, isn't there?' Suping said, glancing down at notes she had prepared. 'I wanted to ask you about Song Lan, the girl from Beijing. They say she had already established herself in the theatre there and now she's here for the silver screen. What is it like to work with her?'

'Wonderful,' Feifei said, her lips drawing tight. Julia turned to Suping and told her to return to the office and transcribe the interview. The Chinese girl obeyed, one eye on Feifei as she left the hotel.

'Thank you for the interview,' Julia said. 'How are your English lessons going?' she asked carefully.

'English lessons?'

'At the Cathay you told me Will was teaching you English.'

'Oh, yes, very well. Though I am a terrible student,' she said. 'If I may take you into my confidence,' she added, in the voice of a smooth operator used to the vagaries of the press, 'I was more or less illiterate before. My husband taught me to read. But in Chinese I already knew how the words sounded. In English it is doubly hard.'

'I can imagine,' Julia said. She had no idea if Feifei was having an affair with Will. The actress possessed all the tricks of a seasoned interviewee, offering up common knowledge about her illiteracy in exchange for silence on the lessons or affair or whatever was going on. 'And is Will a good teacher?' Julia tried.

'Will is a wonderful man,' Feifei said softly. 'We get on very well. His Chinese is impeccable and he has a lot of patience with me. We're friends too, I would say.'

'Is that who you were meeting in the coffee house?' Julia asked. Feifei looked behind her, the paranoid hallmark of celebrity.

'This is not for printing, but yes. People think there might be something ... untoward going on. But if there was, wouldn't we meet in a hotel? Shanghai is full of people having ... affairs. Oh, I've spoken too frankly.' She sighed. 'Sometimes it gets to me, though, all the moralising here when we know what most people get up to at night.' She fingered the tablecloth in front of her, her face set in a frown. Suddenly she looked up brightly.

'Say, Julia, you're American. Do you know anybody here related to Hollywood? I'd like to learn more about the industry. As we've just been saying, we Chinese have a lot to learn from America.'

'I'm sure I can find someone. We Americans like to stick together. Let me think about it. I'll be in touch about the photographs too. When are you free to shoot the cover?'

Watching Feifei leave, Julia asked for the bill. She realised that despite herself, she was quite charmed by the actress. Whatever Suping said, Feifei was the ideal model for the cover of *New Woman*.

Feifei took a cab outside the hotel, feeling happy with how the interview had gone. Yes, the young girl had been a bit difficult – and did everyone always have to mention Song Lan? – but the write-up would be good, and Director Xu would be pleased. Stepping out of the cab at home, one elegant foot after the other, she suddenly thought of Will. She wondered if he would be angry that she had stood him up, if he had seen what was written in the newspaper. She pushed open the door and met her husband's eyes. He was sitting at the bottom of the staircase in a navy three-piece suit, Lili balanced on his lap.

'Hello, darling,' he said. 'I'm home.'

'So I see,' she said, smiling uneasily. 'Isn't that wonderful, Lili? Daddy's home.' Lili nodded and planted a noisy kiss on her father's cheek. 'Now, why don't you run upstairs and play?' Feifei knew Longwei was there for a reason. The little girl's chubby legs scampered up the stairs leaving the two of them alone.

'I have something for you.' He produced a box from his pocket. Feifei opened it carefully. Inside was an emerald set in a bed of diamonds. 'I've had a bit of luck this week.'

'It's beautiful,' she said, breathily, just the way she knew he would like. 'But darling, we could have put this money towards something other than a ring. Something less – frivolous?'

'It's not frivolous. It's beautiful, like my wife. I don't want anyone to forget you're married to me.' His mouth was set in a firm line, and Feifei understood. She slid the ring onto her middle finger.

'Thank you, darling.' She followed her husband through to the lounge where he opened the drinks cabinet and poured himself a whisky. Dusk was setting in and the clouds in the sky had turned pink. Feifei lowered herself into an armchair, watching Longwei. Their marriage was one of silence and tactics. There would be no head-on confrontation. She played with the ring on her finger, feeling a sudden uncomfortable envy for the youth and promise of Song Lan.

Amelia tried not to betray her shock at Tamara's quarters. The dancer lived in a damp apartment above a bookshop on Avenue Joffre. The Russians had established a tiny colony in this corner of the French Concession, where shop windows spelled in Cyrillic boasted of fur coats and sugar-coated pastries. Paint fell off the walls in big, greasy lumps and Tamara's bed was tucked into a dark corner. The sad little space didn't seem right for a dancer – Tamara's limbs seemed too long for its tight dimensions. She had scattered evidence of another life around the flat – faded photographs of a smiling family, an imposing man in uniform and most heartbreakingly, three portraits of Tamara on stage.

'Not quite your Spanish villa, I know,' Tamara said and Amelia was once again struck by how Tamara always seemed to see right through her. 'I'll just be a minute.' She slapped lipstick the colour of blood across her mouth and tugged her bun tighter. 'I'm impressed you're really going through with this,' Tamara said, slipping her feet into dainty ballet slippers. Amelia smiled at this. That was love for something – soaking your toes in Shanghai's filth just to be true to the person you once were.

'Of course,' Amelia said, her jaw clenching. She hadn't told Tamara about the day she'd had. After leaving Julia's office she had stormed through the International Settlement, each footstep growing harder and angrier, but with no direction in mind. Through a blur of hot tears she was blind to the beggars, the Shanghai ladies, the aggressive carriage pullers. She soon found she had circled her house three or four times but couldn't bring herself to go back. When she finally returned she spent the afternoon in bone-cracking stretches, straining her muscles to find the dancer zipped up inside her skin. It was the only thing that calmed her body and sedated her mind.

Tamara led Amelia down the dirty stairwell. Harsh Russian sounds emanated from the pockmarked walls around Tamara's flat.

'I really wanted to live by myself,' she said by way of explanation as they reached the front door. 'I know this place isn't ideal but I couldn't face sharing with other people, especially as the only people I could share with were other White Russians, each with a story sadder than the last.'

'Did you come alone from Russia?' Amelia asked. Tamara

opened the door to the street and the last dust of the day trickled down on weak sunbeams.

'I came with my parents and my sister.'

'Oh.' Amelia regretted asking.

'Do you mind paying for a taxi? There have been stories about thieves outside the Harbin. We shouldn't walk there.' Amelia nodded her assent, letting Tamara continue with her story.

'My parents died on the way. My father was killed before we even made it out of Russia. My sister made it to Shanghai.'

'And you don't live with her?' They made for a taxi.

'She died too.' Tamara drew the conversation to an abrupt stop and they travelled to the Harbin without speaking.

The Harbin advertised itself with a flickering neon light. Amelia wasn't sure what the subtitle read in Chinese, but in English it said, 'Dancing. Cocktails. Jazz. Girls.' Her stomach churned when she read 'girls' advertised as another night-time commodity, something extra to be enjoyed after an aperitif. Inside the bar was dark, and Amelia was glad. She and Tamara were certainly unusual customers here. Every other patron was a man, it seemed, uncouth and sweating alcohol.

'Let's sit close to the front,' Tamara said. She ordered the pair a cocktail each and then surveyed the gaggle of dancing girls. There were a few Chinese women among them with scarred faces and sagging breasts.

'They've seen better days,' Tamara said, with the cold-heartedness of a farmer sizing up pigs. 'But only the roughest Chinese girls work here. Ones past their prime. The reason we're here is apparently there's a young Russian who doesn't know any better. Started working last week. Daddy's got no money so they're selling the family's young flesh to make ends meet. She'll eventually realise what her stock's worth in Shanghai, but I hope to catch her before she does.' Amelia nodded, beginning to feel nervous. Her skin crawled with perspiration. A sad-looking band tried to rouse jazz from their bones, but produced only discordant rhythms. Some men approached the girls for dances, and the women obliged with heavy eyes and loose limbs. Amelia watched the way they let the men bend them back, or thrust them forward, and unwillingly she thought of Will and the Chinese actress. The lights dimmed and a chorus line shuffled out to the front of the room. When the spotlights flicked back up the dancers, most of them white, strutted forward and back, covering crucial body parts with feathers. They fell away suddenly and a skinny girl came forward, fans coquettishly covering her breasts. She dropped them gently and the rabble in the Harbin rose to a satisfied roar. She stuck out a blushing behind encased in silk and scuttled off stage.

'There's our girl.' Tamara stood up with grim determination and made her way over to a Chinese man sitting in the corner with a stained shirt and a perky pot belly. Amelia strained to hear her. They were negotiating in Chinese. Tamara came back.

'We've got an hour of her time. Upstairs, now.'

Amelia followed Tamara up rotten wooden stairs. The upstairs of the club was like a run-down hotel, with weak lamps, puddles of sad damp and doors with long-broken hinges. Three girls, their lips and cheeks painted bright red and their hair teased into elaborate twists, sat on the stairs, breasts pushed up under their chins. Their eyes followed Amelia and Tamara all the way upstairs. Tamara knocked on one door and pushed it open.

'Valentina,' she started but the girl was already on her feet, shaking her head and wagging her finger. The girl, now draped in a dressing gown, shouted at Tamara, her eyes wild. Amelia took a step back, watching Tamara grab the girl's wrist and force her to sit down on the bed. The pitch of their conversation lowered, but Amelia felt Valentina's tone still unfriendly. They talked rapidly for ten minutes, then Valentina reached under the bed and produced a bottle of vodka. She drank some and then held it out to Amelia.

'Hey, English lady, you want some?' she said. Before Amelia could answer, Tamara had yanked the bottle out of the girl's spindly fingers. They spoke for another two minutes before Tamara rose slowly and gestured to Amelia to follow her out.

'Goodbye, ladies,' Valentina called out. A Chinese prostitute was waiting outside the room, looking guilty as though she had been eavesdropping.

'Have you finished with Valentina?' she asked, pouting. 'One of her regulars is here.'

'Yes,' Tamara said curtly. She did not turn to meet Amelia's eye until they were at the exit of the club.

'Well,' Tamara said. 'What do you think?'

'What happened up there?' Amelia asked. 'And why do you have this?' She pointed at the bottle of vodka tucked under Tamara's arm.

'We lose many girls to alcohol. Having witnessed this, I'm sure you can understand why they turn to drink.'

'Of course,' Amelia said, watching Tamara set the bottle down and light a cigarette, the blue lights of the club colouring half her face. 'Tamara, I would really like to help these girls. It's just terrible. What that Chinese girl said about a regular ...'

'I'm glad,' Tamara said, smoke curling between the two women. 'I wasn't sure you would last the night, but I was wrong. She was difficult, that Valentina. Lots of the girls are. They don't want pity, they pretend to be self-sufficient. But she used to dance in Russia and she's beautiful. I've persuaded her. She's coming tomorrow at ten.' Tamara glanced at her watch, which showed it was approaching eleven-thirty. 'Let's hope she isn't too busy tonight.'

Amelia opened the front door quietly, waving Tamara off in the taxi. The lights were all out. The servants must have already gone to bed. But where was Will? She stepped into the quiet darkness, feeling relief that he wasn't home yet. His shoes weren't neatly lined up by the door where they usually resided. She walked into the kitchen and took a long sip of cold tea, a drink introduced to her by the servants. The earlier cocktail had gone to her head a little. She tried to piece together the night. She was shocked by what she had seen, but also energised. She almost felt like dancing herself, and spread her toes across the floor and twisted her wrists in imitation of some of the girls she had seen tonight. The latch on the door suddenly sounded and she froze, ashamed. No longer was she safe in the darkness. Will crashed upstairs and she sat at the table, feeling fluttery. She heard heavy footsteps bring him back downstairs and he crashed into the kitchen.

'Amelia! What are you doing hiding here in the dark?'

She prayed he wouldn't see her clothes. She had not over-dressed for the Harbin, but she had still tried for a little glitz. After all, she and Tamara were meant to blend into their surroundings, not look like moralists out to ruin everyone's fun. She didn't answer him.

'Amelia!'

'Are you …?' She almost asked him but realised she wasn't ready for the truth.

'What?'

'I was out with a Russian ballet dancer. At the Harbin.'

'The Harbin? Jesus Christ, Amelia, you can't go to places like that.'

'I can go anywhere I like. Just as you can teach English to whomever you choose.' She was cold and solid on the outside, enjoying the secret warmth of the cocktail in her veins.

'I don't know what you're talking about. I've half a mind to slap you if you continue like this! You promise me you will never go to a place like that again. You're my wife and you're to go nowhere at night alone, do you understand me?' He pushed his face close to hers and she recoiled from the smell of alcohol.

'You're drunk. Go to bed,' she said. They stared at each other's faces illuminated by the silver of Shanghai's moon. Without a word he turned and went upstairs. Heart jumping, Amelia took another calming sip of tea, more determined than ever to carry on Tamara's work.

Amelia had risen early and was cheerily eating breakfast by the time Will made it downstairs.

'I don't have time to eat,' he said, gruffly, and picked up his hat.

'Have a wonderful day, dear,' Amelia said sweetly and he saw she wanted to pretend last night hadn't happened. He decided to play along for now, though he would not tolerate her going out with unknown Russians to dive bars.

'Thank you, darling.' He kissed her on the cheek and Qi waved him off without breakfast.

He took the brisk walk to work in big, leaping strides. How had everything turned against him in the space of a few short days? After Feifei failed to show up for their lunch meeting he had been counting every ticking minute as he waited for word from her. The first night he had gone out to eat with Rollo, hoping to take his mind off things. They went to a new French place on Bubbling Well Road called *Le Marais*. Rollo promised it was going to become the most fashionable place for at least the next month or so, and in hushed voices pointed out the captains of industry, spooks and celebrities dotted around the room. When they were tucking into their starters, Will saw Rollo's eyes grow wider.

'What? You look like you've seen a ghost.'

'A ghost of a marriage,' Rollo said grimly, nodding to the left. Will turned in his chair and saw Feifei, resplendent in an intricately patterned dress of swooping gulls and rising reeds being shown to a table. With her was a Chinese man he hadn't seen before, his hand on the small of her back. He wore two chunky gold rings on the hand that guided Feifei and his suit was cut so exactly it seemed moulded to his athletic body. Feifei's eyes drilled right through Will to the patterned pastel wallpaper behind him. As she settled down and placed her handbag on the table, he saw a glinting jewel on her finger and a simmering rage rose in his throat.

'Who's that?' he asked Rollo hoarsely.

'Her husband. Very unusual for them to be together.' Rollo shrugged and forked more food into his mouth. Will knew

Rollo found his connection with Feifei flimsy, the stuff of schoolboys and sad old men, but Will knew it was more. He lost his appetite, unable to drag his eyes away from her as she listened attentively to her husband with wide eyes, sometimes reaching across the table to touch his hand.

'Anyway, I wanted to talk to you about Manchuria. Will, for God's sake, focus. We could have a war brewing here and you're mooning over a film star. Can't you just go and watch Garbo films like everybody else?'

And so Will had returned to the Paradise the past few nights, hoping to see Feifei there but finding her stubbornly elusive.

The halls of the consulate ticked with the sounds of productivity when Will arrived at work – fingers gliding over typewriters, drawers opening and closing, the occasional scraping of a chair. But no one lingered with a cigarette, or chatted in the hallway, trying to avoid work for a few minutes more. The door to his office was already open when Will arrived. Ralph alone was sitting at his desk, hunched over it, his forehead resting on top of a pile of papers.

'Oh, Will,' he said, lifting his head. 'It's bad.' Will looked around the office. Everything looked normal. Tidier than usual, but normal.

'What's happened?'

Rollo tapped on the door.

'Good, you're here. Something important to discuss. Follow me.' Will obeyed, walking behind Rollo's authoritative steps until they reached a small office. Rollo pulled the door behind him and gestured to a seat.

'Are you going to tell me what's going on here?' Will asked, lowering himself into the chair.

'Harry MacDonald. Before I say more, is there anything you should tell us?'

'About Harry? No, nothing. Nothing at all. He's a good enough worker, doesn't go out of his way to be helpful but not bad. I've no complaints.'

'Will, he's been working for the Japanese. You know

they're crawling all over Shanghai, trying to get information on everything and everyone, hoping to expand their empire down here. He's a spy. He used his position in the translation department to gain access to all kinds of confidential documents. Not to mention the fact that the press reports, supposedly written by you, have suddenly become very relaxed about the Japanese presence in Shanghai, and sometimes go as far as to mention the improvements the Japanese have brought about in Manchuria. Did you have any idea this was going on?' Rollo was still standing, blocking the door with his wide shoulders. Will sank his head into his palms.

'Of course I didn't. I had no idea.'

'Yes, Will, it would appear you have little idea about anything these days. When you arrived I saw real potential in you, I imagined you as a leader one day. But you're so caught up with some Chinese harlot you can't even do your job properly. Harry MacDonald, would you believe it? You've put your career on the line for a reprobate like that.' Rollo paced back and forth, frustrated that the room was too small to contain his anger. He laughed harshly. 'So Harry obviously believes it. Believes the Japanese line that they're here to help their Asian brothers unite against Western colonial powers.' He shook his head. 'Little Harry.'

'Rollo, what the hell am I going to do?' Will thought of Amelia. How would he tell her this? His parents, his uncle, everyone. Shanghai was far away, but Will knew rumours could run thousands of miles if they were scandalous enough.

'I'll tell you what you're going to do, Will. You're going to leave this to me. I still have confidence in you. I can fix this. But I need you to make a promise to me.'

'Anything.'

'You need to give her up. Wu Feifei. You're not to see her anymore. From now on your only purpose in life is to come here and work. Do you understand? I can't protect someone I don't trust. You missed something this big because you're so caught up thinking about her. Not to mention you've been

highly indiscreet, which doesn't reflect well on any of us.'
Rollo looked solemn and Will rose to shake his hand.

'Do you think I'll keep my job?'

'I dare say you will. But they'll be watching your every move. You can't let something like this happen again, do you understand?'

'Rollo, how can I ever repay you for this?'

'You'll have a chance one day, old chap. Now, leave the consul-general to me.' They left the room and as he walked back to his office Will was aware of meaningful looks shot in his direction. Everything was crumbling around him.

No news was good news, Will supposed, grabbing his jacket at six p.m. Ralph had already left and no word of punishment or reprisal had come throughout the day. Rollo really must have taken care of it. He left the consulate, waving cheerily in the face of his colleagues' concern, dismissing all of them as vultures for misery. He decided to take a leisurely walk home, enjoying the last of the sun's rays. He walked down the Bund, realising suddenly that this lively strip of buildings had become if not a home, then at least something familiar and comforting to him over the past few months. Even the hawkers and the squealing street children were part of his everyday existence and he realised now Shanghai was something he didn't want to lose. He turned down Bubbling Well Road, heading for home, when he had a thought. He'd promised Rollo he would work hard and stay away from Feifei but he hadn't said he would never go out again, or have a drink. He deserved a little something after that long day, and the thought of Amelia's heavy silence in their Spanish villa weighed on his heart. He decided to go to the Paradise. The barmen there knew him well now, greeted him with warm smiles and offered meaningless compliments while he emptied his wallet. It took him a brisk fifteen minutes to get to the cabaret. Slipping inside, he took off his hat and inhaled the dusky melancholy of the white-suited band playing for the taxi dancers who wound round in lazy circles with the earliest clientele. Ordering a gin, he settled himself at the bar and watched. Could he really give up Feifei? It had been days now since they'd spoken and almost as long since he'd seen her with her husband. Her husband looked weasely, Will thought, not someone who could be trusted. But they had the appearance of a couple very much in love and it had to be admitted that there was something brilliant about the man's looks. Longwei had the energy of a young man glossed over with the calm of someone who has achieved everything they need to in life. Will still didn't understand what Feifei wanted from him. He knew now he should have taken the opportunity when he had it, a moment to whisper between grammar structures that he loved her. He bolted up in his chair. He loved her. It wasn't just the alcohol making him soft. He really did love her. And now she had gone. The Shanghai he had come to own, the job, the movie star, were dancing away from him, spinning flirtatiously out of his grasp. He ordered another drink, sinking further into melancholy.

'A dance, sir?' one of the bartenders suggested. If he had to give up Feifei, Will should at least be afforded a dance. So he stood up, shook his stiff limbs and ambled towards the girls. He saw the dark, intense-looking one from his first night, the girl who reminded him of Amelia. He bought a ticket and walked towards her. She accepted the dance gracefully, manoeuvring the two of them around the other dancers with expertise.

'I remember you,' she said. 'I saw you talking to Wu Feifei in here once. You know her?'

'Very well,' he replied with a sad smile.

'It was so exciting when she came in here!' the girl replied. Looking at her nonchalant beauty, Will suddenly felt a rage inside him. He wanted to feel the bounty of youth again, to be a master of joy.

'Do you offer anything apart from dancing?' he found himself asking, already feeling like he had left his body and been replaced by someone else.

'Follow me.' Lilya made frantic hand gestures to an older

lady in a corner of the room who nodded and held up fingers. Will followed the girl outside and down an alley, where through closed doors he could already hear the cries of commercial sex. He hesitated, but the girl stroked his arm and led him into one of the rooms. Mechanically, she took her clothes off and lay down on the bed. Will stopped, looking at her, and then turned away.

'Oh, come on.' She sat up and reached her arms around his waist. 'Is this your first time, sweetheart?'

He unbuckled his belt. Lilya smiled encouragingly, two fingers hooked on the waistband of his trousers.

'What's wrong? Something on your mind?'

'I've had a bad day.'

'Well, this is the best way to relax.' She helped him pull off his trousers. He looked at her pink skin, ribs threatening to puncture her soft, protective layer.

'No, no, I can't. I'm sorry.'

Lilya sighed heavily. 'Come on,' she said pulling him down onto the bed.

He twisted away from her. 'No, really, I'm sorry. I can't.'

Lilya rose, pulled on her dress and went to the door. Before opening it she turned to him and said with a sneer: 'I hope you know you're still paying.'

As soon as the door closed behind her, he vomited on the floor, wringing out the despair in his guts. He felt tears rise to his eyes in the little room, a trail of his cold vomit streaking the rotting wood. He hiccupped, feeling he might be sick again. That was close, he thought. He had almost lost himself.

V

Feifei found the sudden presence of her husband wearing. When she woke in the morning it was to see Longwei looking at her with heart-shaped eyes, when she came home in the evening it was to find him playing with Lili in the reception room. At night, he poured long drinks for her and asked about the new film, making sympathetic noises in response to her complaints about Song Lan. The fragile domesticity of their arrangement made Feifei's mother content, but Feifei's mind continued to race. Now Will was locked away from her, she realised he had become much more than just an introduction to Richard Cable. The way he looked at her, like a sheltered country boy exposed to a metropolitan beauty for the first time, made her realise he could function as an escape plan in his own right too.

One evening Longwei suggested they go to the casino together. This was no surprise to Feifei, who knew her husband's artifice as a family man wouldn't hold up for long. So she agreed, putting on one of her most sparkling dresses and wearing her hair swept to one side, curls tickling her shoulder.

When Longwei went out with Feifei he liked her to be a precious jewel, something to show off to others. She knew how to act – demure, adoring, the perfect little wife. They had done it millions of times, despite all of Shanghai having seen her play whores and rape victims on screen, her hair tossed and wild like an animal's fur. The Empire was three storeys tall, with each ascending level offering more privacy for gamblers. They started on the bottom floor, watching the dance show and drinking together, Longwei nodding solemnly to familiar faces around them.

'I don't want to talk business with you by my side,' he said to her, in a low voice that had once stirred her heart. 'You look so wonderful, I just want to be with you.' She reached for his hand and clasped it tight, her new ring grazing his skin.

After two cocktails they moved up to the third floor where Longwei joined a game of craps. Unneeded, Feifei hung around the sides of the room with the other wives and mistresses. Some gossiped with each other, listing complaints about department stores and domestic staff, while the others gazed into space, happy to endure a man's vice for a little respite at home.

A young Eurasian man rose from one of the tables and came over to introduce himself to Feifei.

'Miss Wu, I just wanted to tell you how much I love your work,' he said seriously.

'Oh thank you,' she said. He was childlike, with a rosy countenance. She extended her arm and he bent to kiss her hand.

'Your husband is a very lucky man,' he added.

'If you say so.' Feifei laughed politely, but she wanted the young man to leave her alone now. The other women were staring, she was hot again under the familiar burn of envy and resentment. He was only a boy, but out of all the glittering butterflies in the room, draped and dressed by the wealth of husbands, once again Feifei had been chosen as the centre for all attention.

'Although I suppose a woman as beautiful as you knows how many admirers she has. I've met a few of them myself,' the young man said.

'Oh no, really–' Feifei protested, aware two of the women had locked their heads together in jealous whispers.

'Harry MacDonald.' He thrust his slim fingers towards her and they shook hands.

'A pleasure, Mr MacDonald.'

'Not at all. Your husband is also a very interesting man. We've been enjoying his company immensely. We have some Japanese friends with us tonight.' The young man slipped back to the table and Feifei shifted uncomfortably in her chair. She saw Longwei order another drink and decided to go home.

He didn't return for two days. One night at the casino and he had reverted to the Longwei of the past. She could write the story herself – too many drinks, big losses, more games, a little recoup, a curvaceous dancer and more alcohol. Feifei was surprised at how angry she found herself at him, how much she resented his absence. Time and time again Longwei swooped back in and reminded her of when they had first fallen for each other, when she was the maid's daughter, practically mute, her only participation in the public life of the family the sweeping of the floors. He had pursued her, always with that same intensity in his eyes, the same promise of more. And she had relented. For almost ten years now they had been playing the same game. But Feifei was not the type to sit at home, licking reopened wounds. She phoned Will's office from the studio.

'Hello? Translation department,' a voice said in English.

'*Wei?* I would like to speak to Will please.'

'Speaking.'

'Will, can we start English lessons again? I'm so sorry about everything. I think, I think that maybe we should do it at my house. That way no one will see us.'

And so they made an arrangement that the next day at five

thirty, Will would go to Feifei's home and they would take up their grammar books and word lists again. Feifei hung up, lingering over the phone.

'You're learning English?' It was Song Lan, draped in expensive furs for a scene set in the frozen north. Feifei looked at the girl's impassive face, her neatly dimpled features so soft and sweet, and wanted to scream.

'Yes.'

'But why?'

'It's the language of the whole world, isn't it?' Feifei said coolly. 'I think it's important.'

'But you're a silent movie actress. You don't need to speak any language.'

Feifei flared with anger.

'Get out, Song Lan. What do you know? Get out.' Her voice trembled, betraying the lack of control she felt over everything around her. Song Lan bowed her head.

'I'm sorry, Miss Wu. I didn't mean to upset you. Perhaps we should all learn English.'

'Not a word of this to anyone, Song Lan, do you understand? What I do outside the studio is my business. Learn French if you want, it suits you better.' The young girl, looking wounded, turned on her heels and left the room. Feifei noticed her hand was still on the receiver.

Tamara was stretching when Amelia arrived at the studio, pulling her toes up towards her temples.

'You're late,' Tamara said.

'Well, you're still wearing your ballet clothes,' Amelia said, feigning a lightness she didn't feel. Will hadn't even come to bed last night, sleeping on the couch when he got back from wherever he had been. In the morning he had left without a word. Amelia had done nothing wrong, nothing that she could pinpoint, and she wondered if that was the problem. She was nothing to him now, just a faceless figure taking up space in his house.

'You look tired,' Tamara said and swung her leg back down

to the ground from the impossible height it had reached beside her head. 'Today's the big day. Every company needs a principal dancer and I've got my sights set on Polina. She's well-paid with much higher status than the other girls, she doesn't need to do this. So we need to be especially persuasive.'

They left the studio together, Tamara's steps long and graceful where Amelia felt hers short and clumsy. They cut through Frenchtown, Tamara blind to the stares the two of them drew, Amelia young and dewy, Tamara dry and imposing.

'Keep up, Amelia. I want to make sure she's still there. They're always sleeping, these girls. But it's almost eleven.'

'So she's a dancer too?'

'Polina?' Tamara dodged a rickshaw and looked back over her shoulder. 'No, no. She's a *hostess*.'

'What's a hostess?'

'My God, you really are an innocent, aren't you? Well, there are the taxi dancers, you know all about them now. Then there are the girls who don't dance with men, but entertain, you know, singers, chorus girls. And there are the girls that don't even get the dignity of dancing half-naked and just service men all day and all night.' Amelia winced. 'But Polina, well, Polina's another story. She's very beautiful. Started as a dancer, but that didn't last long. She's fluent in several languages, a well-educated girl. People just like to be near her. She runs a club now, greets the guests, makes sure they are all enjoying themselves, watches that the dancers don't steal from the customers.'

'That doesn't sound so bad.'

'No. But it's still precarious. You need a pretty face and a kind boss to maintain that kind of situation.'

They were close to the hubbub of the Bund when Tamara pointed at a sweeping mansion block in front of them. The entrance was grand, outlined with swirling metal vines and the busts of goddesses set in concrete. Tamara nodded her head at the porter.

'I'm Polina's aunt,' she said. 'She's expecting me.' Amelia

followed, admiring the sparkle of the marble and the gentle curve of the staircase.

'I didn't expect this. What a wonderful place to live,' she commented and Tamara nodded vigorously.

'That's what I mean. We're going to have to be very persuasive.' They knocked on a door on the second floor. No one opened it, but there were dim sounds from inside.

'Polina,' Tamara called, sounding warm and maternal, while her face was set in hard lines. She said something in Russian and the door creaked back.

'Hello?' The girl peering through the crack in the door was so perfect she looked painted. Her hair was an icy blonde falling below her shoulders, her eyes the blue of a winter sky. Her skin, which may once have been alabaster, retained some of its summer glow. Her body was slender, leading up to the gentle swell of her breasts, hidden by the drapes of a silk dress.

A rapid-fire conversation in Russian followed, with Amelia hanging onto every unintelligible word, her eyes swerving between the two women. Polina stood back and let them in.

'Now we'll speak in English,' she said to Amelia. 'I'm Polina.'

'Amelia Graves. A pleasure to meet you.' The three sat down around a glass table littered with books and magazines in Russian, English and Chinese.

'My goodness, you have this whole place to yourself?' Amelia couldn't help but ask, mentally comparing the huge apartment with its wide windows to Tamara's shabby lodgings.

'Yes. I'm very lucky,' Polina said, crossing her legs modestly. 'So, Tamara tells me you have something important to discuss with me?' Amelia cleared her throat.

'We're starting a ballet company. And we'd like you to be part of it. In fact, we were thinking of you for the principal dancer. A *prima ballerina*, if you will.'

'How did you know I danced ballet?' Polina asked.

'Lilya told me,' Tamara said.

'You know Lilya? Gosh, I haven't seen her for ... a few months, at least.' Polina shook her head, and Amelia understood from the expressions on the two women's faces that they were all to feel sorry for Lilya.

'Yes, she is part of the company already. She told me you were the best dancer in Shanghai, that you trained in Russia.' Tamara smiled broadly and even careful Polina had let a little smile cross her face.

'Yes. But I was young. We left before I could become a real professional. My sister, though, she danced in Moscow.'

'Don't worry, you're professional enough for us. We want to start rehearsing next week. Can you?' Tamara said.

'Oh ... I don't know if I can join your company. My contract with the club means I can't work elsewhere. I'm sorry.' Polina looked down at her hands, which she had crossed over one creamy thigh.

'I can't pay you right now,' Tamara said. 'Therefore it's not a job and it's not a problem. This is a big chance for you. Once the company is up and running you'll never have to go back to the club.'

Polina kept up her protestations but Tamara kept digging in further, unwilling to give up on the promise she saw in the blonde beauty. Amelia could understand her thinking. Polina had the face of a doll and the body of a ballerina. People would queue all the way down Bubbling Well Road to see her delicate feet jump in the air, her slim calves smack together as she leapt.

'Let me speak to someone about it,' Polina said, rising to indicate the conversation was over. 'And thank you for thinking of me.' She squeezed Tamara's hand and both women lingered over their goodbyes, which were tinged with mutual regret.

'He'll be jealous, I'm sure,' Tamara said after Polina shut the door behind them. 'We'll just have to cross our fingers that he likes the arts, or at least the idea of Polina taking a starring role somewhere other than his bed. A very demanding boss, if you understand what I mean.'

It was a short walk for the pair to the consul's house. Cordelia had been charming on the telephone and said Amelia and Tamara were most welcome to join her for lunch.

They ate in a mahogany dining room cluttered with antiques and paintings of rural idylls. Over soup, Cordelia made chit-chat about the consulate and Shanghai's social scene, musing on upcoming parties and rehashing gossip from soirées past. When the main course was served she cleared her throat and fixed her eyes on Amelia.

'So, tell me, my dear, why did you want to meet today?'

'Well,' Amelia started, suddenly feeling self-conscious. She should have told Will she was organising the meeting. But she never had a chance to tell him anything these days. 'Tamara and I are starting a ballet company.'

'I say!' Cordelia cut a sliver of meat and popped it in her mouth.

'Yes, it's a very special venture because we're looking to help some of Shanghai's less fortunate. Russian refugees, in fact. As you know, Russia has a long history of ballet and there are many accomplished Russian dancers in the city.'

'They're accomplished all right,' Cordelia said, dabbing her lips with a napkin.

'Well, we want to offer them an alternative. That's why we're doing this,' Amelia said.

'Do you mean to say that this company will be comprised of … taxi dancers?' Cordelia asked.

'They only work in the clubs because they have no other option,' Tamara said swiftly. 'I was saved by my art. My wish is for the other Russians to be saved by the beauty of ballet. Don't you think it's time Shanghai embraced something a little more artistically challenging than the foxtrot?' Amelia smiled to herself. Tamara had spoken beautifully, but Cordelia frowned.

'You have very noble intentions, I must say. But why are you telling *me* about this?'

'We need support from the community for this. We thought you might have some advice,' Amelia said. 'We would like to raise money. Perhaps our first show might be a benefit and it would be wonderful if you could encourage some of the international community to come along. We won't get anywhere without them. Ballet's not so alien to them and they like to go out and enjoy themselves. The Chinese don't know anything about ballet. Really, if you saw the conditions these poor Russians live and work in, you'd see it's just the kind of cause the international community should be willing to help.'

Cordelia rested her chin in her hands, mulling over Amelia's words.

'Does your husband know you're doing this?'

Amelia's stomach darted. 'Not exactly,' she admitted.

'Yes, well, I imagine after the pickle he's got himself in he'd like you to keep your head below the parapet.' Cordelia sniffed and then sat back in her chair. 'It's very enterprising of you, dear, but we already have several projects–'

'Pickle? What are you talking about?' Amelia's first thought was Feifei.

'The Japanese spy he had working under him. Very unfortunate incident. But these things can't be helped and he does seem determined to get back up and on with things. Oh, have you finished, my dear? I hope you've kept some room for pudding.'

The rest of the meal was like a sped-up film reel for Amelia. She was present, aware that words were being exchanged and pleasantries being had, but she understood nothing. Her husband was a foreign country. He had said nothing about a Japanese spy working for him or any kind of trouble at the consulate. And Cordelia didn't seem willing to help with the ballet. It had been a very bad idea to come back to this bastion of Britishness, this reminder of all Amelia hadn't liked about England. They left, Tamara waving cheerfully.

'What's wrong with you? You haven't said anything to the old bitch for the last half hour.'

'Didn't you hear what she said about my husband? I had no idea.'

Tamara reached out for Amelia's wrist, stroked it and then turned away.

'Nobody in Shanghai has any idea what their husbands are doing, darling. It's better that way.'

Feifei rushed home from the studio, giddy as she burst through the door, heels clattering.

'Ma, my English teacher is coming soon,' she called out. Her mother stood at the entrance to the kitchen, sour-faced, her belly sticking out defiantly.

'And your husband, when is he coming home?'

Feifei waved the question away. 'Why do you want him here anyway, Mama? He only upsets Lili. And me, not that you seem to care about that much. We're going to do the English lesson in the lounge. Can you ask them to make some tea? I'm going to get changed.'

Upstairs, Feifei considered taking off the heavy make-up from filming but saw her sparkling eyes and sensuous lips in the mirror and decided against it. She was embarrassed by her choice, which forced her to recognise she was seducing Will one way or another. She had no intention of touching him, she had never been intimate with anyone except Longwei, but she wanted to live in his mind, to occupy his every thought. It was a different sensation to what she had with Longwei. She changed her *qipao* for a more toned-down tunic and put on a pair of slippers to compensate for her painted face.

As she went downstairs, she heard the bell ring. He had arrived right on time. She opened the door slowly, anticipating his blond awkwardness, his English stiffness. He was as upright as ever, handsome in a tailored navy jacket.

'Hello,' he said in English.

'Hello,' she said back, leading him to the lounge where a pot of tea had been set out. Will's eyes wandered around her silk furnishings and dangling chandeliers and Feifei hoped he was impressed with the modern European style they had chosen for the house.

'I must apologise for my appearance,' she said softly. 'I had a long day filming and I wanted to be more comfortable for our lesson.'

'Nonsense,' Will said. Then looking dreamily out the window at the neatly manicured garden behind the house he recited:

'Since the whole empire appreciates beauty,
'How could Xi Shi stay at home?'

He paused, skipping some lines of the poem.

'None of the girls from the neighbouring homes'
'Could imitate her beauty, no matter how they arranged their faces.'

Feifei slipped into the modest laugh of those habituated to compliments.

'What a beautiful poem,' she said.

'Wang Wei wrote it. He's one of my favourite poets.' Will's complexion had turned pinkish, but Feifei wondered if it was from the hot tea rather than the sudden intimacy of the poem. 'Anyway, where were we last time? Future tense, I believe. Do you remember it?'

'I will,' Feifei said determinedly and Will laughed, though she didn't understand why her choice of words struck him as funny. 'You English with all your tenses. It's so troublesome.'

'Yes, it can be a bother. But let's look at *will* again.' Will pulled the grammar book out of his bag and placed it on the table between them. Feifei recited the sample sentences, stumbling over each letter. Her reading was poor, but she could imitate Will reasonably well, though her vowels were covered by a Chinese burr. He heard an unexpected chirrup as she read and spotted a bird in a beautiful golden cage in one corner of the room. She followed his gaze.

'My father kept birds and it just … reminds me of him.' There was such tenderness in her face he didn't know what to say and pressed on with the lesson.

'Now,' Will said. 'Tell me what you will do in the future.'

'I will go *Haolaiwu*. I will work actress. I will happy. I

will speak English.' Will clapped childishly, pleased with her progress.

'When will you go?' he asked her.

'I will go when can.'

'When *I* can,' he corrected gently. 'Excellent work, Feifei, you're doing so well.'

'Last days I have time. Husband not home,' she said, smiling over her beating heart. 'I happy study English. Also happy friends.'

'Happy to have friends?' She nodded uncertainly, noticing that Will was shifting his position in the stiff-backed arm chair. He leant across the space between them and she could taste his breath, milky, with a hint of the jasmine tea he had just drunk. Her throat pulled tight as a rope. In a split second, he had placed his lips on hers. Feifei felt her body go soft, the way it had done all those years ago with Longwei. When she felt these foreign lips upon hers, it reminded her of the first time her husband had kissed her, when she was just sixteen and her body had become numb and supple as he slipped an exploratory tongue past her teeth and then laid her down on his mother's best seat. Feifei let her body drift away from the moment now too, as Will increased the force with which he kissed her, opening her lips. She gasped and broke away, coming conscious to the moment. Will's lips were streaked red. She wiped them quickly.

'My husband, he doesn't like,' she said, feeling remorse. 'You go now.'

'No. Feifei, I can't go,' Will said in desperate English. He was aware of the moving shadows in this house, just like in his own. Other bodies, other ears, pressed into corners, seeing everything, saying nothing. 'I won't do it again. I just couldn't help it ... you're so beautiful. Let's just be friends. Please?' He grasped her hand, sending a shock through her body. She nodded warily. As much as she regretted it, she didn't want to see that navy jacket walking out the front door. Will was a lifeline to another existence, a life that didn't mean being a washed-up silent movie actress while Song Lan dominated Shanghai's theatres with her serene features and peach breasts.

'Let's study the negative future tense, then. I will. I won't.' The lesson lasted an hour and when Will rose to leave, tea leaves floating mournfully in his cup, he pressed his hands to Feifei's.

'I'm sorry. I shouldn't have done that. See you soon for another lesson?'

'Of course. Thursday? Same hour?' Feifei smiled reassuringly at him. 'I will do my homework, teacher!' She led Will to the door, her chest heavy when it closed behind him.

'Very young, your English teacher,' Mama spat from the kitchen. 'I suppose all the old lady teachers were already busy?'

'He's a translator at the consulate. He's very qualified.'

'Be careful with these foreigners, little Fei. You have no idea what you're dealing with.' Mama appeared in the hallway, her face as tired as her grey bun.

'Mama, I am not a child anymore! I'm learning English to keep a roof over all our heads. You have no idea what's going on at the studio. Some bitch from Beijing is threatening to take my position. What do you want us to do? Rely on Longwei? He'd have gambled the house away by now if I didn't have the money to pay his debts. I've done fine by us so far. I don't see why you need to start complaining now.' Feifei took a step back. Suddenly she felt ridiculous, her face painted like a doll and her clothes so casual. Her mother could probably see right through her, the coquettish actress flirting with her teacher.

'You would be nothing without Longwei, my dear.' Feifei's mother crossed her hands across her chest. 'Don't you dare act so ungrateful. Think of the sacrifices we have all made for your career. You finally get a bit more time off from the studio and what do you do? Learn English! What about Lili? Why don't you play with her?'

'I'm too old for games, Mama. I am too busy taking care of this family so my daughter can have a future. Excuse me, I am going to rest before dinner.' Feifei tore up the stairs, only then noticing Lili sitting halfway up them, sucking her thumb and holding a blonde-haired doll in her other hand.

'Mama,' she mewed softly, and Feifei scooped her up and took her to the bedroom. There she curved her body around the little girl as Lili cried softly.

'I'm sorry, I'm sorry,' Feifei said over and over again, though she wasn't sure who she was apologising to.

Julia stood outside the photographer's studio, drawing her coat tighter around her. The damp cool of a tropical winter was setting in. Every year she forgot how Shanghai turned, how it betrayed you with its humid chill. Feifei was late. Julia had Charles Rigg waiting for her inside. She wasn't sure if it had been the right thing to do. Feifei wanted to meet people from Hollywood but Julia wasn't sure why. All she knew was that she wanted to keep Feifei on side, to keep a connection to the China Star studio for the magazine. Charles Rigg also made Julia's skin crawl. She had met him at a party a couple of months ago. He worked for a film distribution company and was clearly well-fed on it. He was all jowls and paunch, his head almost entirely bald despite the fact he wasn't yet forty. But he still looked at women with the hunger of a good-looking young man.

Feifei hopped out of a taxi. Her face was bare and Julia felt the unusual sensation of jealousy rise through her. This woman was extraordinary. Even without any of the tools of deception of the actress, she was beautiful.

'You look like a movie star,' Julia said as Feifei reached her.

'So they tell me,' she said coolly.

Julia pulled the door open. 'Before we go in, I have a surprise for you. There's someone from Hollywood here.' Feifei stopped still, her eyelashes flickering nervously.

'Really?' A smile crept across her face.

'Really.' Julia placed her hand on the small of Feifei's back, pushing her through the door.

Charles Rigg was chatting amiably with the photographer, an old German, when Feifei descended the stairs to the studio, tugging at the white fur around her neck.

'Hello.' Julia was surprised that Feifei was speaking in English. The actress offered her hand to Charles, in the American style, and he pumped it up and down enthusiastically.

'A real pleasure to meet you, Miss Wu.' He bowed his head.

'Happy meet you,' she stammered. Those English lessons with Will must be going well, Julia thought. Feifei turned to Julia and admitted in Shanghainese that her English might not hold up. Julia told Charles, who shook his head.

'Not at all,' he said. 'I should be apologising – imagine living in China and not knowing Chinese!' He had been in China for just four months and he didn't know how long he would be expected to stay. Julia had the feeling that they weren't missing him too much in California.

The German positioned Feifei on a chair and photographed her in several different poses. Everyone agreed the best photograph would probably be Feifei looking flirtatiously over her shoulder, the silk of her *qipao* straining under her, her eyebrows questioning.

'What a remarkable woman,' Charles said to Julia as they watched Feifei drift through the poses.

'She should come out to Hollywood,' he added, watching Feifei laugh with the photographer between takes.

'Oh, please, Charles. She's beautiful but she could hardly star in a Hollywood film.'

'Of course she could,' he said, his voice distant as he watched Feifei.

'Well, in that case, things have changed a lot since I was in America.'

After the shoot Julia walked back to the *New Woman* office, Charles and Feifei trailing behind her, speaking in pidgin English, Charles' laugh booming. She left them by the corner of Avenue Joffre and went upstairs to the office.

'There's someone here to see you,' Suping said, glancing up as Julia entered the cramped room. She saw Amelia sitting in the corner, peering at a stack of past issues.

'Amelia!' Julia called out, but she felt guilty. She had been consorting with the enemy – the beautiful, smiling, fur-trimmed enemy.

'I need some advice,' Amelia said. Julia sat down opposite her, aware Suping was trying to hear their conversation. 'I'm sorry, it looks like you might be in the middle of something.'

'No, no we've just finished shooting Feifei for the cover.' Julia tried to control her voice, keep it neutral. She saw Amelia's lips tighten.

'Oh. I see.' She shook her head. 'Anyway, I went to see Cordelia about the ballet company. She didn't want to help at all. I don't think we can rely on her to rally the international community. If she's against us, we're on our own.'

'Well, there are plenty of less uptight types in Shanghai too. She was probably the worst person to try to win over,' Julia said with a shrug.

'I just really want this to be a success. Finally, I have some purpose. I am just so happy to be involved with dance again. And Julia, you have no idea how these girls live. I want to help.'

'Why don't you write a piece about it for the magazine?'

'What?'

'An article. Lots of *New Woman* readers would probably support this kind of thing. I know the Chinese are mostly ignorant about ballet, but the Chinese who read our magazine like to embrace foreign things. That should secure some support.'

'But I can't write,' Amelia said lamely.

'Don't be silly, Amelia.' Julia stood up. 'It's decided. I think it'll be a very interesting piece. Maybe we could even interview some of the girls. When is the first performance?'

'Not for a couple of months, at least. Tamara needs to train everyone properly and we have some new girls. We're aiming for January.'

'Perfect! Something of a pick-me-up after Christmas. Let's run it in the December issue. You had better get writing.'

'Oh, thank you,' Amelia said. 'I knew you would know what to do.' She suggested they get some lunch together, but Julia declined. She was meeting Ju Wei at home.

Julia and Ju Wei's relationship was so public it couldn't even be called an open secret. She often ate with his family, played with his children and joined his cousins for days out in the country. His wife, a small, bird-like woman, seemed to genuinely like Julia and never caused a fuss when she came to the house. In the beginning Julia had only been conducting a sincerely platonic relationship with Ju Wei, but while things had changed between the pair of them, nothing ever shifted in her relationship with the family. She was always welcome to drink tea in their airy drawing room or to read stories in English to the children before they slept.

But today something was different. The servant who opened the door didn't meet her eye. Instead, he led her silently to the dining room, where Ju Wei sat quietly, his wife beside him. Seeing Julia, she rose and left, giving Ju Wei a meaningful look.

'Julia, please sit.' Julia sat down opposite him, feeling hard and uncomfortable. There was none of the usual laughter, the lightness of atmosphere she always felt in the Ju household. She focused on the dust catching the light in the air to avoid his gaze. Another servant came through and placed a plate of chicken before each of them.

'We must talk.' Although Ju Wei's English was excellent he usually spoke to Julia in Chinese. His choice of English suggested he didn't want the other members of the household to understand what was going on.

'What's wrong, Ju Wei?' Julia didn't touch her chicken, fear suddenly seizing her stomach.

'My wife.' He paused, and took a shallow sigh. 'My wife is not happy about the nature of our relations.'

'You and me?'

'Yes. She is embarrassed that I am ... *involved* ... with a foreigner. She has given me an *ultimatum*.' He took so much pleasure over this word that Julia suspected he might have looked it up in the dictionary with their meeting in mind.

'An ultimatum?' Julia felt her skin turn cold. Ju Wei couldn't leave his wife for her. That was why she had chosen a married man, so she wouldn't be trapped, cosseted into a monogamous, dull existence as someone's little woman. 'You can't leave your wife,' she blurted out.

'I have no intention of leaving my wife,' he said calmly. 'That is not the ultimatum. You see, here in China, we don't have to choose one woman over the other, as I'm sure you're aware. You Westerners pretend that love is forever while seeking pleasure elsewhere. In China, we have a very efficient system of concubinage.'

'Concubines? What are you talking about, Ju Wei?'

'She wants me to stop seeing you or to make the relationship official. You can become my second wife.'

'I refuse! A concubine is even worse than a wife!' Julia picked up the chopsticks on the table and pierced the chicken's frail skin. 'Is this a joke?'

'Not at all. There are many benefits to being a second wife. For example, you will be recognised as a wife under Chinese law and protected in case something happens to me. You can't be alone forever, can you?' Ju Wei was stately in everything he said, measured as though he had practised these words. Julia didn't recognise him.

'This is outrageous. You must know this goes against everything I believe in.'

'In that case, we will end our relations today. It will pain me, but if that is the only option, it is what we must do.' Julia felt Shanghai draining away from her, the existence she had built around Ju Wei fading and blurring.

'I can't not see you,' she said quietly.

'Well, you understand the situation. Why don't you take some time to think about it?' Ju Wei raised his tea cup to his lips, taking a noisy sip. Julia couldn't believe how calm he was. Inside he was churning, she was sure, but the big presence of his wife filled the room. They finished the meal in silence, Julia chewing loudly to express annoyance. Clearing the plate, she rose, pushed her chair into the table and met his eyes haughtily.

'I will be in touch,' she said, and turning on her heels she hoped he hadn't seen her mouth quivering in preparation for ugly sobs.

VI

They had a dance company of sorts. In total there were twelve performers, including Amelia. The other dancers were all Russian, with the exception of Plum, a gifted Chinese dancer discovered by Tamara. With a dozen dancers, preparations were to begin in earnest for the Shanghai Ballet's first show, which Tamara had provisionally scheduled for January.

It was the first Monday rehearsal that would bring them all together and Amelia was already dressed in her dance clothes, eating a boiled egg, when Will appeared at the foot of the stairs.

'Amelia,' he called.

'I'm here,' she said. 'Won't you join me for breakfast? Today is the first rehearsal we'll have together. Tamara's –'

'You're not going,' Will interrupted her icily, walking into the room.

'Don't be silly, darling. I can't stay at home all day with nothing do. Besides, you know I adore ballet.'

'You're an embarrassment to me,' he said, his voice

growing louder. 'I've heard all about your little project, spending your time with common whores! You are not to go.'

'You can't forbid me, Will. What's happened to you? I'm here in Shanghai for you. Please just let me have this one thing.' But she was watching his back, watching him slip away from her.

'If I come home this evening and find you have gone anywhere near that Russian and her coterie of whores, there will be trouble,' he said over his shoulder.

She heard the door close behind him. It was too late to turn back now. She would go. She couldn't let Tamara down.

Polina was already there when Amelia arrived, practising tiny *pliés*, her eyes focused on the mirror. Amelia smiled to herself that despite her protestations, Polina had come. The other girls trailed in, all alike in their skinniness though their faces differed. Some had weathered the lifestyle better than others, she thought, looking in particular at Lilya's weak frame. Valentina, the girl they had visited at the Harbin, was there too, her posture challenging as the girls lined up at the barre. The presence of Polina, with her expensive leotard and natural poise, had led to a shift in atmosphere. When they were all assembled Tamara clapped her hands.

'It is ten-fifteen. I will not tolerate lateness.'

'Speak in Russian,' Lilya moaned, her voice thick with yesterday's alcohol.

'I will not. We have Plum and Amelia here and they are as much members of the company as you are. This is not only for Russians.' She paced up and down in front of the girls, her small frame suddenly menacing. 'Take a look around you. This is the Shanghai Ballet. I am taking a chance on you girls. I told you we would meet four days a week at ten a.m. and that I expected everything from you. My hope is to make you professionals but for that to happen, everyone must do their bit. That includes arriving on time. Right, let's welcome our new dancers, Polina and Plum, and start with the basic positions.'

101

It was clear the new girls were used to dancing, the way they arranged themselves so easily into first, second, third, fourth and fifth positions. When Amelia took first position she felt a little thrill run through her as usual, enjoying the sensation of her feet sticking out at opposing angles, her legs turning out neatly from her hips. It was immediately obvious that Polina had received far superior training to the other girls. Her movements were fluid, her arm arcs of light, soft and elegant. Amelia watched her, trying to imitate her ease. She wondered if Polina practised alone at home, if she ever thought of who she should have been.

'You're all too stiff,' Tamara barked at one point, hitting Lilya's leg. 'I need grace, I need movement. Stop.' She turned to the piano player and held up a hand. 'You're all dancers. So let's just dance. Forget ballet. Just dance.' The old pianist played a popular Chinese number that was doing the rounds in all the cabarets at the time. The beats were fast as bullets and the dancers, shrugging away their embarrassment, moved away from the barre and let their feet run to catch the counts. They were spinning and twisting and rocking, sometimes brushing against each other. Amelia stood frozen, watching how they swung their bodies with ease, and then felt herself stepping into the fray. Some of the girls were bumping into each other, the room was so small, and laughter bubbled through the air. Amelia found it infectious and suddenly she was laughing too, and they were all dancing crazily around the room, giggles almost turning to tears. Tamara clapped and they all stood still. The piano stopped abruptly. Amelia waited for Tamara to reprimand them but instead she smiled.

'That,' she said slowly, 'is what I need from you in ballet. Energy, emotion. Let's go through the positions again.' The girls, limbs still shaking with laughter, took their places, the ice between them melted by the music they could all dance to.

The room filled with the classical overtures of ballet and Amelia felt something shift in her. As she lifted her leg in a *ronde de jambe en l'air* and stretched her fingers high above her head she realised she was herself again – a girl she had packed away in a box in London, hidden in the attic of her family home, a girl that once dreamed of nights at the ballet and a marriage built on laughter and trust. Will's morning threat was forgotten, it passed to a deeper layer inside her as a former Amelia rose to the surface. They practised for two hours, sweat gathering under their ribcages. Amelia saw in the eyes of the other girls a certain glint that hinted they felt the way she did, that they had discovered the secret selves buried deep inside their bodies.

Towards the end of the class, Tamara whispered something to the old piano player, who stood up and left the girls to stretch in silence. They sat down, legs wide apart, their fingers reaching across the floor in front of them. Polina was flat on the ground, like the worshippers Amelia had sometimes spotted through the dust clouds of the Buddhist temple. The other girls looked on in envy, willing their spines to become supple like hers. The pianist came through the door, a wide smile on her face.

'*Vatrushka!*' Tamara called out and the girls clapped as she placed the round buns on the floor. Scampering out of their splits all but Amelia and Polina grabbed for chunks of the sweet discs. Polina reached her arm into the scrum and the other girls stopped grabbing and instead looked up at her in jealous silence, watching as she delicately broke off half of one bun and handed it to Amelia.

'It's got jam inside,' she said, her English arch and correct. 'A preferred Russian snack.' The graceful ballet girls of ten minutes ago had gone. Now the Russians were back to being taxi dancers, their foreign words boisterous, their teeth sinking into the buns. Tamara watched them, a maternal light in her face that surprised Amelia. Feeling left out, she rose to leave and was surprised when Polina followed her.

'They can be a little unfriendly,' she said quietly. 'Don't worry. It's not personal – one day not so long ago they thought they would end up a lady like you. It's very hard for them to accept their fate. I can teach you some Russian if it would help you feel more at ease around them.'

'Oh, there's no problem. I'm just glad to be back to ballet.'

'I can tell you've trained too. You've got talent,' Polina said. 'Well, I'll see you tomorrow.' She disappeared down the stairs to the midday bustle of Frenchtown. Amelia wrapped her arms around her, feeling a little less alone. The Shanghai Ballet was real.

Feifei couldn't help herself smiling these days. Of course, Longwei was once again missing, but that didn't bother her. She heard on the circuit that he was working hard, and she knew that meant he was also playing hard. But her stars were aligning. She had Charles Rigg now. Of course, he was a fat little man, an American who believed he was far more important than he was, but he worked for a Hollywood company. Feifei had seen him once since the photoshoot. Infatuated, he had invited her for dinner at *Le Marais* and she had choked down the heavy French food while he regaled her with tales she only half understood. But that didn't matter, because she could tell all he wanted was to look into her eyes and dream her a goddess rather than a woman. Feifei had been in this position so many times she knew how to make it easy for the admirer, how to smile just so and dab the corners of her mouth with a napkin, each action at once genteel and unabashedly erotic. He had brought another friend from his company to the dinner and although Feifei hadn't quite understood the man's position, she had smiled along to his stories too. She told them about the film she was working on, her role as the prostitute that sacrifices it all and the cheerful patriotism that ran through the movie.

'Fascinating,' Charles said, leaning over the table towards her. 'In America, people go to the movies to escape politics, to escape war. In China you hold the mirror up to reality and face it head-on. Admirable, I would say.'

'The Japanese,' Feifei said slowly, carefully, enunciating each word the way Will had taught her, 'have *ravaged* the

north of our country. It is our *duty* as artists to show that.'
Will had been through this phrase with her twenty times, not
understanding why it was so important for her to learn. For
some reason, she hadn't told him about Charles Rigg yet.

As well as the promising dinner with Charles, there was
the film, which was progressing well. Song Lan's part had
been expanded to give her more screen-time but Feifei knew
she would still be the shining star at the centre of what was
sure to be a hit. How could people not love a story that saw
justice meted out to those Japanese bandits? And then there
was Will. Dear Will, who sat opposite her in the lounge, his
hand shaking when he poured her tea, his eyes desperate and
wanting. Sometimes Feifei felt that she was cruel, that she
was playing with him. But she was learning. And there was
something else about him that she couldn't let go of. His gentleness, his love for poetry, his neat blond hair. His fascina-
tion with her was enduring. It seemed to go beyond the fun of
flirtation with a film star. Feifei had never had the luxury of
choosing a man, Longwei had taken that option away when
he laid her down on the chaise and planted Lili inside her, but
if she had been able to select someone herself, she might have
chosen someone like Will.

On Thursday evening Will came over at seven p.m., his
face drawn and serious.

'What's the matter?' she asked in Chinese, leading him to
the lounge.

'Work,' he said. 'It's nothing.'

'Tell me.' She poured tea for him this time, watching the
leaves settle at the bottom of the cup. 'I want to help.'

'We lost someone from the department earlier this month.
A Eurasian chap called Harry MacDonald. He was secretly
working for the Japanese. I almost lost my job.' He sank his
head into his hands, avoiding Feifei's careful gaze after his
admission. 'Now the work is just piling up and I'm worried
I'm not doing a good job. I don't want to go back to England
with my tail between my legs. And my wife–' Feifei gulped
at this first open recognition of his wife, '– she's a stranger.

Running around with whores from cabarets, learning *ballet* of all things. I honestly don't know what's to become of us. She's unhappy too. We simply weren't made for one another.' Feifei took a deep breath. She didn't know how to respond to his candid confession. She was unhappy with Longwei too, lonely and frustrated. But at the same time there was freedom in an unloving relationship.

'Many of us are in unhappy marriages,' she said, close to whispering. 'But that's the way of the world. You have to do what you can.'

'She came all the way to Shanghai for me.'

'Yes,' Feifei said, feeling a strange haziness fall over her. 'Remember that. Remember what she did for you.' She reached out for his hand and gently stroked his fingers. He smiled at her, a smile of regret and lost possibilities. That name he had said, Harry MacDonald, was strangely familiar to her.

'So, today we're going to look at the conditional, aren't we?' He turned business-like and Feifei nodded. She was not paying Will for these classes and sometimes she wondered if she should. But she saw now in his soft vulnerability that he would be there whatever. The best thing for now would be not to tell him about Charles Rigg, she decided.

Around ten p.m., when Feifei was removing her make-up and getting ready for bed, she heard the door slam and Longwei clatter into the hall.

'My wife!' he called from downstairs. Drunk. Thinking of Lili, Feifei leapt up, her face half-painted, and scampered down the stairs.

'Longwei, you're home,' she said softly. He looked like the young man of all those years ago, a boyish grin on his face, a stray hair tickling his forehead, a smart suit outlining his trim figure.

'I have something for you,' he said, pulling a box from behind his back.

'Oh,' Feifei said, fingering the box. It looked expensive.

She eased it open to find a long chain of emeralds, a dazzling necklace that must have cost a fortune. 'Longwei, you shouldn't have! Did you have a big win at the casino?'

'No, my darling.' He grabbed her waist and kissed her, and she found herself guiltily thinking of Will doing the same thing. He pulled away, evaluating her with fresh eyes. 'Business is going very well. I've made some new contacts who are trying to make inroads into Shanghai. They appreciate my connections and are paying me quite handsomely.'

'Oh, I'm pleased,' Feifei said, embracing him, and wondering for the thousandth time if perhaps this could work, if maybe Longwei could hold down a job, if his family might take them back into the fold, if someone other than her would be the guardian of Lili's future. Then it came to her. Harry MacDonald. She stepped back. 'Japanese,' she said. 'You're working for the Japanese.' He looked at her coldly.

'What makes you say that?'

'Harry MacDonald. The man from the casino – those are your new business contacts, aren't they?'

'Yes, I'm helping some Japanese. They're doing a lot for Shanghai.'

'But Longwei, you *can't*. They're raping and pillaging all over the country! People will call you a traitor.'

'So you don't like the necklace.'

'It's nothing to do with the necklace. The necklace is beautiful.' Feifei felt stung. How could her husband work for the Japanese? Better to live in noble poverty than rich serfdom to an evil people.

'I'm helping Chinese people,' he said. 'At least the Japanese are able to give them jobs, unlike the bloody British. What have they ever done for us?' He shook his head. 'The world is changing, my darling Fei, we are going to become a united race. Asian brothers together. Forget these distinctions, Chinese, Japanese. We're all one.'

'Don't you read the newspaper?' She looked again at the necklace, accusing in its sparkle.

'Imperialist propaganda from those British pigs. You have to meet them for yourself,' Longwei said. 'We'll have dinner with some of my Japanese colleagues this weekend.'

'I refuse.'

'You are my wife. And you will not refuse. I'm going to bed now and I expect you to join me.'

With heavy legs, Feifei climbed the stairs to their bedroom. While Longwei turned away from her to undress she eased open the bedside drawer and saw the promising eyes of Anna May Wong looking up at her. She had to get to Hollywood. She lay down to dream of America, her thoughts mixed with pictures of Will's wife dancing ballet with Russian prostitutes and his sadness, like a crack in precious porcelain, that afternoon. Longwei leant over to kiss her and she breathed in the alcohol on his breath, found herself wondering if it was sake.

Will walked back from Feifei's house, his heart lightened a little by her kind words. But what he had told her was true. He felt everything slipping away from him. This damned city really was the whore of the Orient, part promising temptress, part unrepentant destroyer. Work was piling up in the translation department and Will soon realised that Harry, with the goal of siphoning off information for the Japanese, had been an extremely efficient translator. He needed someone else in the office but there was no way to ask. After the Harry fiasco, the Chinese freelancers were all being thoroughly vetted and there was no one to help. Harry had been employed before Will arrived in Shanghai, alleviating him of most of the blame, but he still felt silently accused by his stern higher-ups.

Rollo took him for lunch the day after he had exposed his sadness to Feifei.

'You've taken a hard knock, but it's time you got back on your feet,' Rollo said to him. 'Tell me what you're reading about the Japanese. How concerned should we be?'

'The Japanese are further entrenching their position in Manchuria. The local warlords, hard as they try, are powerless to stop them. There's resistance but I fear the Chinese aren't much up to it.'

Rollo nodded. 'Interesting. And do you think they have plans to invade elsewhere?'

'I'm a translator, Rollo, not a spy. But I can't imagine all the Emperor wants is the frozen north, can you? Shanghai's the jewel in the Chinese crown.'

'There's hope for you yet, Graves. Let's order another round.'

Rollo was pleased with him again and that set Will at ease. He felt slightly guilty that he had broken their deal and was still seeing Feifei, but it wasn't affecting his work. No one would find out either, now that the visits were strictly domestic.

When their food arrived, Will noticed Rollo looking at him with a quizzical expression.

'I spoke to Lilya the other night,' Rollo said.

'Who?'

'Lilya. At the Paradise.' Will felt lunch protest in his stomach. He hadn't been to the Paradise since that night.

'Oh, right. One of the dancers?'

'Don't act so coy, Will. She's one of my favourites too. Amelia not keeping you happy at home?' Rollo laughed. 'She did always look a little … cold to me, shall we say.'

'Rollo, please, I –'

'Will, don't worry. Everybody does it. It's natural. She looks a little like your wife, anyway.'

'Things have been so strained between us,' Will said. 'Amelia's got these fanciful ideas about saving Russian dancers and she's learning ballet alongside a troupe of whores. I've tried to stop her but she doesn't listen and honestly, in some ways, it suits me better to have her out of the house, to have her come back exhausted, not able to argue with me.'

'Oh yes, I heard all about that. Cordelia's been entertaining all the ladies with details of Amelia's little project. A trifle embarrassing for you, I imagine, but as you say it gives you time alone. Time for girls like Lilya.'

'It was just one time. And I didn't –'

'It always starts as just one time.' Rollo drained his glass and smacked his lips together. 'I thought you and Amelia were a lovely couple though.'

'We were, we are, I don't know. She was so keen on me and she ... she just became part of my life. But Shanghai's opened my eyes.'

That evening, Will found Amelia in the parlour, her back hunched over the desk. She was writing furiously. He could see the curve of her spine sticking out from under the leotard she had taken to wearing around the house. He was always finding her stretching and spinning in some corner, her leg muscles growing harder by the day. She was losing the enthusiastic curves of the unmarried woman, ossifying into an unloved wife instead.

'Amelia, what are you doing?' She looked up, frightened to meet his eye. It made him feel terrible, to see how his wife had become afraid of him. He softened his tone. 'You're writing something.'

'It's nothing.' She put her pen down and placed her hand over the paper. Will could see the ink from her words leaking over her fingers. He calmly removed her hand to see what was underneath.

'Saving Shanghai's Russians – All You Need Is Art,' he read aloud. 'For the past month I have been involved in a very special project to save Shanghai's dancing girls from their dangerous and sometimes fatal destinies. White Russians – and one Chinese – from several Shanghai clubs are studying under the tutelage of–' He broke off. 'God damn it, Amelia! What is this?'

'Nothing.'

'Answer me! Since when did my own wife lie to me?' he barked at her, the collar of his shirt suddenly feeling uncomfortably tight.

'Since you didn't tell me you had a Japanese spy working

under you and you almost lost your job. Since you started coming home late every night. Since you tried to stop me from going to ballet when it's the only thing I have of my own. Since you started having an affair –'

'That's enough!' Will erupted, throwing his hands up in the air. He was momentarily distracted by what he thought were sniggers coming from the servants next door, but he brushed them away. 'Not another word from you. Are you intending to publish this ... this *article*, if that's what we're going to call it?'

'Yes.' Amelia stood up, pressing the paper to her chest. 'In *New Woman* magazine.'

'I forbid you, Amelia. You've become out of control since we got here. Where is the girl I knew back in England?'

'I'm standing right here,' she said slowly. 'But you – I don't even recognise you, Will.'

They stood silently, each taking in the other's flustered appearance, wondering who was right after all.

Will stormed upstairs, anger suffocating him. In his bedroom, he stamped around heavily, picking up books and throwing them on the floor for dramatic effect. Breathless, he sat on the edge of the bed and thought of Feifei, perhaps the only person he really knew in Shanghai. It would all be fine, if he could just see her again.

The next morning Will saw Amelia ready to leave the house, her practice clothes bundled into a bag, her hair pulled into a neat chignon.

'Where are you going?' he asked.

'You know where I'm going, Will. To ballet.'

'No you are not. You're staying at home. We have already had this conversation and you have continued to ignore my wishes. Under no circumstances will you dance again or even *think* of publishing that article. I will have you on the first ship to England if you dare disobey me.' Coldly, he put on his jacket and turned away.

'Please, Will. I can't let them down.'

'Well, you seem to have no trouble disappointing me with your behaviour. You should be ashamed of yourself.' Only his back faced her.

'Then send me to England. There's nothing here for me anymore without the ballet. I'll just be a prisoner in the house.'

'You don't mean that, Amelia. If I find out you've taken a step – one tiny little step – out of this house, there will be hell. See you tonight.' Will left, not looking back, knowing there would be a broken expression on his wife's face. But he had to take control of the situation. It was shameful enough that Amelia had decided to dance with ladies of the night, and it was unthinkable that she might announce the fact to the international and Chinese communities in a widely-read magazine.

He walked quickly to the consulate, noticing how people on the street steered clear of him in a city where there wasn't room to distance oneself from a leper with flaking skin. But people felt his radiating anger and gave him space. Impatient, he ran up the stairs to his office to find Ralph already there, combing through official documents. He opened the first newspaper on his desk and looked through it, the pages choked with hateful accusations about the Japanese and the story of a Chinese businessman murdered for his association with an executive from Tokyo in Shanghai to cream off the city's best garment businesses. What a world, Will thought, reading how the Chinese man had been tortured to death. The phone rang. Ralph answered in halting Chinese and gestured to Will.

'It's me,' Feifei said. 'I'm afraid I have to cancel our lesson later. And in fact until further notice.'

'But why?' Will felt his chest split in two. He couldn't go on without the happy thought of Feifei at the end of a long day. 'Please.'

'I'm very busy here at the studio. I am so sorry. I will review what we've learned. I'll let you know when we can start again. Sorry again.' The connection clicked and Will knew she was lying. He rifled through the newspapers to see if there was any gossip about her but found nothing. In fact, Feifei had more or less disappeared from the press in recent weeks.

Feifei decided to visit Ling at home. She liked going to the room her friend shared with a Eurasian taxi dancer just off Avenue Joffre. There was something about their chaotic and feminine space that made Feifei feel she was witnessing a stage of life she had missed, that the pair of them truly were modern girls. Ling served Feifei some tea.

'I'm so tired. I was at the Paradise 'til three last night. I wish Director Xu would give me a bigger part and pay more. I love singing but the hours are horrible.'

'Mmm.' Feifei knew she needed someone to speak to, that Ling would be the one to tell her what to do. Despite her sometimes naïve straightforwardness, Ling had a stronger head on her shoulders than Feifei did, and could silence her heart more easily. Ling's flatmate, Coco the taxi dancer, was rarely home, usually out spending her earnings on European fashions or in popular cafés, hoping to meet a man to take her away from dancing. 'Coco's not here, is she?'

'Ah, you want to talk. Tell me.'

And so she did. Feifei told Ling about corpulent Mr Rigg and her lessons with Will and that she was sure he was in love with her. She held back Longwei's involvement with the Japanese. Which one should she choose, she asked her friend.

'No,' Ling said firmly. 'Longwei gave you everything. Lili, your career. I know he plays around, Feifei, but he's a *man*. That's what they do. You can't work in the entertainment industry for a day without realising that men and women, we're different. They're built to roam free and we're made for the home, for love.'

'Do you really believe that? Because I feel that maybe I am capable of loving more than one person at a time.'

'Oh, Feifei. You've watched too many Hollywood films!' Ling laughed and Feifei found herself laughing too. 'If I had a husband who bought me emeralds, I would be the happiest woman in Shanghai. Instead, I have men pawing at me, thinking because I sing that I'll lift my skirt for them.'

Feifei sighed, and looked around the room, checking they were alone. She lowered her voice.

'But, Ling, you don't understand. Longwei is working for the Japanese.'

'What?' Ling's eyes grew round. 'The Japanese? Never. I don't believe it.'

'I'm serious. He's helping them get into business in Shanghai. He's a traitor.'

'Have you not heard about the businessman who was tortured to death because he was helping the Japanese? It was the talk of the Paradise last night. Some said the Green Gang did it.'

Feifei felt a chill in the room and wrapped her fur tighter around her. 'Why would the Green Gang do it?' The notorious gangsters meted out violence for all kinds of perceived misdemeanours. Feifei thought of Longwei tortured, giving a final gasp as some scar-faced gangster slit his throat.

'Well, them or the Communists or ... I don't know who. An embarrassed family member. Everyone in Shanghai is a potential killer these days.' She shrugged and then took Feifei's hand in a firm grasp. 'But it's dangerous, Feifei, not just for him, but for you. Not to mention that Director Xu would go mad if he knew. What about the film?'

'The film. I hadn't even thought about the film.' Feifei felt little desperate tears prick her eyes but she fluttered them away. 'What should I do, Ling? I feel like you're the only person I can talk to.'

'Would you really run away with that man to America?'

'Only if he can get me a role.'

'And Lili? And your mother?'

'If I go to Hollywood, I'll have money to send for them later.' And suddenly she was laughing again, thinking of the golden shores of America, bills falling from the sky like leaves in California.

'Go to Hollywood then, if you can. Before Song Lan

makes sure none of us have a job. Forget about the English poet. They don't have enough backbone to abandon their wives, the English, that's why they come to watch us at night instead.'

Feifei left to keep her appointment with Julia. She was going to approve the final photographs and article at the magazine office. She found the American arranging blocks of text on a page.

'Come here and take a look,' Julia said, without rising from her seat. Feifei walked over and ran her eyes over the photographs, which glittered with movie star perfection, and the dense sentences, which she still laboured over.

'It looks beautiful, Julia. I can't wait to see the magazine. When does it come out?'

'Towards the end of December, so not long to wait.' Julia still hadn't lifted her eyes from the papers in front of her.

'Julia, is everything all right?' Feifei asked. 'Is there a problem with the article?'

'No, no problem. Feifei … what do you think of concubines?' Julia turned her face up to Feifei's. The actress shook her head.

'Very old-fashioned. I wouldn't like it,' she said.

'But what if the concubine really loves the man? Can it ever be justified?' Feifei looked at Julia, the underneath of her eyes hollowed out and dark. She understood. That writer, Ju Wei. All of Shanghai knew they were carrying on. Feifei placed a hand on Julia's shoulder.

'In the case of true love, anything can be justified,' she said. 'The problem is recognising love. Think with your head and your heart. What do both of you want?' She smiled to herself, Hollywood flashing through her brain.

'Thank you Feifei, but please don't mention this to anyone.'

'Of course not.' Feifei left, feeling strange as she walked down the stairs. Julia was the international adventurer, the American not bound by convention. The idea of her becoming a Chinese concubine should have been laughable but, instead, it made Feifei carry a heavy sadness around with her for the rest of the day.

That evening she was surprised to see Longwei's brother sitting in their lounge, leisurely smoking a cigarette.

'Beautiful Feifei!' he said, standing up and straightening his three-piece suit. 'It's been far too long.' Feifei felt immediately uneasy. Second Brother hadn't been to their house in years. Longwei's family had made clear they disapproved of the marriage, his mother suggesting they abandon Feifei and Lili to fend for themselves on the city streets, a fate that Feifei sometimes turned over in her head before falling asleep at night. She could have ended up one of the women she played in the movies, rather than the pretty face paid to portray their sad fates.

'Second Brother, what are you doing here?'

'Why, we're all having dinner of course!' Feifei's stomach clenched. The dinner with the Japanese. And Second Brother was involved too!

'I'll go and get changed,' she said, passing Longwei in the hallway.

'Wear the necklace,' he said, squeezing her waist.

Three severe-looking Japanese businessmen were already waiting for them in a private room in one of the Chinese restaurants on Bubbling Well Road. Feifei, coiffed to wifely perfection, sat between Longwei and his brother, facing the three men like an interrogation panel. Talk was gentle, about the weather, how the foreigners missed Japan, and there were some veiled allusions to business that passed Feifei by. At one point, the middle gentleman placed down his chopsticks and nodded at Feifei.

'You must excuse us, talking about business when we have the prettiest flower in all of Shanghai sitting at the table with us.' Feifei wondered if he knew that prostitutes were often referred to as flowers in Chinese, but decided to think the best of the enemy and smiled gamely. 'Please, tell us about the film you're working on now.'

'It's called *Shanghai Dreams*,' she said, wondering how much to divulge. 'Actually, gentlemen, you may find it very interesting because it is about the tensions between our communities. I play a prostitute whose son goes up to the north to join the Chinese resistance.' The room was filled with electric silence, save for the aggressive chewing of one of the Japanese.

'Well, that's a small part of the movie, isn't it, Feifei?' Longwei shot a daggered look in her direction and suddenly the emeralds, those dirty jewels, weighed heavy on her chest.

'It's not a small part of the movie. It's ... it's the whole point, I suppose.' She dipped her head, looking at the beef congealing on her plate. Her heart was beating so loudly she wondered if the others could hear it. She had broken the rules. Model wives smiled, nodded, ate the food set down in front of them and showed off expensive presents from their husbands. They did not talk politics.

'What she means,' Longwei said, 'is that to bring in the crowds the cinema makers try to make films ... controversial. Add a political dimension. Actually, she brings up something that is very important for us to think about. The image of Japan and how it is being skewed by the Chinese and Western media.' One of the men nodded vigorously, cracking a crab shell between his teeth.

'That's why we need someone like you, Longwei, to help us address the problems. Even better, you're married to the star of a propaganda film! Not everybody has connections like that.' All the men laughed heartily together, the tension dispelled by the faith that Longwei, one man from Shanghai, would stop a whole social movement against the Japanese by controlling his little wife. Feifei's eyes ached with tears she couldn't set free. Longwei would be furious.

At the end of the meal, Second Brother accompanied the Japanese to a cabaret. Longwei declined to join them, saying he wanted to go home with his wife.

'Naturally,' one of the men joked. 'If my wife looked like that I wouldn't have left Japan.' They all laughed rowdily and Feifei felt suddenly chastised, like a common prostitute. She followed Longwei to a taxi. He didn't turn back to look at her. They rode in silence, his unspoken accusations in the air.

He slammed the front door behind him so loudly the frame of the house shook.

'Ssh. Don't wake Lili,' Feifei said, walking away from him, thinking if she could just find Mama, or one of the servants, that whatever storm was brewing might blow over.

'Stop there,' Longwei said, his slender frame suddenly seeming to fill the whole foyer. 'You disgraced me tonight. I let you run around town, appearing in films, going to cabarets with your friends, I don't say anything when the gossip pages tell me you're meeting mysterious foreigners. But this, Feifei, this is too much. You may have ruined a deal for me and my family.'

Feifei swivelled slowly on her feet and met her husband's eyes, which were squeezed closed in anger. 'Since when does your family care about you? Since you became a traitor? Longwei, you're the one working for the Japanese. You're bringing shame upon all of us.'

'You are not to make that film.'

'I told you about the film months ago, Longwei. You knew the plot.'

'I forgot. Things have changed since then.' He placed a heavy hand on her shoulder. 'You go to the studio on Monday and you tell them you can't be in that film.'

'No, Longwei, my whole career, everything, it will be destroyed. We're almost finished. They can't afford to re-shoot with a different actress. Please.' The concealed tears now spilled over onto her cheeks. Feifei knew Longwei had no time for tears, but she didn't care anymore. She let out a low howl.

'Shut up!' Longwei suddenly slapped her across the face, and Feifei reeled back, knocking into a vase of lilies, which toppled over. It cracked loudly on the floor. No doubt everyone else in the house could hear what was going on. Longwei had never hit her before. He might have stabbed her with words and strangled her with silence, but not once had he hit her.

'You pathetic man,' she said, her voice holding steady. 'Hitting your wife to please these bastards tearing your country to pieces. I hope you're proud of yourself.'

'Don't talk to me like that.' Longwei hit her again, this time harder. Feifei tasted blood in her mouth. 'There will be no film. Those 'bastards' will make me enough money that you can sit at home in leisure, like a *real* wife.'

'I don't want to be a real wife. I want to be me.'

Longwei snorted.

'Enough. Get out! You're a danger to me and my daughter!'

'You're telling me to get out? But, Feifei, this house is mine. Where would you be without me? You'd be nothing more than a prostitute. Lili would have died or been sold long ago, you know that. So don't you dare tell me to get out of the house my family and I have provided for you, you ungrateful bitch.' Staggered by his words, Feifei collapsed onto the table that had previously displayed the lilies.

'Longwei ...' Her voice was as broken as her spirit. They needed to stop fighting. Lili would be upstairs, her teeth chattering. She looked at his face, at the contempt he felt for her and she bolted upright. 'Fine. I'll go.' And she stormed out the door, pulling it shut even more loudly than he had done.

Outside the breeze was chilly. Feifei started running, her tears mingling with mucus as she clattered down the road in high heels. It was midnight and she realised she must look ridiculous, like an empress running from her palace. Feeling like something was chasing her from behind, though she knew Longwei would probably be turning down the sheets, confident of her return, she pounded her heels against the street. She hadn't been thinking where she was going, but suddenly she knew. There was only one place for her now.

Amelia slept well these days. Her muscles always ached sweetly in the evenings and she spent half an hour before bed stretching herself out, contorting into the ballet dancer she had always wished to be. She hadn't gone to the studio for two days after the argument with Will, instead telling Tamara she was sick. She planned to go back, and even thought of sneaking out after he had left for work, perhaps arriving a little late to the class. But she was terrified she would be seen. He was still hardly talking to her, so she spent her days going through the routines that Tamara had drilled into the dancers. Next week was important, because Tamara was going to decide what they would perform for the benefit, the first public outing for the company, which was scheduled for January. Amelia had to return then. So on Friday night, although her mind raced with what the next week held, her body lulled her immediately into a soft sleep.

It was a soft mewling noise like an injured animal that first stirred her, a keening coming from outside. Then she heard the staccato gunshots of high heels on the road and lifted her head from the pillow. The low crying continued, its pitch growing higher. Amelia placed her head back down. They lived on a residential street but this was Shanghai – anything could be going on outside. But something tugged at her as the muffled wail continued, something maternal and instinctive. Amelia's limbs unfurled themselves and she went to the window, where she could see nothing but the exaggerated growth of a shadow in the weak light on the street. The crying person must be standing on their doorstep. Amelia shivered and pulled on her dressing gown. A short, sharp shout came: 'Will!' There was no doubt about it, the woman outside was calling Amelia's husband's name. The final consonant was burred in the Chinese way, but it was his name. Amelia approached the door to her husband's room and knocked on it, cracking it open slightly.

'There's a woman outside calling your name,' she said. Will shifted slightly and groaned.

'Sleeping,' he said.

'Can't you hear a woman crying?'

'Go back to sleep.'

Shaking her head, Amelia made her way downstairs, each step filling her chest with another layer of dread. She paused at the stained glass pane of the door and looked through it. A pair of eyes stared back at her through the coloured glass, rimmed in smudged black and hauntingly direct. The woman didn't move her gaze, didn't flinch at the appearance of Will's wife. Amelia opened the door slowly, taking in the visitor. It was Feifei, but not the Feifei Amelia had seen before. This woman's hair fell out of her low bun in messy clumps of curls, her lipstick was smeared across her chin and there was even a small rip in the collar of her *qipao*. Amelia took a step back from the door and crossed her arms across her chest. She wanted to shout at the woman, at this husband-stealing actress, to demand what she was doing screaming other people's loves' names in the streets at night, but she found no words rising to her throat. Feifei watched Amelia wordlessly too, glassy eyes sweeping over her rival's pastel night gown.

'I'm ... I'm sorry,' Feifei said softly and Amelia allowed herself a flash of hope that the English lessons story Julia had told her about Will and Feifei was true.

'What happened to you?' Amelia asked, but Will cut her off, thundering down the stairs, shouting loudly.

'Amelia, get away from there. I thought I told you to go back to sleep.' At the bottom of the stairs he swung into Feifei's view and she bit her lip nervously looking at him.

'Will, it's Wu Feifei,' Amelia said, noticing how her husband had started at the sight of the actress.

'I'll take care of this, Amelia. The woman must be drunk. This is nothing for you to worry about,' Will said, placing himself between his wife and the actress. Amelia took an unwilling step back, as Will moved out with Feifei onto the porch, their voices low.

'What on earth's happened to you?' he demanded in Chinese.

'Longwei hit me,' she said matter-of-factly.

'I'm so sorry.' He looked at her face, mangled by her husband and felt rage surge through him. 'This is outrageous.'

'I didn't know where to go,' Feifei said.

'I understand. But you can't stay here. I'm sorry. Here, I'll give you some money and you can stay somewhere safe.' Feifei nodded at this suggestion. 'I'll be back in a moment.' He went in wordlessly, passing Amelia and going upstairs.

'Don't be cruel, Will,' she called after him. 'We can't leave her on the streets in this state.'

He called that he was going to get her money, but the actress was already limping away down the front path in her treacherous heels.

'Feifei!' Amelia called, and the actress turned to meet her eyes. 'Come back.' Feifei nodded like an obedient daughter and let Amelia's hand guide her through the front door. 'We've a guest room you can stay in for the night. But first, let's find you something comfortable to wear and clean up your face.' Amelia didn't know if Feifei understood, but the woman smiled while slipping off her shoes and followed Amelia to the bathroom.

Amelia shone a light on Feifei's face and found what she had before believed to be lipstick staining her skin actually had the rough, dry texture of congealed blood. Feifei's smooth face wrinkled as Amelia applied alcohol to a couple of small cuts.

'What happened to you?' she asked and little crystal tears dotted Feifei's eyelashes.

'My husband.' She shrugged and Amelia wondered if it was because she had no more words in English, or just no more words at all.

'I'm so sorry,' Amelia said, dabbing her face gently. Where she had expected to feel hostility towards her competitor, she found a great gentleness. She wanted to cradle Feifei. She understood. Feifei loved someone incapable of loving her back, at least of loving her in any real, tangible way, just as Will couldn't love Amelia.

'I come here –' Feifei spoke English haltingly, but with an

eagerness that made Amelia hurt even more for her. 'Here ... because you ... husband-Will ... he is a good ... friend. My teacher. Sorry to disturb.'

'Please don't worry. I'll fetch you a night dress. Let me show you the guest room.' As Amelia walked out of the bathroom she found Will waiting for her.

'I was going to give her money for a hotel,' he said weakly.

'Well, she was already leaving. Besides, what hotel would admit a woman like that? She looks like she's been in a battle.' She felt a sudden exhilaration as she pushed past him to go upstairs. Now Will's mistress had come to the house, he had brought more shame to them than Amelia's dancing ever would. Feifei, the wounded warrior, had done Amelia a greater service than she would ever know.

Amelia tried not to dwell on the image of her husband's lover in one of her own night dresses climbing under the sheets in the guest room. She tucked the sheets up around Feifei and touched her swollen cheek.

'Will you be able to sleep?' she asked.

'Yes, of course. So sorry.'

'Does your husband do ... this to you often?' Amelia asked, gesturing vaguely at Feifei's face, pale and lifeless, the bruises underneath a ghoulish purple.

'Oh, no. First time. No problem.' Feifei fluttered her eyes shut and Amelia left the room for a sleepless night.

Feifei immediately fell asleep in the guest room. The bed was comfortable, the sheets as warm as an embrace against her skin. She had cried all her energy out, there was nothing to do but submit to sleep and think about the consequences tomorrow. She woke two or three times in the night, each time seized with panic when she recalled what had happened. She thought of Will's hard, steely face when he told her she had to go elsewhere.

Morning came quickly and Feifei woke to the door bursting open.

'You need to leave now, before my wife gets up.' Will stood in the doorway, his Chinese barking and harsh.

'*Wei'er*, I'm so sorry,' Feifei said flatly.

'Hurry up. Where are your clothes?'

'My dress is ruined.' Feifei would meet him with the same coldness, if that was what he wanted. She rested her head deeper into the pillow. 'Your wife is so kind I thought she might lend me some clothes today. She really is a lovely woman, Will.'

'Yes, yes. A lovely woman. Come on. Where is your dress?'

'She took it.' Feifei saw that Will was getting impatient. He strode over to the bed and Feifei wondered for a moment if he might strike her, if he might colour the bruised palette of her face again. But instead he sat down on the bed beside her and took her hand.

'I'm sorry, Feifei. I don't mean to be cruel. I simply panicked last night and I'm panicking now. What were you thinking of coming here?' Feifei reached long fingers out towards his wrist and rubbed it gently. There was no point, she thought, in making an enemy of Will, not when everything else remained so uncertain.

'Longwei hit me, Will. We had a terrible argument. He told me I can't be in films anymore.'

'What?' Will seemed genuinely shocked. 'How can he say that?'

Feifei let her eyes close and sighed. 'I can't tell you, I can't tell anyone. But it's a disaster, for me, for my daughter, my mother.' She had been trying to elicit sympathy from Will but was surprised to find tears, real, ugly ones, spilling out from under her closed eyes. She let her body go slack as Will leant over and held her.

'Ssh, ssh. Everything's going to be all right. You've still got Hollywood.' He laughed softly and she did too, hiccuping into his shoulder.

'Morning, Feifei. I brought a dress that might fit you … oh!' They both turned to see Amelia in the corner of the room, a blue dress crumpled over her arm. 'I'll just leave it here.' She set the dress down on the back of a chair and pulling her spine straight left the room, closing the door hard behind her.

'Will, I'm so sorry.' Feifei looked at him, stricken. She reached to touch his face but he pushed her away.

'Get up, Feifei, you need to go.'

'I'm sorry.' She frowned. 'Will we start our lessons again?'

'I thought you had to stop.'

'Because of Longwei. But I don't think he'll be home for a while now.'

'I'll call you.' Will turned and left her in the weak morning light, the cosy bedroom now icy. She shivered as she pulled the dress over her head, noticed how it hung too loosely off her shoulders, how the waist gathered in the wrong place.

Downstairs, she put on her heels again and tottered to the living room, where Amelia sat with a heavy book in her lap.

'I want say thank you,' Feifei said softly. 'You very kind to me last night.'

'Oh, it was nothing.' Amelia didn't look up from the book and Feifei peered down at it. The page was split in two, with Chinese characters on one side and English on the other.

I avoid the shame of daylight with a silk sleeve,
The spring depresses me, I am too listless to rise.
It is easy to find priceless treasures,
But hard to come by a lover with heart.

Feifei stepped away from Amelia and the book, her breath catching. Once again these poems by old men hundreds of years ago had come to haunt her, the quatrains that Will recited, the haunting truth that trickled through the centuries.

'I'm sorry,' she said, placing a hand on Amelia's shoulder, but the English woman pulled away.

'Goodbye, Feifei.'

Feifei turned to leave her, the woman whose heart she had broken, feeling utterly wretched. There was no one left in this world who loved her, not Will, not Longwei, not her mother, maybe not even Lili. And she had driven a woman who should have had it all, should have been a queen in her Shanghai castle, back in time to the laments of dry old sages. Well, she thought, closing the front door quietly behind her. Maybe there was one person who still loved her.

When Feifei had gone, Amelia threw the book down on the floor. She knew Will drew comfort from these poems, from the fact that humans had been running in the same emotional circles for hundreds of years, never learning to co-exist harmoniously. He had told her some of the poets retreated to nature with just wine and the moon for company. Right now that was a very appealing idea. But she didn't want to retreat into the wilderness. No, Amelia wanted to hide herself in dance and she would do it now. She rose to find Will but collided with Su who yelped when she saw Amelia.

'Missy! Wu Feifei here? In your home?'

'Unfortunately, Su, it would appear that she was indeed here,' Amelia said drily, leaving the maid trailing behind her, not understanding. Amelia had no time for the petty gossip of the servants this morning. She climbed the stairs, feeling an echo of dread from the night before when she had descended the same ones, knowing in her most secret heart what was waiting for her downstairs.

'Will,' she said, rapping on the door of his bedroom. He was sitting on the bed, looking out the window. Amelia thought of him watching Feifei making her way down the street, ever elegant even in a dress that didn't fit her. She felt anger bubbling but swallowed it back, savouring the acidic taste. She had to stay in control. Her mother had played marriage like a game, forgiving in order to be forgiven, and Amelia would do the same.

'Amelia,' he said, his head hanging on his neck like it was too heavy for him to hold up anymore. 'I can explain everything. I'm giving Feifei English lessons. She really must have nowhere to turn if she came here. I have no idea–'

'I don't mind, darling. Don't worry.' She settled herself on the bed next to him. 'But I hope you understand that after

126

the events of last night I will be returning to the ballet on Monday.'

'Amelia, we've discussed this.'

'It was different then. If you are going to behave in this way without even considering the impact of your actions on me, on our extended family, then I have the right to do the same. I know you'll continue to give her lessons, to see her, God only knows what you were whispering about with her this morning in bed. Under our roof, Will! While she was wearing my night dress.' Amelia felt her voice verge on hysterical and took a steadying breath. 'This is the end of the discussion, Will. I will go to the ballet on Monday and you will continue doing whatever it is you do with that woman.' She left him still staring out the window and thought to herself how what they said wasn't true. Victory was sour, not sweet. But still, it was victory.

When Amelia arrived at the academy on Monday morning, she found Julia in the corner watching the girls limber up at the barre, notebook in hand. Julia, who was attractive in a more strapping, sporty way, looked as though she might give way to laughter at any moment, watching the tiny limbs of the dancers flail close to each other's faces, petite noses gracing shins as they stretched.

Julia waved to Amelia, who smiled warmly in return, removing the layers that had shielded her outside. After her discussion with Will on Saturday she had gone to Julia's house to tell her what had happened. Pragmatic Julia had agreed with her that she should leverage the Feifei situation to continue with the ballet but the news had somewhat subdued her.

'You know, I'm surprised. I didn't think they were having a real … affair. I introduced Feifei to another friend and she seemed quite taken with him,' she told Amelia while the maid set down tea in front of them.

'Who knows how many men she has?' Amelia said, her joyful victory giving way to wifely spite as she thought of the film star trotting down the road in her clothes. She had tried to avoid telling Julia about the embrace she had witnessed, but her friend had drawn it out of her.

'But do you love Will? Don't you want to fight for him?' Amelia was surprised by the question, imagining Julia to be the kind of woman who pooh-poohed the idea of love, thinking it was nothing more than a diversion between work and parties.

'Of course I love him. But Shanghai's changed him. I think we need to leave ... but as long as we're here, I need to have my life, my independence. I have a real chance now with the ballet.' Julia raised her eyebrows and took a too-hot sip of tea, spluttering slightly.

'The first day I met you, Amelia, I never would have imagined you saying something like that. You still wanted to tow the line, to cover up all the wonderful gifts you had. It was me who wanted to bring you out of your shell. But oh my, how the roles have reversed.' She fingered the rim of the tea cup.

'How?' Amelia asked.

'Ju Wei asked me to marry him.'

'Oh, Julia, congratulations! I shouldn't be telling you all these awful stories about marriage.' Amelia moved to give her a hug, but Julia pulled away.

'He's already married. I'd be wife number two,' she said, deadpan, her hands fidgeting and her eyes unwilling to meet Amelia's.

'You can't do that,' Amelia said confidently. 'What kind of life would that be?'

'Like yours,' Julia said sadly. 'But official.' Amelia had left soon afterwards, but not before confirming that her friend could come to the ballet on Monday to get some details to add into the piece Amelia had already written.

Tamara entered the room and clapped her hands.

'I see we have company,' she said pointedly to Julia.

'Yes, for the article,' Julia said. 'I'll go wherever I'm not in the way.' Tamara pointed to the furthest corner of the room and started the warm-ups. Amelia went to take her usual place at the barre next to Polina. The first week they were together Tamara had rearranged their positions every day until a hierarchy became clear. Polina and Amelia, both with ballet experience, were the best, though Amelia trailed Polina by a long way. But today she found Lilya, the young girl with long brown hair, in her place.

'Lilya, that's my place,' she said and Lilya met her with a sneer.

'You don't come, you lose your spot. Sorry.' She shrugged and shifted her feet into first position.

'I was sick, Lilya. I always dance behind Polina.'

'Tamara said if we missed two days in a row we wouldn't be part of the company anymore. But you come in, like a queen, and demand I move aside for you. The treatment isn't the same for the Russian girls.'

'Lilya, please move.' But Amelia's voice wavered and Lilya heard it.

'Or what?' She put her hands on her hips like a man preparing for a bar brawl. Tamara clapped her hands angrily and growled at Lilya in Russian. Lilya snapped back at her and the exchange between the two rose in volume until Lilya slid back along the barre, making a small space for Amelia to slip into. When Amelia had slotted into her position, Lilya said something in a low voice in Russian and all the girls tittered, except Polina and Plum. Amelia knew Plum only didn't laugh because she didn't understand. She was a taxi-dancer too, one of the crowd. Amelia felt hot, embarrassed tears sting her eyes. It wasn't fair, she thought, these girls didn't have husbands to answer to. They didn't know that Feifei had burst into her home on Friday night and left her loveless and alone in a city far from home. They went through their usual *pliés, relevés* and *rondes de jambe,* all the time with Tamara watching carefully, adjusting chins, straightening shoulders, cracking hips as she moved legs higher. They were going through the second drill when Amelia felt a sharp kick to her shin. It might have been a mistake, so she carried on, dipping lower into her *pliés,* trying to feed off the competition, to raise her legs higher, to turn around with more grace, to make each position as perfect as if a sculptor had placed her there. But then came another kick, this time against her buttocks. She turned around to glare at Lilya, but the other girl had fixed her gaze on the wall, a beatific smile on her face. On the third kick, Amelia stopped dancing.

'Lilya, I know what you're doing,' she said, loudly, wanting the others to hear. Lilya looked at her innocently.

'Nothing. I did nothing. Please, Amelia, continue dancing.' But Amelia stood still until Tamara came over to her.

'What's going on here?'

'Lilya keeps kicking me,' she told Tamara, feeling like the teacher's pet at school. Looking at Lilya, her lip raised to her nose in ugly haughtiness, Amelia knew that to survive in the class she would have to become one of them. 'But I'm sure it's by mistake,' she said pointedly, wanting to send a warning to Lilya, who just smiled sweetly in response. Tamara walked away and they continued. But when the next kick came, a single tear worked its way down Amelia's cheek. There was no magic in music today, no remedy in repetition. Amelia was other and she was never good enough, not for the girls, not for Will, not even for cosmopolitan Julia, who had condemned Amelia's marriage so bleakly. Tamara called that they would take a break for five minutes, after which she would announce the dances they were to perform at the benefit.

All the girls gathered in an excited circle, trying to guess what the ballets might be, occasionally dipping into English or Chinese for Plum's benefit. Amelia made her way over to Julia who was scribbling furiously.

'None of them have any shoes!' Julia exclaimed, laughing. 'It's a beautiful image. I'll get one of our artists to do that for the story, a picture of a barefoot ballerina.'

'Tamara needs to know people are committed before she makes a major outlay. It's all going to be expensive. But some of them dance in socks or stockings,' Amelia said, sitting down beside Julia, her heart leaden in her chest. Her face was flushed from her near outburst, but luckily the other girls had been sweating and were pink-cheeked too, their ardour steaming up the windows to the street.

'But still! No shoes!' Julia was shaking her head, still laughing to herself. She looked at Amelia. 'Are you all right? You look exhausted.'

'It's hard work.'

'They're competitive. But you have to remember the lives these girls lead, Amelia. They don't want anyone to dance better than them. Every step means a cent to these girls, and they bring that mentality here, I suppose.'

'Mmm.' Amelia felt she might cry again, she was so desperate for someone to be kind to her. Polina walked over to the two of them.

'May I join you?' She elegantly folded her legs under her, crossing her hands in her lap. Many of the Russians in Shanghai claimed to be from noble lineage, and while the other foreigners doubted the origins of some, Polina looked like exactly the kind of woman who would be at home on gilt-edged chairs, talking to heads of state. 'Don't let them bother you,' she said quietly to Amelia. 'They do the same with me. They see it as unfair that we have the lives we do.' Amelia thought of her life, her marriage to someone in love with a film star, her long, solitary afternoons reading Will's poetry books and practising *developpés* in the lounge. At least those girls had each other. And Polina's life? Subject to the whims of a gangster, chained to a club she had to entertain in every night, tolerating the chatter of men with alcoholic breath. 'After all,' Polina continued, 'you did miss two days. You broke the rules and there's no punishment for you because you're necessary for this whole thing to happen. They know they are dispensable. Tamara said to us on Friday, 'You think I can't find Chinese girls half the size of you lot and three times as graceful? You must behave if you want this opportunity.' They don't think the situation is fair.'

'I know, but ... What did Lilya say? The thing that made all the girls laugh?' Amelia asked, lowering her voice to match Polina's.

'I don't remember,' Polina said, but her face was too open for lies. She clutched her hands together tightly, too tightly, in a sign that the words would hurt.

'Just tell me. It was about me. Don't I deserve to know?' Amelia eyed Tamara, who was still talking enthusiastically with the old pianist. 'Please.'

'Well, it's not true. She said you act high and mighty, as though you were better than all of us, but actually your husband spends all his nights in cabarets and that she slept with him once. She said ... she said that if she's good enough for your husband she should be good enough for you.' Polina winced at the last part, not able to look at Amelia. Julia took a sharp intake of breath.

'What?' Amelia's head felt light, the room was suddenly unbearably hot.

'I shouldn't have said anything. Of course it's not true. She is a little unbearable, this girl. But she has worked in that business since she was thirteen. It's made her very hard.' Tamara stepped away from the piano and shouted to the girls to gather round. Polina gave Amelia's hand a squeeze, but she felt her heart pull tight. Amelia watched Lilya scamper to the front of the room, settling at Tamara's feet, eager for news that she would be dancing an important role. Amelia felt her eyes narrow and her jaw harden. Everywhere was a battlefield in this city.

Tamara surveyed the twelve young women in front of her, in their mismatched clothes, with grey stains under their eyes and hair thick with secrets of the night.

'Girls, I am pleased to announce that we will be dancing pieces from two ballets, *Giselle* and *Swan Lake*. I am even more delighted to announce this in front of Julia Hart, who is writing about us in *New Woman*.' Some of the dancers made excited noises, their eyes growing more sparkling.

'I wrote some of it too,' Amelia said to them, but only Polina acknowledged her with a curt nod.

'Yes, well, it's going to be fantastic publicity. Now, let me tell you about the ballets. Unfortunately we will not be able to put on a whole ballet, rather a sampling of what we are capable of, but it is important you know what they are about. The first ballet will be Giselle, about a peasant girl who dies after being deceived by a nobleman who is already promised to another. The Wilis, the spirits of jilted women who dance men to death, rouse Giselle from her grave and she joins them. They try to kill Giselle's lover, making him dance all night, but he survives because Giselle forgives him.' Julia was making frantic notes. 'Most of you will play Wilis, but there are two important roles that must be filled for the parts we are to perform.' All the dancers sat up straighter, as if catching Tamara's eye now would guarantee them the part. 'Polina will play Giselle.' Polina nodded, smiling graciously. 'And Amelia will play Myrtha, Queen of the Wilis.'

'Me?' Amelia momentarily forgot Feifei, Will, Julia's concubinage and Lilya's kicks. She glowed with the idea of taking a lead role. 'Oh, thank you, Tamara.' Tamara gave a soft, professional smile and continued.

'I am sure you are familiar with Swan Lake, a beautiful love story about a cursed woman who is a swan during the day and a woman at night. Odette and Odile, her nemesis, are played by the same dancer, which in this case will be Polina. This is where the real work begins, girls. It is approaching the end of November. We must be ready in two months. Polina and Amelia, you must take extra classes with me from now on in the afternoon. Right, stand up! Let's begin with the Wilis.'

Julia watched the dancers, transfixed as Tamara led them through the steps. She wrote copious notes, about the condensation on the windows, the pinpricks of sweat on the girls' necks, the ropey calves that lifted them up and out of the Shanghai gutter. When the class was over she asked Amelia to lunch.

'You too, Polina, if you like,' she said, noticing the blonde standing to the side. The three of them went to a Russian restaurant Polina knew nearby. Outside of the studio, the earlier dread Amelia had felt rushed back. She picked at her food.

'Do you want a drink?' Polina asked.

'I have one.'

'No, I mean alcohol. You look terrible.' Amelia shrugged and let Polina order her some vodka.

'It should be champagne but they told me they don't have any. We have a lot to celebrate. We've got the best roles! Myrtha, that's fantastic. Oh, I can't wait.'

'Do you think it's true?' Amelia asked both of them and Julia placed a maternal palm on her back.

'Amelia, I doubt it. Lilya was just being spiteful. But that … that's what men do. You know that.'

Polina agreed.

'You shouldn't think about it.'

'But-but … he already has Feifei! How many women does he need?' The drink had freed her tongue, made Amelia forget who she was with, that she barely knew Polina, who was so graceful and lovely that no one could desire anyone other than her.

Julia steered the conversation gently away from Will.

'Polina, you work in the Blackbird, don't you?'

'It's a terrible name,' Polina said. 'I keep telling him he should change it.'

'Maybe we could have the benefit there!' Julia said, pleased with her idea.

'Oh, no, I don't think so. All the acts are booked months in advance …'

'Yes, but come on, you're the star there! Just one night.'

'I don't think so,' Polina said, draining the last of the clear contents of her glass. 'I'm sorry.' She patted Amelia's hair. 'Come on, we've got extra classes now, Myrtha. I don't think Tamara will be pleased if I take a weeping drunk with me.' Amelia followed her, limbs and mouth numb from the vodka, which she had never drunk before. She did feel a little better, actually, with her two friends beside her, leading her out the door to the street. And soon, maybe, she allowed herself to think, the whole of Shanghai would know who she was. She might be on the cover of magazines just like Wu Feifei.

'It's genius, really,' Julia said as she waved them goodbye. 'Taxi-dancers dancing men to death! Genius!'

VII

Will was working hard. No one at the consulate could question his dedication now. It didn't matter that he had come to China in the first place after being awarded a job he had never truly desired. He knew that he had come close to losing Shanghai. He couldn't bear the thought of going back to London now. Shanghai was his drug – it dragged him down and lifted him up and living without it would be impossible. He left for work earlier and earlier, mostly to avoid seeing Amelia and arguing with her about her dancing, and since Feifei had cancelled their lessons he often stayed in the office long after Ralph had left. But despite his best efforts to show the others at the consulate he was a good worker, he noticed the offers to go out for drinks were drying up and even Rollo seemed to be losing interest in training him as a protégé. As a result, Will often ended up touring the cabarets and bars alone at night, confident he would usually find someone to talk to. But he hadn't been back to the Paradise, not since the night with Lilya.

This morning Ralph was noisily clearing his throat while

translating legal documents. Will flicked through the newspapers in front of him. Almost all of them had the same story about a burned down factory in the Chinese settlement, complete with pictures of charred wood, rubble and machinery spread across an empty street. 'Arson by the Japanese', 'Devils destroy Chinese business'. The *North China Daily News* was more objective in tone, but still suggested the malevolent forces currently occupying Manchuria were likely behind the pile of ashes that had once employed hundreds of Chinese people. Will folded away the English-language papers. After all, his job was to report on the unseen things happening in Shanghai, the Chinese sentiment and what it meant for the British and their international partners. Although he sometimes doubted how helpful the reports he wrote were, he enjoyed analysing each individual Chinese character, linking them to connotations and poems the journalists themselves may never have read. He started to write his report, quoting the angry words from the Chinese newspapers, taking too long over every word, the way he used to with classical texts at Oxford. Rollo rapped on the door lightly.

'Good morning, chaps. How's the report coming on, Will?'

'You heard about the factory?' Will asked Rollo.

'I saw something in the paper, yes. Is it important?'

'I don't know, Rollo,' Will said earnestly. 'The rhetoric in the Chinese papers is getting stronger. Tolerance is fading. Some of this vocabulary is quite … war-like.'

'Well, who would know better than our eminent Oxford scholar?' Rollo laughed and sat at the edge of Will's desk. 'I have a task for you, Will. Sent from up high.' He pointed at the ceiling, as though the consul-general himself might be somewhere in the celestial sky. 'They want a special report,' he said, dropping his voice to stop Ralph from hearing. 'About Chinese-Japanese relations.'

'Well, I'm hardly an expert. There are political officers like you, there are spies out there in the field, Rollo. Although I'm flattered, I think someone else should be writing it.'

'You see, Will, that's not what they want. They want to gauge public feeling. *Chinese* feeling about the Japanese. Rate the likelihood of a war. Oh, and they'd like some information about the Communists too. You can get your hands on some commie publications, can't you? In Chinese?' Will shook his head.

'Rollo, there's a witch hunt for radicals all over the city, I can't go buying those magazines,' he said. 'As I said, I'm sure there are spies raking through them as we speak. I am pleased they thought of me, but I don't think I'm the man for the job.'

Rollo frowned.

'It seems to me, Will, that you may be forgetting what happened with Harry. Perhaps you shouldn't be so quick to dismiss an opportunity like this.'

Will mulled it over for a moment, while Ralph coughed nervously.

'Fine. When do they need it by?'

'You can have a few weeks. But please do keep me up to date on your progress. They want something fairly long and detailed. I'll do all I can to help.' Rollo rose and left. Will called him back.

'Why don't we go out for a drink soon?'

'Of course,' Rollo said quickly, waving at Ralph as he left.

With a sigh, Will went back to his report. At least more work would keep his mind occupied, he thought. It had been a few days since Feifei's appearance at the house. He felt shame rush through him when he thought of how he had dismissed her, how he had claimed to Amelia that Feifei was drunk, though he hoped she hadn't understood. He thought of the sad trail of blood down her chin. He had no idea Longwei was beating her. Sometimes he allowed himself to imagine an alternate future, one where he and Feifei could be together. But that required a different past, a history without Longwei and Amelia. He rose to find a telephone where he could make a call without Ralph hearing him. Out in the corridor he walked quickly, not pausing in case he talked himself out of it. He found an empty office and slid through the door, his finger turning the telephone dial quickly. He knew the studio number off by heart.

'Hello, could I speak to Wu Feifei, please?' he asked.

'She's not here. Hasn't been in all week,' a bored-sounding young man said. 'Do you have any idea where she might be?'

'No. None at all.' Will's heart seized with fear. Cold, dead fear, stronger even than what he had felt when he discovered Harry MacDonald was a spy.

'Want to leave a message for when she returns?' But Will had already hung up. After work, he would go to her house. It didn't matter if that bastard Longwei was there.

As he walked back to his office he heard two confident, bubbling voices.

'Yes, well the Chinese rhetoric is getting stronger. War-like … yes.' Will stopped and cocked his ear but he couldn't hear the rest, just little bursts of laughter and the agreeable tone of mutual compliments. Had that voice been Rollo? It certainly sounded like him. It reminded him to finish his report, and he rushed back to the office.

Feifei was home alone. Truly alone, or as possible as that was in her household, now that Lili was at school and Mama had gone to run some errand, unable to shake off the bustle of a maid even after years as the matriarch of a wealthy home. That left just the servants downstairs, crashing around noisily in the kitchen. Feifei lay on her bed, the side of her face still throbbing. It was no surprise to her that Longwei had disappeared for the weekend after she ran away, but he returned on Monday morning to make sure she didn't leave for the studio. She watched, exhausted, as he barred the door with his hand.

'You heard what I said,' he told her sternly and feeling her muscles go weak she had obeyed, going upstairs where she lay on the bed. Ten minutes later he had come through, concern across his face.

'I just want to keep you safe,' he said, lying down next to her. 'I'm doing this for you and Lili. I'll make money for us and then you don't have to appear in politically dangerous films.'

'*Shanghai Dreams* is not dangerous, Longwei. It's uplifting. The whole country besides you is united against the Japanese.'

'We don't know how things are going to turn out, Feifei.' She sat up, resting the side of her head on her hand.

'Do you know something I don't?' she asked him.

'Look at Manchuria,' he said, closing his eyes to indicate the conversation was over.

'What is it that you're doing exactly? How are you helping them?' But Longwei didn't reply.

He had gone out on Tuesday night and two days later still hadn't returned. Feifei didn't feel sure enough that his absence would be long-term, so she continued without contacting Will, who she was losing faith in anyway. She hadn't heard anything from Charles Rigg either. She groaned, leaning over to open the drawer and look at the picture of Anna May Wong. What would Anna May do, Feifei asked herself, and decided to phone Julia.

'I wondered if I could come to the office and see the final photographs and text for the interview,' Feifei said when she got through to the American. 'And perhaps I could take you out to thank you again. You and that young girl – Suping?' Feifei heard her voice strain, aware that this was bizarre, that the chase should have been in the other direction.

'Of course.' Julia sounded distracted. 'How about next week?'

'Fine. Perhaps you could invite your friend Charles Rigg? I, um, I recently saw an American film and I'd like to discuss it with him.'

'I'll ask him,' Julia said, hiding her suspicion, if there was any.

When she heard loud, insistent knocks at six-thirty, Feifei went to the door. Mama was upstairs and Lili was at a friend's house. She wondered if it might be Longwei but was surprised to find Will standing at the door, hat in hand, eyes downcast.

'Feifei,' he said. 'I've been so worried.'

'Please, don't be,' she said, ushering him in. 'I'm fine. But I don't know if you should be here, my husband …' Will looked tired, she thought, anxious in a way a young man shouldn't.

'Why haven't you been at the studio?'

Feifei hung her head. 'I can't talk about it. Don't tell any of them you've seen me, please.'

'Feifei, what's going on? Is this because of your husband?'

'Yes. But it's not what you think.'

'You looked terrible on Friday. I'm so worried. I can't stop thinking about you.' His despair seemed genuine, but Feifei couldn't forget the panic on his face on Friday night, when she had arrived at his doorstep, his urgent desire to rid himself of her and her inconvenient wounds. Still she found herself raising light fingertips to his face. She had to keep him around.

'I scratched Longwei quite hard too, you know,' she said quietly. 'He never normally beats me. Please don't worry about that. It's something else. But I can't talk to you about it. I can't talk to anyone. It's dangerous.' She held her breath, knowing she sounded dramatic. 'Please go, Will. I will be in touch when we can meet again. My husband is keeping a close eye on me at the moment.'

'Feifei.' He grabbed her hand and pressed her bony knuckles to his lips.

'Please go.'

'Let me help you.' She shook her head, her ring scratching Will's palm as she pulled free.

'By leaving you'll help me.' Then she leant in close to him, let her warm breath tickle his neck. 'I want to see you too. Just wait.' He nodded solemnly and left, placing his hat back on his head as he stepped into the weak, grey light of late November. She looked at the clouds in the sky and wondered if it might rain later, suddenly stricken by the feeling that Will was a good man, better than she thought. It scared her what he might do.

Will went home, his pace choppy, his mind racing with questions. He hurried, thinking all the time that there must be something he could do to help. Walking down Fuzhou Road, he scanned the bookshops, remembering the report Rollo had told him about. He should keep an eye out for communist material. One of the shops displayed a large sign in the window offering discounts for students. He slipped through the door, to the surprise of the old man hunched over the till.

'No foreign-language books here,' he said.

'That's fine. I'm looking for political texts in Chinese,' Will replied in perfect Mandarin. Often these days he used his imperfect Shanghainese, but he wanted to knock back this superior intellectual. The man's face softened.

'Are you one of our Russian friends?' He looked delighted so Will nodded almost imperceptibly. 'In that corner.' He pointed to a messy stack of books and magazines at the back of the shop, covered with a layer of innocuous romances and detective novels. Will sifted through them and picked out two radical publications, paid the man and with a duck of his head left the shop, slipping the magazines inside his coat. They seemed to weigh him down even more than Feifei and her problems.

Amelia was already home when he got back, playing with the food on her plate. He sat down opposite her and called to Qi to bring him some dinner too. Amelia said hello to him, a smile playing at the corners of her lips. He saw suddenly in her the burning intensity that had first attracted him. He thought of when he read the first poem to her, about the lady on the jade stairs ... her face had glowed in the same way. After that she had thrown herself into Will, his life and his family with unexpected fervour. Despite Feifei's unexpected appearance, despite the fact they had turned into two strangers under one roof, he realised that Amelia was something close to happy.

And it made him feel even worse. Quickly clearing his plate he went to the study where he pulled down one of the new collections of poetry he had bought since coming to China. One of the verses would please him, soothe away his concerns. Every time he was anxious, Will translated a poem. It was something about going back to his roots, recovering the person he had once been, that serious, good-hearted young man tucked away safely in the draughty libraries of Oxford, sure he knew how the world fitted together. He sighed, turning the pages until he found a poem that made his heartbeat slow as he read it. Lifting his pen to the page, he wrote out his translation:

Carefully she weaves delicate clouds,
Shooting stars reflect her grief,
The couple crosses the remote Milky Way.
Meeting once a year in the golden wind and jade frost,
It is a scene that surpasses all those on earth.
Tender and soft, flowing like water, their union like a dream,
How can they bear to think of their route home?

He gripped his pen tightly as he wrote the last two lines:

When two feel love genuine and enduring,
How can it matter that they are not together morning and night?

Feeling sentimental, Will pictured Feifei's pale hands, the elegance of those ten fingers loaded with glittering rings.

'Good night.' Amelia peered round the door. They were talking now, not as husband and wife, but in a neighbourly way.

'I won't be long,' Will said, waiting until she had closed the door before he pulled out the magazines he had bought. Sleep would not come easily tonight, he thought, so he might as well start on the report, his second chance.

Julia was hunched over her desk, looking at the lay-out for the interview with Feifei. She was pleased with the article, which she had sprinkled with references to Feifei's private life, little nuggets of information the actress had dropped during the interview at the Metropole. She had also finished the article about the Shanghai Ballet and was especially pleased with the headline: *Shanghai's Barefoot Ballerinas*. She forced herself to read the piece again, searching for errors. But she couldn't get the dinner at the weekend out of her head.

'Good morning.' Feifei strode across the office, wrapped up in delicious white fur.

'Oh, Feifei, hello.' Julia invited the actress to sit down, thinking that her interest in this one article was excessive. It was all about Charles Rigg – big, fat Charles and his big, fat promises. Feifei started reading over Julia's shoulder.

'Uh, Julia. I hate to be difficult but perhaps we could cut down the references to *Shanghai Dreams*? There are some … problems with the film.' Julia looked up at Feifei, her face still as tranquil as the monks meditating at the Jade Buddha Temple in the mornings.

'What kind of problems?' she asked.

'Nothing serious. It's just, well, the release date might be pushed back. I don't want to give people false hope,' Feifei explained.

'But everything's already finished.' Julia was suddenly cross, feeling the familiar fluster from Saturday of not knowing what to do, of thinking that maybe she would never understand this place and its people.

'Please, Julia. I'm so sorry to trouble you.' Feifei sat beside her and picked up the piece about the ballet dancers. She read silently, her fingers sometimes tracing more complex characters, her lips softly spelling out the words.

Julia turned away from her, her face flushed. On Saturday morning she had gone with Ju Wei to sign the papers to make her concubinage official. She had wanted to be a little romantic about it and even bought a new dress, which her distracted lover failed to notice.

'Just a formality,' he said as they left the office. That night the women of Ju Wei's family had organised a dinner to welcome Julia into the clan, serving huge steaming plates of seafood and noodles. She could see there was kindness in this matriarchy but simply couldn't enjoy the dinner. The women drank wine, their diamonds glistening in the low candlelight, their tipsy gossip filling the air with incomprehensible words. Julia spoke passable Shanghainese – shopping Shanghainese, drinking Shanghainese – but not bosom-of-a-family Shanghainese. Ju Wei's wife was seated as far away from Julia as possible and refused to meet her eye. At a dinner held in her honour, Julia felt like an intruder. As she piled her plate high with food to avoid talking, Julia couldn't help but think of her mother. She would have to write to her, the woman growing more knitted with wrinkles by the day, and tell her that her wayward daughter of almost thirty had finally tied the knot. She wouldn't tell her she was a second wife, that would break her mother's heart. Since her father had died, Julia knew her mother was waiting patiently in their roomy New York apartment, hoping for Julia to give up her adventures, for young Helen to return from college, and ultimately, for death to claim her and take her to her husband. Between two mouthfuls of crab, Julia's eyes filled with tears. But she knew that she wasn't homesick. They were tears of wounded pride. After the meal she had been shown her room in the house, beautifully made up with silk across the bed. She had settled in this annexe for second wives, feeling suddenly like a virgin. She heard Ju Wei talking in fierce whispers with his wife, then the sound of his slippered feet down the corridor.

'You know you don't actually have to live here,' he said, closing the door behind him. 'You're a modern woman, you can continue to live at your own apartment. But stay tonight, of course.' Julia started crying again, this time for shame, thinking that no modern woman would ever allow herself to be a concubine. She had felt daring and glamorous with her writer lover, with the sleepless nights they spent together at her apartment, him filling her head with sweet words and delicate rhymes. But now she was an aged virgin, a ridiculous woman not even worthy of wife status. Ju Wei lay beside her and they slept on top of the elaborately made-up bed, Julia's hot tears swaying them both to sleep.

Feifei placed the paper down. 'Very interesting,' she said. 'I'd like to help in some way.'

'Sorry?' Julia felt annoyed with Feifei today. She wanted to be left to wallow.

'With the ballet. You know I could have ended up with a fate like that myself,' she said, pointing at the article.

'You mean you want to dance?' Julia said, challenging, wanting this beautiful woman to reply that of course she wanted to be part of the company, she was so talented, so desirable that she could do whatever she wanted.

'No, of course not! Just to support it. Why don't you remove one of the references to *Shanghai Dreams* and say that I am backing the project.'

'And how, exactly, are you going to do that? With money?' Julia sighed thinking of the rewrite of the article, of getting Suping to translate it again.

'I can give a little money, perhaps,' she said, surprising Julia. 'And of course I would attend the first performance.' Julia felt herself relax and gave Feifei a small smile.

'Fine. That's very kind of you.' She decided not to tell Amelia right away.

Julia had suggested a French restaurant not far from the office for lunch with Charles Rigg. Feifei sat with Suping and Julia, watching the door carefully, willing Charles to arrive as the other two perused the menu, Suping occasionally exclaiming at the exotic names of foods. Charles came in at last, draped in a heavy winter coat. Feifei noticed to her approval that it looked expensive. He took his seat at the table.

'Miss Wu,' he said, sliding a box across the table. 'For you.' Feifei picked up the thin box and opened it to find a perfect circle of a bangle, dotted with diamonds.

'Thank you,' she stammered, aware her English was disappearing without regular lessons. 'I cannot ... cannot take.' She slid the box across the table towards him, wondering how he would react to her modesty. He cackled loudly, drawing disdainful looks from diners around them.

'Miss Wu, it's nothing. You have lit up Shanghai for me and I want to light up your wrist the same way. Like the lights of Hollywood,' he added, gazing across the table at her. Julia quickly translated what Charles had said and Feifei nodded curtly, removing the bangle from its box and slipping it onto her slim wrist. 'It's broken my heart not seeing your pretty face,' Charles continued. 'I was up in Tianjin. My God, you're even more beautiful than I remembered!'

'Thank you very much,' Feifei responded, admiring the way the light caught the diamonds around her wrist.

The group ate together amiably, Charles regaling them with tales of a traveller's Shanghai. Feifei felt Suping grow impatient in her seat as Charles told story after story about dirty-cheeked orphans on the streets reaching into his pockets for coins and Russian dames rhythmically removing their clothes by night.

'City of contrasts,' he repeated. 'You show us Americans what a good time really is.' Feifei strained to understand everything, but whenever she felt weary she looked at her wrist, the sparkling diamonds winking back at her.

'If I may call you Feifei,' he said at one point, reaching across and stroking the jewels that now circled her arm, 'I wonder if you would take me for a walk, Feifei, after lunch, show me some sights I might not have seen.'

'I would like,' Feifei said, dipping her head to hide her smile from him.

'Fantastic!' Charles banged the table like a bad-mannered boor, but Feifei chose not to notice.

'She's married,' Julia said to Charles when Feifei had excused herself from the table. 'You know that, don't you?'

'She doesn't seem very married,' Charles replied.

'Well, she is. Her husband belongs to an important merchant family. A very powerful dynasty you do not want to cross. Believe me.'

'Julia, I'm leaving town in a couple of months. It doesn't matter.' Charles shrugged. Looking at his juicy lips it struck Julia that this was a man that set out to enjoy life, to overindulge in everything be it food, women, or music. He rubbed his significant belly and sighed. 'What a wonderful lunch, eh, Su ... I'm sorry I'm hopeless with these names.' But Julia wouldn't stop.

'Charles, you don't know what you're getting yourself into. Buying her jewellery! You don't even know the woman.'

'You secretly in love with me, Julia?' He hooted with laughter again and even Suping giggled, though the other diners, wishing themselves in an upmarket *arrondissement* of Paris, were clearly irritated by his gusto. Julia turned her face away from Charles. After all, Feifei was on the front page of her magazine and was now the first patron of the Shanghai ballet. Julia would just have to let them get on with their business.

Telling Suping she would meet her back at the office, Julia walked briskly to the hairdresser's, where a no-nonsense woman with sharp scissors knew to chop just an inch or two off the bottom of Julia's sensible hair, worn neatly below her shoulders.

'The usual?' the woman asked.

'No, thank you. I'd like a bob.'

'A bob?' The woman's face creased in the mirror. 'Very short, yes?'

'I want it to be short and I want it to ... swing. Can you do that?' The hairdresser looked unsure but nodded. The customer was always right in this salon.

'As you like.' And she proceeded to lop off huge chunks of Julia's hair, which fell to the floor with the soft sound of celebration.

'I just got married,' Julia said to the mirror and the woman smiled slightly, not lifting her eyes from her work.

'Shall we go down to the Bund?' Charles asked Feifei as they left the bistro, his fingers grazing the diamonds around her arm.

'You not mind walk a little far?' she asked, wincing at her poor grammar. The Bund was the last place she wanted to go. It had been more than ten days since she had gone to the studio and even longer since she had appeared in the press. Perhaps people thought she had died, and they wouldn't have been far wrong. Charles walked proudly beside her as they cut through the streets of the French Concession, Feifei leading him towards somewhere she guessed he had never been.

'I was so pleased when Julia told me you invited me to lunch,' he said as they walked the backstreets, past the *lilongs* where families gaped at their expensive clothes. Occasionally someone shouted out Feifei's name and she ducked her head, not turning to look. She picked up her speed, willing them away, hoping to get to a place where no one could afford the escape of cinema.

They finally reached the neighbourhood. She hadn't been here for years, afraid of confronting that old Feifei, filled with dread at what the young girl might ask her.

'Welcome to Zhabei,' Feifei said, carefully picking her feet over the rubbish that littered the ground. Charles wrinkled his nose at the smells that hit them – human waste, fried food, livestock.

'Why did you bring me here?' he asked, looking at the squalid houses, built from the materials of misery, edifices of too much work and not enough pay.

'Follow me.' The narrow street strewn with washing lines was so familiar to Feifei. The place they had lived after her father died, crammed into an apartment with three other families. 'Here. I used live here.' She pointed to the third floor of the building, which looked close to collapse. Charles looked at the stained, crumbling building and back at spotless Feifei, obviously shocked.

'But why did you live here?' he asked.

'I tell you story.' And so she did, to the best of her English ability. Her father had run a small tailoring business, making enough for them to live decently in Shanghai when they had moved there from Guangdong. But when he died, in a traffic accident when Feifei was thirteen, he left the family destitute. With no safety net to fall back on, Feifei's mother took a job as a domestic helper to Longwei's family. They left Zhabei when the family decided to take on Feifei's mother as a full-time servant. Then she told him about Longwei, about the secret afternoons and evenings on his mother's favourite recliner until Feifei's stomach grew big and round and he said he would marry her. She tried to explain how, as an educated youth, he had hoped to break down class barriers but had instead been cut off by his family.

'But now, marriage is not good,' she said solemnly. Charles nodded and gripped her wrist. Feifei had watched enough Hollywood movies to know that Americans were obsessed with ideas of love and destiny and togetherness. Americans considered marriages without love to be a violation of their rights and Feifei knew she could exploit Charles' cultural sensitivities. 'I am in danger. I cannot explain but danger. You said before that Hollywood … it is possible for me. Still?' And Charles, looking visibly moved by the story, wrapped a chubby arm around her shoulders and said: 'More than possible. I don't want a beautiful woman like you in danger. We'll get you to Hollywood.'

'Thank you,' Feifei said, suddenly noticing tears trickling down her face. These were real tears, salty and sour, and she hoped Charles didn't think this was a performance. 'Let's leave,' Feifei said, leading him down the street. He followed obediently.

DECEMBER 1931

子夜歌

还从何处来
端然有忧色
三唤不一应
有何比松柏

Night Song

Where do you come from,
With such a sorrowful expression?
I call three times and receive no response,
Why aren't men reliable as pines and cypresses?

VIII

It was ten past ten on a Wednesday morning when the Shanghai Ballet discovered the problem.

'Valentina,' Tamara barked, questioning her students in rapid Russian. The dancers shrugged their shoulders. Polina and Amelia, in their prime positions at the barre, went on stretching, readying themselves for a morning of drills and an afternoon of practising solos. 'I asked a question, girls,' Tamara said, switching into English. Polina brought her body still and Amelia followed suit. The other girls stood listlessly at the barre, mostly looking at their feet, which were growing stubbier, bloodier and harder by the day. 'Somebody must know where she is.'

Lilya cleared her throat.

'She is in prison.' She looked away, not daring to meet Tamara's eye.

'Prison?' Tamara gave a gruff laugh.

'Yes.' Lilya shrugged. 'If you like, we can try to find another dancer for you. There is a girl at the Paradise–'

'It's too late for that,' Tamara said, raising her hand. 'What is she in prison for?' In a city of opium addicts and prostitutes, Amelia found it hard to imagine what transgression was deviant enough to warrant arrest. Lilya slowly lifted her head to meet Tamara's eye and said something in Russian. Whatever she uttered was not news to the other girls, the swans from *Swan Lake*, the village girls from *Giselle*, the bulk of the company. They didn't react to whatever Lilya said.

'What happened?' Amelia whispered to Polina.

'Communism,' Polina said through gritted teeth. Tamara groaned and threw her hands up in the air.

'Polina, lead the drills this morning,' she said. 'I'm going to try to sort out this mess.' She left the studio, banging the door hard behind her. The pianist started and Polina led them through their exercises.

Tamara arrived back after the usual drills, just in time for rehearsals for the show. She came into the studio still shaking her head, her face furious. They practised Swan Lake first, all the girls teetering on their toes, necks long and lithe. Polina usually picked everything up with ease, but that day her timing was off, her spins shaky. When they stopped for a break Amelia reached for her friend's hand.

'Polina, are you all right?'

'I just don't understand why Valentina would do this. Let's go outside.' Polina led Amelia to a café nearby, where she bought the pair of them pastries, 'for energy', she winked. Money was never a problem to Polina, unlike the other girls. Amelia never saw them consume anything or show off new purchases, unlike Polina who bought countless sweet treats and always came to rehearsals wearing new clothes and jewellery.

'Valentina was part of an underground communist group, mostly Russians, I think,' Polina explained. 'The police broke up one of their meetings and she was arrested. It seems she was an active member. Though I can't imagine how she managed to fit it in with ... everything else she does.' Polina shrugged. 'The show will go on, I suppose.'

'You seem upset. Did you know her well?' Amelia thought

back to the night she had first seen Valentina in that dingy room at the Harbin with a bottle of vodka hidden under the bed. Nothing about Valentina suggested she would be political, but maybe Amelia had underestimated the women around her. She saw them as only as pretty, pitiable ornaments.

'I am upset,' Polina said, delicately nibbling the last of her cake, 'because I don't understand how a Russian girl could do this. Not one like me. Valentina went through the same things – losing all her possessions, her social standing, most of her family ... it's just her and her mother in Shanghai, I believe. And she goes to join the oppressors? Some Russians, they believe–' Polina broke off, her voice tearing. 'They-they want to go back now, they think things will be better in the motherland. We are second class citizens here but they don't understand that there we are capitalists. We are the bourgeoisie. They think our compatriots, our so-called comrades, will welcome us back with open arms? Shanghai is bad, but it's all we've got.' Polina's perfect exterior was cracking. Amelia moved her fingers gingerly to Polina's shoulder to comfort her. 'My sister worked in a place like that. I know how bad it can be. My sister, a ballerina! Letting men enjoy her, the way Valentina has to as well.'

'But your sister's doing something different now?'

Polina snorted. 'You could say that. She killed herself.' Amelia felt stricken, realising suddenly that her friend was completely alone in the world. She reached to embrace Polina, but her friend pushed her away.

'Come on. Time for *Giselle*,' Polina said, standing to leave. For the people that had lost, Amelia saw, routine became a religion, the last constant to cling onto. She knew because she hid her misery like them, losing her thoughts in the repetitive movements of ballet.

Will had shared the first part of his report with Rollo and thought his friend seemed pleased. 'I'll let them know you're doing a good job on this, Will. Your future here is once again looking bright.'

153

So far Will had composed an outline of the general political situation in China, supposedly united under Chiang Kai-shek's Nationalist government, but really tearing apart at the seams. He analysed the warlordism that plagued the country, making it victim to the petty desires of individual men, as well as the groundswell of new political ideas in Shanghai. Will had painstakingly translated articles from the communist publications he had purchased, trying to assess how much of a danger radicals posed to unification. The magazines urged urban workers to realise the extent of their exploitation and rise up in revolt against the existing social hierarchy. Looking around him at the irreparable gap between rich and poor in Shanghai, at the garish wealth of the upper echelons and the obscene poverty of those living in the gutter, he could understand the appeal of such revolutionary ideas. But he was careful to downplay the importance of the communists in the report, making clear they had few funds from Russia and that Chiang Kai-shek's intolerance made it unlikely the party would gain a real foothold in China's cities. Will enjoyed the work and felt that by looking at China as something separate from himself he was beginning to see how it all fitted together. His labours brought him a satisfaction similar to that he gained from translating poems. He would begin the section on the Japanese soon. Rollo hadn't said who the report was for, but Will had a feeling it was destined to land on the desk of the consul-general himself.

He went straight home that night, skirting the nocturnal offerings of Shanghai's bars. His hard work was making him too tired for cocktails and besides, he increasingly only had one woman on his mind – Feifei. She said she was in danger and the more research Will did for his report work the more he had the sensation that the whole city was in danger, that Shanghai was balancing delicately on the edge of a disaster, held together by loose pins. His mind still on Feifei, Will found Amelia waiting for him in the drawing room.

'What are these?' In her hands were the two magazines,

their jolly red characters declaring class war from across the room.

'Amelia, for God's sake, put them away!' Concerned about the servants snooping, he had been considering how best to dispose of the incendiary material.

'So, you're a communist now?' Amelia's voice was steely. She set the magazines down on the table next to a vase of wilting yellow flowers.

'If you must know, it's for work. I'm writing a report on the political situation in China. It's very important. I may be promoted.'

'That's good,' Amelia said, softening. 'So the consulate gave you these?'

'Oh, no, I bought them myself on Fuzhou Road.'

'You did what?' Amelia stood up, her face burning close to his.

'Why are you so concerned about this?' He didn't know how his wife had found the magazines nor why she was so incensed by his possessing them.

'We lost a dancer today, Will. A communist. The police rounded them up and put them in prison. Tamara went to get her out, tried bribes and everything. But the communists are a menace to society, so greasing someone's palm isn't going to help. This is dangerous, Will, get rid of them.' Amelia picked up the two publications and thrust them into Will's hands. 'Now.'

'It's consulate work, Amelia. No one's going to arrest me. They'll arrest a little Russian tart for anything, and all the better. I'm going to be fine.' But he felt shame remembering going into the bookshop, cocksure and excited about his report. You never knew the nationality or the motive of the person standing next to you.

'A little Russian tart? Maybe you'd feel differently if I told you it was Lilya.' Amelia had a sneer on her face as she spat out the name. Will felt the deepest layer of his skin turn cold. Lilya. Amelia knew. 'But don't worry, your friend Lilya still has her place in the ballet.' Will saw his inability to deny, to

155

challenge, to repeat the name as if it was a mysterious code, had served only as confirmation for Amelia. She turned on her heels and he wordlessly watched her climb the stairs, her buttocks high and energetic, her slender limbs disappearing onto the upstairs landing. He found himself wishing suddenly for the Amelia of incessant chatter and soft kisses and silly enthusiasm. She was still that person, he saw, but not for him. He was trapped miserably between a wife whose love had dried out to a painful scab and a woman he might never be able to call his. Filling his gut with resolve, Will went to his study to do more work on his report. He found one of his poetry books gone. That must have been where Amelia found the magazines. No doubt she had also found his latest translation tucked in between the pages of another collection lying open on his desk:

In the hall hangs a painting of a goddess;
A beautiful woman emerges from the palace.
Both of them painted so beautifully,
Who can tell which is real?
With clear complexions and bright eyes,
Their slender waists are as one.
How does one distinguish between them?
One is always in high spirits.

Folding the poem away in favour of a stack of local newspapers, Will wondered if Amelia had realised he had been so drawn to the verse because of the two Feifeis – the one Shanghai saw on the screen and the one Will knew in her most vulnerable moments.

Feifei had not been to the studio in over two weeks. The longer she left the problem, the bigger it grew, until she couldn't even think of what to do. She remained mostly in the house, where she could shut out the world – Director Xu and Song Lan, Longwei and his Japanese friends, the growing, coarse anger of a patriotic people for whom she had once considered herself a noble spokeswoman. Once it was public knowledge that she wouldn't be in the film, Feifei would become a fallen heroine, a traitor of the people. She asked Mama's advice, but her mother told her just to follow her husband. She was too scared to tell anyone else about Longwei's involvement with the Japanese and after he had hit her, she dared not disobey him. She thought of how Lili had cried when she had returned from Will's house, trailing her blonde, blue-eyed doll down the stairs with her, wailing that she thought her mother was never going to come back. Every time someone called for Feifei the servants told them she wasn't there. 'No, I don't know where she is. I've been in my village, I just got back an hour ago ah,' they would lie, Feifei impressed at their protestations when the callers told them they had already heard that line. 'Last week? That was another girl!' But today when the doorbell rang and one of the maids, Lin, came to tell her that a man called Xu was waiting downstairs, Feifei rose from the chair where she had been listlessly flicking through a magazine and told Lin to bring him upstairs and serve some tea.

'So, you're alive.' Director Xu stood in the doorway, his face serious.

'Director Xu, I'm so sorry.' Feifei looked at the floor. The director moved towards her, inspecting her face, and she wondered if he was looking for wounds inflicted by Longwei. Nonsense, she brushed the thought aside, no one knew what happened in this house. 'Please sit,' she said, taking a step back from his searching eyes. He obeyed, but watched her with an intensity that Feifei found discomfiting. Lin served tea, her eyes swivelling between the two, hoping to catch snippets of scandal. Feifei dismissed her.

'I can explain,' she started.

'I hope so. You were spotted last week in a French restaurant.' Damn it, Feifei thought, Shanghai was like a little village sometimes.

'Oh, I see.' She took a too-hot sip of tea. 'Director Xu, I am in danger. I don't want to be dramatic. I had no idea what to tell you. I cannot continue with *Shanghai Dreams*.' Feifei felt the salty sting of tears in her eyes.

'Feifei, we have worked together for many years. You know you can tell me anything.'

'Not this.' She shook her head and took a deep breath. 'Longwei has banned me from the film. He is my husband and I can't disobey him.' Director Xu raised his eyebrows at this.

'As far as I can see, my dear, you have done nothing but disobey him from the day you two married. But that's another story. You've never let him hold you back before. Is this something to do with his new acquaintances? He seems to be quite the man about town again.' Feifei felt her heart still. People knew. Of course, Longwei would be incapable of being discreet. He would be flaunting his new-found wealth, trying to impress his disapproving family, desperate to show them that despite his lowly marriage and inability to make it to Cambridge, he had succeeded in the city that favoured only a few.

'Acquaintances?'

'I've seen him with lots of high rollers. And some Japanese, of course.'

'He says I can't continue. But I'm so worried about him too. Did you hear about the businessman that was murdered for his association with the Japanese?'

'Among other things,' Director Xu said drily. 'He was involved in lots of dirty deals, from what I hear. It might not be so clear-cut. I wouldn't worry.'

'I can't bear to read the papers. Every day there's a protest against the Japanese, a boycott, and there's my husband, *smoothing the way for them*, as he puts it. A traitor. And now I'm just as bad.' Director Xu drained his teacup.

'It pains me to do so, Feifei, but I am able to continue the film without you. We have already shot the key parts. Some scenes will have to be altered of course, but your suicide can happen off-camera. Or we use a double and shoot her from behind.' He went quiet and Feifei turned to the window, her eyes tracing a splattering of rain drops. 'I hope we can work together again.' He stood up.

'Director Xu, is it over?' she asked, her voice childlike. If he stepped even just one foot out her door, Feifei knew her Shanghai movie career would be finished. But she saw no alternative but to let him leave.

'No, Feifei, of course not.'

'But Song Lan, and what you told me before, about talking films and my rough voice ... I suppose I'm getting old. Twenty-four already. There are new girls ...' Feifei was choking on tears now. 'And my husband ...' Director Xu looked helpless, as though he wanted to embrace her, to soothe her, but instead he turned away, trailing the stardust of Shanghai behind him.

Feifei sat still, goosepimples pricking her skin. She heard the door close behind him and a pain gripped her heart, knowing that the most important thing in her life had been sealed off. She flashed with anger at Longwei. Every day she hated him more. She thought of all the times she had obeyed him when she was nothing more than a girl, let him touch her with his delicate, soft, rich fingers, first gently, then roughly, how the first time he had penetrated her she had had no idea what was going on. She regretted those afternoons now, the decisions she made at a time when all that mattered was survival, protecting her mother's job and keeping food in their bellies. Of course, there had been good times too, when Longwei had reinforced her dismal elementary schooling by coaching her in characters and, most importantly, the fateful day he took her to the China Star studio, announcing proudly that he had brought them the most beautiful girl in Shanghai.

'She will be the Chinese Garbo!' he had announced and Feifei had marvelled at how his mouth, Chinese like hers, could produce these alien sounds. She also wondered who this mysterious Garbo was. But she didn't thank him for any of it, not now, instead she wished she had never lain down on her back, passively letting him fondle her. A man who disobeyed his family was capable of betraying his country. She should have known all along. Feifei walked through to her bedroom, her feet feeling achey and old. She lay down on the bed and slept, as she spent all her days. Shanghai was empty now. She wanted to sleep for a long time.

She was awoken by the shrill ring of the telephone and buried her head in the pillow to ignore it. Lin knocked on the door and whispered that a foreigner was asking for her. Thinking it might be Charles, Feifei roused enough energy to drag herself out of bed and go to the phone, only to be disappointed by Julia's feminine voice.

'Hi, Feifei, it's me. Listen, you know how you said you would support the Shanghai Ballet? Well, they've lost a dancer and I wondered if you knew anyone who might be good enough. I know that you're friends with lots of entertainment types, and I was thinking it might be good to get someone who is a bit of a name on board ...'

'I'm sorry. I don't think I do. I just want to support it by name,' Feifei said, a rush of weariness taking hold of her. 'I will come to the benefit but I can't find you dancers. Sorry, Julia.'

'Oh, that's fine,' the American said, sounding hurt. These foreigners, Feifei thought, always so demanding. She hung up the phone and went back to bed.

The next day Feifei had another visitor. She told Lin to let her friend in, her heart heavy as Ling entered the small room where the maid had laid out yesterday's tea set. Ling gave Feifei a hard look that didn't suit her round, happy face. She sat down opposite her and lifted a cup to her lips. She paused, inhaled the scent of jasmine and set it down.

'Director Xu says you quit.'

Feifei nodded. 'Ling, let me explain.'

'Before you say anything,' Ling said, straightening out a *qipao* Feifei had never seen before, 'you should know that they have given me some time off. Until after Chinese new year, in fact. As I play your friend in the movie there is apparently no need for me to keep going to the studio. Or to keep getting paid, apparently.' She sat quietly, waiting for Feifei to say something.

'Ling, I'm sorry.' Feifei wished her friend would leave, hoped only to crawl back into bed and sleep again. She had been in bed when Longwei came home the day before but she sensed he liked this immobile, silent wife, that she had finally become the person he had always wanted to marry. A beautiful doll, quiet and sleeping, with limbs that could be manipulated for pleasure.

'Oh, and also, they've suggested I *reduce*.' Ling's cheeks puffed with false pride as she said this. 'Of course, Song Lan is only too delighted you've left. She's going to be the star now.'

Feifei looked at Ling, noticing how her arms had grown slacker, her stomach rounder. Too many late nights in cabarets, Feifei thought, too much good food. 'Ling, did Director Xu tell you what happened?'

'No,' she said coldly. She took a sip of her tea, watching Feifei over the rim of the cup and Feifei felt the pain from yesterday returning. Would all her acquaintances traipse through her house over the next few weeks, taking a final tea with her, staring accusing and silent as they faked cordiality? 'But I can guess. You're too busy chasing foreigners to film. I heard you were seen with some fat man. At least the blond one was good-looking.'

'Ling, it's nothing to do with that.' Feifei realised now looking at her that she needed a friend. 'It's to do with Longwei. He banned me from being in the film.'

'But why? You know he's always banning you from this and that, getting jealous. I'll find him some little dancer from one of the cabarets and he won't care anymore.' Ling's words stung, but Feifei knew it was usually an effective solution.

'It's more than that. Ling, if I tell you something, I have to be able to trust you. Longwei is working with the Japanese.' As the words fell from her lips Ling's expression softened.

'Oh.'

'Yes, I'm afraid of what will happen to us … to him, to me, to Lili. My mother says we should all follow Longwei. She

161

sees him as our saviour. She doesn't care that I have single-handedly supported this family for almost eight years.'

'What are you going to do?'

'I have no idea.' Feifei felt a little relief from talking to her friend, but still her problems loomed up around her, dark and fanged, and she had little clue as to how to proceed. Ling reached over and tenderly took one of her hands. 'Ling, I've had a thought!' She dropped her friend's hand and jumped up. 'Why don't you join the Shanghai Ballet?'

'The what?'

'*Baleiwu*. It's a very elegant European dance. I am helping them and they need a dancer. And, well, it would help you to lose weight too. The Russian girls, they are very long and lean, with nice, hard muscle.' Ling's eyes flickered as she decided whether to be offended or not.

'Dance? I don't know, Feifei. How much money is in it?'

'Nothing at the moment, but they're putting on a show in January. Lots of people will be there. It'll be a chance for you to show Director Xu he's made a big mistake.' Feifei sat herself back down, feeling traces of her old self fizzing inside her. 'Come on, Ling. It's a wonderful idea.'

'I'm more of a singer than a dancer,' Ling said, but Feifei was sure her friend would agree.

After accompanying Ling to the door, Feifei felt better. She would stay awake until Lili got back from school, she decided, and then take her somewhere special. She didn't have to hide anymore.

Valentina was gone. The White Russians, unlike the British, French and Americans, were stateless and therefore subject to Chinese laws. There was nothing that could be done, no strings that could be pulled or friendly foreign judges who could be called upon, so the dancers simply carried on with their drills, their turns becoming softer and more fluent, their turnouts more pronounced, their ballerina buns neater and higher on their heads. Several of the girls had enlisted their best contacts to free Valentina, some had even sent hulking Russian boyfriends who worked as security guards to threaten to beat the jailers, but all to no avail. Amelia felt a strange, grudging respect for Lilya after she told them she had paid for Valentina's release the only way she knew how, only to have the three guards laugh her out the prison after they had enjoyed her services. She told this story with a straight face and the only ones who winced were Polina, Tamara and Amelia. The other girls had nodded solemnly, used to selling their bodies the way market hawkers sold off vegetables, sometimes with painful discounts when times were bad. Tamara was looking for another dancer but told Amelia she feared she had found all of the capable taxi dancers in Shanghai. She had been teaching some young girls ballet but explained they were far too young, the oldest only twelve, to be part of a company.

'In five years,' she said, 'we will rival the Bolshoi. But for now, I need adult bodies that I can try to mould into dancers.'

There were less than two months to go before the fundraiser, planned for January 28th. December had brought real winter to Shanghai and the dancers wrapped themselves in several layers as they practised, the wind clattering against the studio's flimsy windows. It was a Monday when Julia arrived at five to ten, trailing a Chinese girl behind her who looked vaguely familiar to Amelia. These days it was not only Polina and Amelia who arrived early to stretch and there were several girls dotted around the wooden floor, legs contorted at angles and teeth gritted as they worked out knotted hips.

'Morning! I have some good news!' Julia, her hair chopped short, stood in the middle of the room. 'I have another dancer for you.' She pulled on the girl's wrist and the new dancer gave an approximation of a *plié*. She didn't have the body of a dancer, Amelia thought, looking at her broad shoulders and fleshy upper arms, but her cheeks were rosy with excitement. 'This is Ling, a singer and an actress from the China Star studio. She comes recommended by the Shanghai Ballet's new sponsor, actress Wu Feifei, who is not only donating money to the company but will also attend the first show.

163

She should be guaranteed to draw the crowds.' The girls on the floor clapped as Julia spoke, ready to welcome Ling, and stood up crowding around her. But Amelia's face set hard and stony as she stepped away from the actress and made her way directly to Julia, pulling her aside.

'Hi, Amelia!' Julia enveloped her in a hug. 'Gosh, you look more elegant every time I see you. You're really getting slim compared to all those other wives, gorging themselves on gossip and cocktails.' Amelia said nothing, leading Julia to the stairwell outside the studio. An old Russian was carrying steamed buns up the stairs and eyed the two elegant young women suspiciously.

'Julia, why have brought a friend of Feifei's here? It's hard enough for me as it is, with Lilya here.'

'Aren't you going to say anything about my hair?' Julia said, her laugh tinkling and innocent.

'Very nice. But I'm serious. And Wu Feifei is our *sponsor*? The woman is having an affair with my husband.'

'*Au contraire*, my dear Amelia. I have diverted her attention with another man. When we interviewed her for the magazine she saw my article, I mean, *your* article about the ballet and she said she wanted to help any way she could. She's giving money, Amelia, we can't turn that down. Plus, she'll attract people who wouldn't normally consider coming. She's not a problem to you anymore.'

Amelia looked sceptically at Julia. 'Fine,' she sighed. 'We need all the help we can get. But Julia, it just feels that you aren't really thinking of me in any of this.' Tamara poked her head out into the stairwell.

'When you've finished gossiping, please Amelia, we need you in here.' She shrank back into the room.

'I'm sorry, I really am. I've been distracted recently,' Julia said. 'You know I married Ju Wei?'

'Congratulations!' Amelia said, but she knew the words sounded hollow. Amelia had discovered that it was torture being someone's only wife, never mind the runner-up. 'I hope you're very happy together.'

'Yeah, me too. Hey, do you have a venue for the show yet?'

'No,' Amelia said. 'I keep pestering Will to take me to one of the consulate functions so I can meet some more *influential* people but he always makes an excuse.' She made a face and Julia, now a married woman, laughed heartily.

'I'll see what I can do for you, Myrtha, Queen of the Wilis,' she said and disappeared down the stairs.

Back in the studio, Amelia saw Tamara looking disapprovingly at Ling's posture and her figure, but she kept her mouth shut and corrected her gently, manipulating her chin and arms softly. In Shanghai, commerce trumped everything. Whatever would bring in an audience would have to do, even if it was a girl who looked like a farmer's daughter.

Feifei met Ling for lunch in a newly-opened café a week after her friend's first rehearsal with the ballet. The pale winter sun streamed through the window and Feifei allowed herself to feel optimistic for once. She had little idea what Longwei was up to when he was away from home. She saw him once or twice a week when he came back, the magnanimous businessman, showering Feifei in sparkling jewels and Lili in imported toys. Even Mama had been the recipient of a tight dress that made her aged figure look ridiculous. He never asked Feifei to accompany him to dinner or dancing again though, and for that she was grateful. The week before she had seen Charles again when she took Lili to a western shop that sold chocolates. Feifei found the taste too creamy and sweet, but Lili had developed a taste for foreign foods thanks to her French classmates. While standing in line to buy truffles she spotted Charles coming in the door.

'I thought it was you!' his voice boomed. 'And who's this?' He rubbed Lili's head vigorously and her small features knitted in annoyance.

'Daughter,' Feifei said quietly, feeling embarrassed at her poor English in a shop full of foreigners.

'You're going to grow up to be heartbreaker like your

mother,' he said, pinching one of Lili's soft cheeks. Lili scowled.

'I very much enjoyed our walk,' he said, addressing Feifei, who was still trying to work out what 'heartbreaker' meant. 'Would you perhaps join me tomorrow for dinner? We can discuss business,' he said. Feifei smiled warmly.

'I like,' she said and he waved them goodbye, saying something to Lili about not eating too many chocolates and obeying her mother. But the dinner turned out to be something of a disappointment. Without anyone to translate for them, the conversation between the two had been halting and awkward and Feifei was growing impatient. She needed to get her back-up plan in place and Charles still hadn't put anything on the table.

Now it was time to call in a favour with Ling, who said she had already lost an inch or two from her waist thanks to Tamara's strict routine. She told Feifei in rushed, excited tones that not only had her English improved but she was learning some Russian.

'It's unfair that you pick up these languages so easily. I'm really struggling with English, which actually leads me to why I came here today,' Feifei said to her friend. 'I wondered if I could meet my English teacher at your apartment. I never know when Longwei will come home these days and I don't have any opportunity to take classes.'

'You mean you would like to meet that poet who is in love with you at my house?'

'He's not in love with me,' Feifei said, but she felt her face glowing. Her whole life she had been trained to seek adulation and any confirmation of it boosted her heart.

'He is. There are plenty of Russians teaching English, but you prefer him. You must be missing his romantic verses.' Ling teased, but Feifei knew she would agree. She understood what it was like, how sometimes you had to throw yourself into situations you could never have imagined just to keep your life in balance. 'Of course, you and the poet may meet at my flat. But you may not lie on my bed.' Ling dissolved in a fit of giggles, drawing stares from the other patrons. Feifei laughed along with her. Yes, she thought, the sun warming one side of her face, things were changing.

Will approached the address Feifei had given him with a little trepidation. Of course he was excited to see her again, he had been aching for a sign from her, but now it had come he felt only apprehension. Feifei had already told him she was in danger but a little investigation of his own told him that she didn't know the extent of her problems. Walking home down Bubbling Well Road the other night he had spotted that a Hollywood film was showing at one of the cinemas. He lingered outside, reading the sign: *Daughter of the Dragon* starring ANNA MAY WONG. Feifei had told him many times about the grace, beauty and talent of this Chinese actress, so Will decided to buy a ticket. Amelia barely noticed what time he came home these days. Whether he was back at six or eleven, he would likely find her stretching out on the floor or standing, hands thrust above her head, eyes tracing the slow and deliberate movements of her arms. He slipped into a low seat in the cinema and watched the film, which, disappointingly, was about Fu Manchu, one of the old China stereotypes he had come to abhor since arriving in the country and discovering it was not the land of misty-eyed beauties and wandering poets he had once imagined it to be. Anna May Wong as Princess Ling Moy shone, her hair blunt and straight across her forehead, her neck and wrists dripping in jewels. But as soon as she opened her mouth, Will noticed something that made his heart fall into his stomach. Wong had perfect diction. Every time she opened her mouth she formed perfect-sounding words, not so removed from Will's own accent. She was not a Chinese from China but must have been born abroad. There was no way at all that Feifei would ever speak like her.

Ling lived in a block of mansion flats in the French Concession that had fallen into some disrepair in recent years, the grass growing wild and tall on the lawn in front. Feifei came downstairs to let Will in and following her up the stairway with its walls of peeling paint, Will suddenly imagined this as an alternative life for Feifei. It was likely the kind of place a pretty girl with a talent or two could get herself to in Shanghai, but it was the limit. Only by being married to her odious husband had Feifei ended up living in such splendour. Will noticed the light curves of her body in a sky-blue *qipao* as she climbed the stairs in front of him.

'Thank you for coming,' she was saying, though he focused only on the movement of her hips. 'I've missed our lessons.' She opened the door to the room and Will realised suddenly that they were alone. The space creaked with emptiness. Feifei served him tea, her movements jerky as she poured the steaming liquid into his cup.

'So, what shall we study today?' Will asked. 'We were looking at conditionals before, oh, how about this?' He flicked through a grammar book. 'Prepositions. Very tricky.' Anna May Wong's perfectly formed words echoed in his head.

'In a minute. First, I want to ask you something, Will.' She took a deep breath. 'I told you I was in danger. Do you think there is any way you can help me?'

'Of course. But first, you have to tell me what the situation is,' he said slowly.

'Fine. Well, my husband is working for the Japanese. It could be a very dangerous situation for me and my daughter. I think maybe I should go abroad but I don't know how.' She looked down at her lap.

'I'm sure there's something I can do,' Will said, though he knew he had little power at the consulate and certainly wouldn't be able to secure papers for someone after harbouring a spy.

'Oh, thank you.' Feifei took one of his hands and gripped it gently. 'I'm scared for my safety, Will.' She squeezed out a single tear that traced half of her cheek before hardening into a crystal. Will stepped around the small table between them to embrace her. He remembered how he had kissed her before and she had become shy and embarrassed, then disappeared from his life entirely. But seeing her ruby lips quivering below him he couldn't resist her. He lifted his hands to the back of her head, feeling the soft padding of her black curls, and pulled her face towards his. Their lips met and this time she didn't pull away, letting her body hang limp in his arms. He traced her breasts and stomach with fevered hands, his breath becoming ragged. He felt for the slit in her dress and stroked the stockinged thigh underneath. She gently rubbed his neck with her fingers and he sighed, sure that his feelings were reciprocated. He pulled back to look at her, this woman from the screen, fleshy and seductive, held in his embrace.

'Feifei,' he started, when he heard the door open. He shot a look behind him and saw a young girl, who was not Ling, with a look of shock on her face.

'Oh, hello,' she said, in clumsy English.

'We're having an English lesson,' Feifei spat at her. The girl ducked her head and disappeared behind the flimsy partition that marked her side of the room. Feifei sighed.

'Unlucky,' she said, stroking his arm with the tips of her fingers. 'But thank you for agreeing to help me. You are a good man, Will.'

After the lesson had ended, Will left the apartment with one last hurried kiss, his heart dancing. It was mid-December and night was already rolling in, but he basked under imagined summer skies all the way home. Shanghai was beautiful once more.

Now that Will had a plan, he was able to settle into a peaceable routine with Amelia. He was so sure of his folly that he found himself quite able to tolerate his wife and even to admire her, in the manner of a kindly uncle or old family friend. They each had their habits – Amelia returned later and later from the studio, her hair matted with sweat and her figure growing sleeker and more feline by the day, while Will returned promptly from his duties at the consulate to lock himself in the study and work on his report. He also threw himself back into poetry. Reading those old words, he saw that the kind of love he had for Feifei only came along once in a lifetime and if he was to let the actress slip away he would become just another of life's witnesses, destined to watch others savour the fruits of existence. He wanted to drown himself in the beauty of poems, to live the words he knew by heart, at least until he could devote himself to loving Feifei in some kind of permanent arrangement. He translated new poems with gusto and amassed a collection he was thinking of sending to England to seek publication. His new favourite poem was one called 'Remembering' by Su Shi. He found the words *What is our life on earth? Like a flock of geese alighting on the snowy ground* strangely comforting, the way they echoed the futility of life. If all this was nothing more than a snowy claw mark left by a goose, he had to seize it, to squeeze everything out of it he could, and worry little about the effects of his behaviour. So when Amelia asked him to spend Christmas at Julia's he readily agreed, even finding himself looking forward to the idea of a conjugal visit to friends. He socialised little these days, his head full of Feifei and his ever-shifting plans for the pair of them. Singapore was his top choice at the moment, though perhaps they might first go to Hong Kong.

Julia's party was held in her spinster apartment, where she still lived with her old cook for company. But Ju Wei sat proudly by her side, enjoying the freedom of having wives from two different cultures who demanded distinct duties for him for their separate festivals. The cook had made an approximation of Christmas dinner, which the guests swallowed between bites of conversation and sips of champagne. Will had finally been given entry into his wife's secret world. First he took in the unaccompanied Tamara, her face sharp and her tone harsh, noticing she rarely entered conversation, only speaking to dismiss something as useless or uninteresting. Then there was Ling, who thankfully did not show that she recognised Will. She brought a man she had recently met at the Paradise who claimed to have been educated in England, a fact that was plainly a lie given his struggles to communicate with the native speakers, but they decided to indulge her naïve romance. Someone called Polina was due but had yet to arrive. There was a staid English journalist, Edmund, from the *North China Daily News*, and a young Chinese girl from Julia's magazine.

'I may be Chinese,' she said simply when Will enquired as to why she was celebrating Christmas, 'but I am *new* Chinese.'

Their words bounced from politics to gossip, always rounding back to the plans for the Shanghai Ballet. Amelia in particular talked enthusiastically of theatres packed to capacity and front page news stories, with one eager eye on the uninterested Edmund at the other end of the table. Watching Amelia's glowing dark eyes under her shiny hair, Will felt a tenderness for his wife that was fresh and unexpected. Now he knew he was leaving her, he watched her every action as though he were remembering a life once lived.

When the main course was finished, Julia placed her cutlery down noisily and announced that the next issue of *New Woman* would be coming out tomorrow, with none other than Wu Feifei on the cover. Will felt his last piece of dry turkey catch in his throat. What was the point of sanctimonious Shanghai society if not to smooth over the bumps created by the city's inhabitants? He watched men at the consulate who had spent the night before together in a brothel greet each other warmly with banal talk of sunshine and cricket, the vagaries of Shanghai's nightlife left to rest during daylight hours. He hadn't expected to hear Feifei's name and wondered if his wife had planned the ambush. But the pained smile on Amelia's face assured him she had not wanted to hear those three syllables pronounced either.

'But even more importantly,' Julia said, patching over her error, 'is that the Shanghai Ballet is inside this issue! I'm talking about the wonderful article by Amelia Graves, of course, a woman of many talents.' Ling clapped excitedly, whispering to her date who stroked his moustache. She blushed red from the alcohol. Giggly, Ling spluttered: 'Well, it's a good thing Feifei's on the cover this month. You got to her just in time.'

'Sorry?' Julia turned to face Ling.

'Well, Feifei has plans far greater than *Shanghai*.' She laughed again. 'Hey, what is this stuff?' She swirled cognac around in a gold-rimmed glass, which her date removed from her grip and set down firmly on the table.

'Whatever do you mean?' Amelia asked.

'Well, you might see her in the cinema, but not Chinese cinema. She's going to Hollywood.' Will felt the tension in his jaw give way. It was just her old dream. She wasn't going anywhere without him.

'Good for her,' Amelia said, with none of the conviction she might have had if she had been told the news a month or two earlier.

Julia had hosted enough parties to read an atmosphere with the precision of a thermometer. She wished she had never mentioned Feifei. She had simply thrown out the name in a lapse of careless excitement about the new issue. She wanted people to remember she was a magazine editor and an American woman of the world, even with her new husband sitting beside her, their romance officially sanctioned to permit such social appearances. Will and Amelia had shrunk into themselves at the end of the table, each internally praying no one would look in their direction and connect them to Feifei. So she had redirected the conversation only for Ling to revive the corpse of Feifei with careless words. Feeling for her friend, Julia immediately suggested the dancers give a demonstration of their skills. All looking reluctant, the ballet dancers met each other's eyes over the table, daring the others to stand up. Ling flung down her napkin and leapt onto her toes, flapping her arms up and down in an approximation of a swan. Laughing drunkenly, she tipped over to one side just as the cook announced in his hoarse voice that another visitor had arrived.

Polina entered the room, a vision in a swinging coat of black fur that fell gracefully to her shins. Her cheeks were coloured a high pink from the cold outside and her hair had been curled in bouncing spirals to frame her softly sculpted face.

'I'm sorry I'm late,' she breathed and Julia noticed how every man in the room – including Ju Wei – became unnaturally stiff in their chairs, their sexual interest palpable under the hum of female camaraderie that greeted the Russian's arrival.

'Oh, Polina! Not at all,' Julia said, rising to greet the last guest. She had not set a place for anyone accompanying Polina and seeing the most beautiful woman in the room take her solitary seat Julia felt a little pang for her. But glimpsing Ju Wei out of the corner of her eye, Julia scolded herself for pitying anyone. There was just reality, and you took it or you died alone and hungry.

'Would you like some food?' Julia asked but Polina shook her head. 'You have to eat something. I'll get the cook to fix something for you though I'm afraid we may already have finished off the lot. I'll get him to whip you up something Chinese, he's far better at that anyway.'

Julia slipped out of the room, not allowing Polina to refuse. When she came back, Polina was holding forth on the evils of communism. Clearly Valentina had come up in conversation. She only hoped no one would mention Lilya's carnal sacrifice for her friend. Damn Amelia's philandering husband, Julia thought, sitting herself back down, there wasn't a movie star or a communist in town you could mention around the pair of them.

'They lost everything because of these people and now they go running back into their arms? Ridiculous,' Polina snorted.

'Well, Russia is financing part of the Chinese communist movement. Moscow's a model for China's young communists, and many study there, coming home to find fault with everything capitalist and imperialist,' Will said, apparently not awkward, his face flushed with the enjoyment of dissecting the city's political underbelly. 'And it makes sense. Look at the wonderful project you ladies have put together. Many

Russians have met a cruel fate here in Shanghai and when they're told the motherland is now a communist utopia where no one wants for anything ... Well then, what's a few stolen jewels and an occupied mansion? It's history. In Russia you don't have to pay for bread in such ... extreme ways.' Amelia looked surprised at Will's words but Polina nodded.

'You are wise. You can say this because you are objective. But people *died*. People we must never forget.' The ghost of her sister breezed through the dining room and everyone shivered.

'Not another wasted life,' Tamara said firmly. 'Not in our Shanghai.' The cook brought through a plate of steamed beef and peppers for Polina, who launched into the meal with an abandon unsuited to her snowy elegance.

'We were just talking about another group of young Russians arrested for being part of an underground cell,' Will said warmly, turning to Julia. 'There was a lot in the papers about it yesterday. Chiang Kai-shek is certainly feeling nervous about the support for communism here in what should be the *bourgeois* capital of China,' he continued, warming up to his topic.

'Well, you certainly know a lot about politics. All this time I thought you were a poet,' Julia said, which prompted unwarranted laughter from Ling, who clumsily clamped her fingers over her mouth.

'I used to consider myself a real man of letters. But since I've been working at the consulate I've discovered just how interesting modern China is. After all, my favourite poets, such as Du Fu, often wrote beautiful verses about politics –'

'Yes, dear,' Amelia said, silencing Will.

Ju Wei rose from the table then and offered the men cigars. They filed out of the room, leaving the women to watch Polina finish her meal. Julia watched Ju Wei with envy, the way he could hold court in her house, while in his residence she was now forced to curl into herself, make herself as little a burden as possible on every occasion. She watched him until the crinkles of his Western suit had disappeared through the door frame and turned back to Polina, who shovelled forkfuls of meat into her mouth, eating quickly.

'My gosh, Polina, you're starving!' Julia said.

'I've been on hunger strike,' she said. The other women waited until she announced the end of her meal with one final scrape of the knife across the plate and leant back in her chair before daring to speak. 'I have something to tell you. I was late because ... he won't let me do it.'

Tamara jolted upright in her seat. 'Do what?' she demanded, but they all knew the answer.

'Dance,' Polina said, her voice strangled. 'I'm sorry.' Her eyes flashed red and she sniffed, but she seemed determined not to cry. She still had all the pride of a prima ballerina. Tamara let out a burst of staccato Russian, to which Polina only shook her head pathetically.

'But what are we going to do?' Amelia cried with an emotion that surprised them all. 'You're our principal dancer!'

'I know. I'm sorry.' The tears were flowing now, and Ling, with the unabashed affection of a drunk, wrapped one of her arms around Polina's neck. Polina brushed her off.

'I don't deserve kindness. Not from any of you.'

'But what about the venue?' Julia asked. She had been counting on the Blackbird after making several enquiries at hotels and clubs favoured by Shanghai's elite set only to be turned down at every one once the managers understood where the dancers were sourced from.

'The venue? I never said you could use the Blackbird. I never even asked him,' Polina said, her new curls bobbing uncertainly around her.

'Did he know you were dancing with us?' Tamara asked.

'No. I knew he would say no so I just joined the ballet and hoped he would like the idea once it was too late for me to turn back. I wanted him to see I was serious and that it would be good for me ...'

Tamara pushed her chair back and stood up, towering over the table and pointing at Polina, ranting in Russian.

'Tamara,' Julia said. 'Sit down. Let's think of what we can do.'

'I will go and see him,' Tamara said coldly. 'I will be his Christmas present.'

'No, no, you'll make it worse! You can't,' Polina protested, but Tamara folded her arms in a way that let them know the decision had been made.

Feifei rang the doorbell of the imposing house, two tightly wrapped gifts in her hands. She didn't know exactly what these people did on Christmas Day. The whole story about a man being born to a virgin and then going on to be hung from a cross seemed both unlikely and ghastly, but she felt she should probably bring a gift. She was delighted that Charles had invited her to this event and even more excited that he had told her negotiations with one of the studios in Hollywood were under way. Luckily for Feifei, Longwei was going out for a big lunch with some of his contacts and when he left the house a trail of cologne hung in the air. That smell always meant a long day, Feifei knew, one that would likely stretch into the night. It was the smell of hunting for women. So she had changed into a blood red *qipao* and wrapped herself in white furs, feeling very celebratory. Standing on the porch, she shifted the presents from one hand to the other, fretting about making a good impression. The door swung open and a woman with a cracked walnut face stood looking at her.

'Oh my, aren't you just a darling!' she exclaimed, wafting a cigarette in Feifei's direction.

'Hello,' Feifei said, wary at the meaning of the woman's words. *Darling* was good, she knew, but the woman had almost spat when she said it.

'Now, I hate to turn away such a beautiful surprise, my dear, but I haven't got the faintest idea who you are.' The woman's laugh had a tinge of cruelty and Feifei instinctively backed away, the presents she held now feeling large and obtrusive.

176

'She's with me.' Charles loomed behind the woman, wearing a new navy suit tight across the shoulders. 'This is Wu Feifei, the most famous – and most beautiful – actress in Shanghai.'

'An actress!' The woman laughed again, waving Feifei through the threshold. 'I should've known you film types would bring *actresses*.' She disappeared down the corridor and Feifei warily stepped to Charles' side.

'She doesn't like me,' she said quietly but he shook his head, planting a firm hand on her back.

'She's jealous. A bad hostess.' And he chuckled away in that easy way of Americans. Feifei handed him one of the gifts.

'For you. From me.'

'Can I open it now?'

Feifei watched as Charles tore off the wrapping paper and marvelled at the forthrightness of these foreigners. He hadn't even pretended to decline the gift. 'Oh, what's this?' he asked.

'They're jujubes. Very good to nourish body in the winter,' Feifei explained. 'And that … that is a mah jong set. Now you are living in China you can learn our games!' She beamed at him but saw only puzzlement on his face.

'Well, thank you. Did I tell you, you look absolutely ravishing?' Feifei didn't know what ravishing meant, but that didn't stop the word lighting a little glow inside her as they went into the main room, where they found the party, stagnating in its sedate stage, everyone lulled quiet by drink.

There was a table laid out with food, and men and women, all European and American, circled the room, clinking glasses and talking in low voices. Feifei felt the heat of a hundred stares on her face when she entered the room with Charles. The other women at the party looked dowdy, she thought, and were at least ten years older than her. Clutching the other gift, she approached the wrinkled hostess again and proffered the present.

'You really are a darling,' the woman said, placing her permanently attached cigarette down on an ashtray as she tore through the paper. 'You didn't need to bring a present.'

'I want,' Feifei said, and internally cursed herself for getting the tense wrong. Her English rose and fell depending on who she was speaking to. With Charles, it was relatively good, and with Will it flowed smoothly, thanks to his boyish encouragement. But with strangers she always stumbled over the words. At least in Hollywood she would have a script. The woman shook the box of ginseng, the same confusion on her face as Charles' had shown just moments before.

'Well, it's very *authentic*,' she said, turning back to the party. Some of the women gave stifled laughs and Feifei felt her face flush again. 'I suppose that's what happens when the natives get involved in our traditions. What a *wonderful* culture clash.' The woman's words were swimming in Feifei's brain, knocking into each other and losing all meaning. It was like watching a film without understanding the plot. Charles came up behind her and offered to introduce her to people, placing a glass of fizzy wine in her hand. But Feifei felt acutely uncomfortable. People gawked at her and their sophisticated words flew over her head, their meanings distant and obscure. She stumbled behind Charles as he made his way around the room, managing to shake hands and smile as she was expected to but feeling like a shadow. She wanted to shout at these people that she was a movie star, someone important. But that wasn't true anymore. Charles led her to another American man, one who looked not unlike him, but slighter and younger.

'So, this is the girl,' the man drawled, reaching down for one of Feifei's hands and lifting it to his lips to mark it with a light kiss. Feifei smiled warmly. He seemed to be the only person at the party pleased to see her. 'You're right, Charlie, she's a knockout. Stunning.' Charles bristled proudly and explained the man was a friend who was also in the film business.

'I go to Hollywood,' Feifei said, her voice slow and careful.

'I betcha Charles will take you anywhere you like. Isn't that right, Charlie? He'll take you to see New York too if you like.'

'No, I go to Hollywood to be actress,' Feifei pronounced and the man hooted loudly, causing other guests to turn and stare.

'She's special, this one,' he said. Feifei frowned. How could all these people live in her kingdom and have no idea she was queen?

After an hour or so of further blustering conversations, Charles said he would see her home. As they left together Feifei heard scandalised titters. She hoped people knew she was married, even if her husband wasn't waiting for her at home. Shanghai was always carefully divided between foreigners and Chinese and it was far from unusual to find a party with not a single Chinese face present, save for the domestic help. But blundering Charles, still somewhat of a Shanghai virgin, likely hadn't picked up on the subtle social mores of two opposed elite sets. Feifei's husband and many of his friends had open, worldly views. They had studied abroad and they wanted to shake up the system. They saw no harm in mixing with foreigners, and more enlightened aliens, such as Julia, felt the same way. Feifei felt fire under her skin as they left the party. Just wait until you see me on one of your Hollywood screens, she thought.

'You're quiet,' Charles remarked. 'I'm sorry the party was a bit of a drag. You're far too young and beautiful to be wasted on a scene like that. Let's get a drink on the Bund. I've got good news for you.'

So over a gin for Charles and a green tea for Feifei, who had felt the fizzy wine go to her head, he told her his big news.

'One of my friends at the studio tells me he's got a role for a Chinese. They start shooting in late spring. It's not a main role, but a nice supporting one. How does that sound?' Feifei stared at him wordlessly, seeing her starry new life reflected in his eyes. 'Are you pleased?'

'Of course,' she breathed. 'What's the role?'

'Oh, they're still ironing that out. They wanted Anna May Wong for it but I told them there would be a new Anna May in town soon.' Feifei couldn't help herself squealing. Now she understood why the foreigners liked Christmas. This was a better present than jujubes.

'I don't understand why I have to come,' Amelia said, trailing Tamara's fast pace down the wide tree-lined avenue.

'Because you're the kind of respectable English woman we want him to think our company is made up of. Hurry up, Amelia!' Amelia wrapped her coat tighter around her. Boxing Day was biting cold and she had been looking forward to a leisurely day at home as Tamara had given all the dancers two days off. Instead, she was following her friend to Jimmy Kang's house to beg for Polina to be allowed to dance. Tamara had explained that Jimmy was a gangster in Shanghai, an opium kingpin with a large stake in the city's nightlife through the avenues of prostitution and cabarets.

'Anyway, Amelia, you were supposed to find us a venue, secure the support of the international community and a million other things thanks to your respectable social position. Do you remember? As far as I can see, you have achieved precisely none of those things. So now it's time for you to help me.' Resigned, Amelia followed Tamara's graceful steps up the driveway of a large, French-style house, with wide-set windows.

'It's beautiful,' Amelia said, marvelling at the size of the building.

'We're not here as tourists. Come on.'

Jimmy Kang didn't just have servants. He had a domestic army, all working as a ring of steel round their master. When Tamara knocked on the door and demanded to see him they all shook their heads as sadly as abandoned dogs, explaining the master had gone and they didn't know when he would be back.

'Then I shall wait,' Tamara said. 'I'm here on business. You can let him know the Russian with the girls is here when he returns.' She took a seat on one of the stiff-backed chairs in the cavernous hallway, indicating that Amelia should do the same.

'That's a funny way to put it,' Amelia said, sinking down next to her.

They waited, a big grandfather clock counting the minutes Jimmy snubbed them. But after forty minutes and two thousand four hundred ticks of the clock, two servants appeared to let them know Jimmy would receive them in one of the rooms upstairs. Following Tamara up the sweeping wooden staircase, Amelia tried not to betray her awe at the splendour of the house.

They found Jimmy sitting comfortably on a soft chair in a room draped with silks and soft fabrics, a Versailles in Shanghai. Jimmy smoked a pipe leisurely, not bothering to rise to greet them, only squinting up at them. The two women sat down opposite him. Amelia noticed a large scar on one side of his face like a claw mark. The man was cold as a lizard and she couldn't imagine Polina's beauty next to his ugliness. It would be grotesque.

'What can I help you ladies with?' he said gruffly. 'Something about some girls?' His eyes drifted over to Amelia and she realised with horror he was sizing her up, deciding if she was worthy for sale.

'It's about one girl in particular. Polina,' Tamara said. Jimmy's eyes narrowed.

'What about Polina?'

'I am her dance teacher and the head of the Shanghai ballet–'

'Ha! You mean you're the head of a troupe of whores! Polina is not a prostitute, she would never go near something like that. Out of the question. Now get out of my house.' Jimmy's face twisted, making him even uglier than before.

'If you would just give me a minute to explain. Polina was our principal dancer. She would become the talk of the town if you would let her take part. She has great talent and could really make this into a career. We don't have another dancer talented enough to take her place.'

'Explain to me please, why I should let my Polina sully her name so you ladies can put those of us who actually *pay* Russian girls out of business? Hmm? Didn't think about that, did you?' He sat back and took another puff on his pipe. 'Now kindly leave my house.'

'Mr, uh, Mr Kang,' Amelia broke in. 'I'm not Russian. I'm not … one of those girls. That isn't the idea exactly. It's just they're really the only women with any dance training. But I'm English, and we have two Chinese dancers –'

'Nonsense! The whole of Shanghai can dance the foxtrot,' Jimmy retorted. Tamara rose first, her face hard as she left without saying anything.

'Thank you for your time, Mr Kang,' Amelia said, following Tamara out the door and back down the grand stairs.

At the bottom they happened upon Polina, deep in conversation with a Chinese servant. She turned slowly at the sound of their voices.

'What on earth are you doing here?' Her jaw stiffened as she looked at both of them, defeated by the power of one man and his pipe. 'Oh no, you didn't speak to him, did you?' Her fingers flew to her mouth, fluttering nervously on her lips. She turned to the servant and said something else. 'We're hosting a dinner tonight and there's just so much to organise,' she said, straining to sound normal. 'Come, I'll see you out.'

'Polina, we had to do something,' Tamara said.

'He won't change his mind. I'm so sorry.' Polina opened the front door for them, waved them out, desperate for them to leave.

'But we need a dancer,' Amelia said. 'Is there no way?'

'No. But … Tamara, you know all the parts perfectly! Why don't you do it?' Polina's cheeks brightened with her suggestion.

'But I'm not young and fresh like you. I don't think so.' Tamara and Amelia stepped outside and Polina closed the door behind them, giving a small wave. Tamara turned to Amelia. 'Well, that was a disaster. But maybe she's right. I could dance the parts.'

'There's our solution,' Amelia said, but both of them felt wrapped in the oppressive heaviness of Jimmy Kang's drawing room.

Walking back through Frenchtown they passed a news stand. There smiling up at them were thirty Feifeis, serene in their identical pose of seduction. Tamara grabbed one of the magazines, swiftly flicking through the pages until the article cried out to them: SHANGHAI'S BAREFOOT BALLET, accompanied by blocks of Chinese translation.

'Wonderful, wonderful!' she said. 'The show must go on! Polina's right, I can dance those parts!' Amelia linked her arm through Tamara's and they walked in the direction of the Russian's apartment, talk of fame and a dozen encores filling the air above them.

Will was desperate to see Feifei again. Whereas before he had buried himself in shallow pleasures to take the edge off his wanting, he now drowned his desire in work. He had completed his new collection of Tang and Song dynasty poems, which he had bound and sent off to a publisher in London. He allowed himself to write a little dedication: *For FF, who helped me to see the poetry in life again. Shanghai, December 1931.* By the time the book was published, if it ever was, Will would be somewhere far away with Feifei. He imagined waking with her in Malaya, rushing to collect the parcel and holding it under her eyes, watching them grow large when she saw the acknowledgement of her importance. He had to tell her his plan. They would leave as soon as possible. His report was due in January and he felt he must do his duty by the consulate so as not to embarrass his uncle too much. Then there was Amelia. She was so happy with her ballet though, and once when he had broached the subject of returning to London, she had dismissed the idea.

'But I wouldn't be able to dance in London!' she said as they ate together one evening.

'Well, I'm sure you could dance somewhere. You mean to say you are quite happy in Shanghai?' She mulled over his question and nodded.

'I'm happy.' She would stay, Will decided, and if not there were always ships home. He had decided not to worry about it too much anyway – marriage was all nothing more than social obligation and he and Feifei rose far above that.

So the night after Christmas he made his way to the Paradise, where Ling was performing in a festive show. Dressed in sparkling sequins, her face made-up and serious, he found her already centre stage, the lonely men of Christmas enraptured by her. At the end of the set Will approached her.

'Oh, it's you,' Ling said playfully.

'Yes. Thanks for not landing me in it yesterday.'

'A friend of Feifei's is a friend of mine,' she said.

'Speaking of Feifei … I would like to see her. Could we meet tomorrow at your house?' Ling crinkled her nose.

'Ah … she is very busy recently. I don't know.' But she promised to ask and told Will to be at the apartment at six p.m. the next day.

He turned back to the bar, deciding to have one celebratory drink now his plan was coming together. Sitting alone and stirring his fizzing gin, he heard a man announce himself by clearing his throat.

'Mind if I join you?' It was Rollo, with two men from his department. He waved the other two away to a table and ordered a drink. 'I can only stop for a moment because we're here on consular matters.'

'Oh?' Will looked at Rollo, a man who savoured job titles and petty tasks, who enjoyed office gossip and low-level politics. Now Will was going to run away with Feifei he felt far above the dull minutiae of 'consular matters'.

'It seems I'm going to be promoted,' Rollo said, lowering his voice.

'Congratulations!' Will felt genuinely pleased for his friend.

'Yes, I'm going to be second-in-command in the department, I think. They wanted to let me know before tomorrow, before we're all back in. Speaking of which, be careful not to get too drunk, old chap.' Rollo clapped Will on the back. 'See you later.'

'Oh, Rollo. The report?'

'Yes?'

'Should I still give it to you? Now that you've been promoted?'

'Of course,' Rollo said.

Will turned back to his drink, enjoying the trumpeting victory sounds of the band. He would miss Shanghai. Swivelling around in his seat he watched two dancers appear on the stage and begin to remove their clothing one layer at a time. The crowd whistled and jeered and Will thought uncomfortably of Feifei and the slit in her dress, the silkiness of the stocking he had felt underneath. Feeling flustered, he finished off his drink and made for the door, waving to Rollo as he left. Tomorrow, he told himself. All he had to do was wait for tomorrow.

Feifei arrived at Ling's apartment at a quarter to six. Her friend was changing out of her dance practice clothes and searching for a dress to wear to a performance that night. She had finally been offered a contract by one of the big hotels.

'You know,' she said, discarding one *qipao* into a pile of rejects, 'it maybe wasn't such a bad thing, the studio letting me go.'

'I'm glad,' Feifei said, but she found it hard to muster encouragement. She was growing impatient with her situation. In just a month, she would set sail for America and a new life. She didn't know exactly why she was keeping Will hanging on, other than out of careful habit. Plans could always fall through. After all, Longwei had proved to be far flimsier than he had first appeared. Soon she would be gone, and she could leave Will in peace.

'You seem quiet,' Ling said, fastening the buttons of an emerald dress. 'What's wrong?'

'I think I feel guilty,' Feifei said.

'About the poet man? Don't be silly. He's your English teacher,' Ling said, a mischievous glint in her eye. 'Well, I'm off. Have fun!' The door closed behind her and a few minutes later Feifei heard bounding footsteps up the stairs, he was taking them two at a time. Her chest acidic, Feifei opened the door to Will, who stood breathless and impatient at the door. She stood back to let him in and he paced the room, unable to contain his energy.

'Right, Feifei. We need to talk,' he said as she poured him a drink. He looked too big, too polished for this shabby little room, his hope filling every corner of it. Feifei felt dread as he circled around her, accepting the drink with a courteous nod. 'I came here today because I need to tell you something.' He stopped beside her and held one of her hands tightly. 'I love you, Wu Feifei. I want to be with you and I want to protect you. That's why I've decided we'll go away together. To Singapore.'

'Singapore?' Feifei knew she sounded ungrateful, like the daughter of a rich *taipan* dismissing a new holiday destination. 'But we don't know anybody in Singapore.'

'Exactly! But if you don't like the idea of Singapore we could go to Macau. It's meant to be very beautiful. East meets West in perfect harmony. Like you and me.' He gripped her fingers so tightly they were turned white.

'Will, I appreciate the idea but ... you're married.'

'So are you! We must say goodbye to convention, Feifei, because what we have is something real.' She sat down and he knelt by her side, laying his head in her lap. Her back stiffened. 'Let me tell you my new favourite poem,' he said and she realised he would not stop. '*Ren sheng dao chu zhi he si? Ying si fei hong ta xue ni.* Don't you see? Human existence is just like a goose taking off from the snowy ground. Sometimes it leaves a little footprint but that's it. What is life after all, Feifei?' She was alarmed. He was ranting like a madman, his veins popping.

'I suppose,' she said carefully. 'I went to a party the other day and nobody knew who I was. Perhaps my career is just a footprint in the snow.' Will looked at her strangely, his head cocked to the side, and let go of her fingers. She wished she hadn't said anything. He must have been able to guess she was with foreigners if no one had recognised China's most eminent actress.

'I'm sorry to hear that. But that's the whole point. We're more than careers, more than a list of achievements.'

'Oh, Will.' Her eyelids drooped as she took in the sight of this man, a colonial reduced to a child at her feet. 'You are a wonderful person.'

'So that's a yes?'

'When do you want to go?' she asked. She still had to play it safe. Anyway, a life in Singapore with a poet couldn't be worse than her life right now in Shanghai, her career amputated, her husband rampaging across town with dancing girls and enemies of the state. Just in case.

'As soon as possible.'

'Well, I am a patron of the Shanghai Ballet. So I cannot leave before the end of January. Why don't we plan to leave in February?'

'Perfect!' He lunged towards her and she instinctively pulled back as he kissed her. 'Oh, Feifei, what about your daughter?' He settled himself into a chair opposite her.

'Lili,' Feifei said softly. She hadn't given Lili much thought up to now, thinking that once she was a Hollywood star Lili would automatically be sucked into her starry orbit. 'Do you promise you'll look after her, Will? Whatever happens?'

'Of course. Your daughter is just as important to me as you are.'

'You promise?' She held his hand again and he nodded solemnly. 'Then we will go first and send for her after, once we have made a nice home there.' Will kissed her again and she let his hand rove over her face and neck.

Will clasped her close to him before leaving. Feifei told him it was safer if they weren't seen together so Longwei would be unlikely to get wind of their plans. It was best if Will went ahead with the planning and they left together at the beginning of February, she told him firmly and he agreed. Closing the door behind him, the atmosphere suddenly felt heavy and dense. Feifei sat down, her heart light and fluttering. It wasn't right, but it was safe. He would forget her as soon as she was gone, she told herself. After all, he had fallen in love with an image, the Shanghai seductress who beamed from painted posters. He had not fallen in love with the girl with dirty feet and ragged clothes who lived in Zhabei with her servant mother, or the shy maid who lay back and let Longwei turn her into a mother. Will thought he loved Feifei, but really he loved the idea of Feifei. Feeling better, she stood up and made her way home, checking in the mirror for tell-tale lipstick smudges around her mouth.

Will almost ran home, feeling his chest might jump out of his chest and fly away on one of the dark December clouds. He would have Feifei. They would leave all restrictions behind and jump into the unknown, love the net ready to catch them. Struggling for breath, he opened the door to the house and heard Amelia talking with another woman in the front room. He wanted to run upstairs to preserve his joy but knew he would be expected to say hello.

He found Polina sitting opposite his wife, her delicate fingers cradling a cup of tea. She looked even lovelier than on Christmas Day, her cheeks shiny and red like a pair of polished apples.

'Hello, Will,' she said warmly. He nodded in greeting.

'Polina came to tell me that she's found a venue for us,' Amelia said happily, and Will felt sure then she would be fine without him.

'Yes, it's not the best place in Shanghai but it will certainly do. It's on the edge of the International Settlement, right next to Zhabei. Hopefully the Shanghai set will be willing to go over there,' Polina said. 'Jimmy's just bought it. He felt so bad about ... well, you know, me not participating, that he decided to make it up to me.'

Amelia clapped her hands in excitement. 'Everything's coming together. Isn't it fantastic, Will?'

'Indeed it is. Now, if you ladies don't mind I have some work to attend to.' Polina smiled politely and he withdrew, feeling the same pleasure as before, though it was a little tempered. Upstairs, he pulled out a new book of poems and traced his fingers over one:

The river bank is lush with green grass,
Willow trees rise above it.
Why then do fresh sorrows return year after year?
As I stand alone on the little bridge,
Wind filling my long sleeves,
The people return to their homes,
And I see the crescent of the moon shine over the forest plain.

People would like the translation, he thought, though he didn't necessarily agree with the poem's sentiments. Not every year had to bring fresh sorrow.

JANUARY 1932

善哉行

来日大难，
口燥唇干。
今日相乐，
皆当喜欢。

Marvellous! A Ballad

The days to come will be very hard,
Our mouths will be dry and lips parched.
Let us be happy together today,
Let us all delight in each other's company.

IX

January was always a cruel month. After the festivities of Christmas and New Year, the Shanghailanders found themselves in a social desert as their friends nursed their health and sorted their finances for the month, preferring the warmth of the family circle to the bitter winds outside. The Chinese had their New Year to look forward to, but those far from home were listless. Amelia thought this lucky. Now the dancers had a venue organised – Jimmy Kang's new Peking Club – they were able to paste flyers around town and spread the word to their friends and families. While many of the Russian girls had little in the way of family, they were well-acquainted with Shanghai's high spenders and they promised them that ballet was just the kind of thing their wives would like to see. Julia had managed to insert a small piece in the *North China News*. Amelia had even swallowed back the sour taste of pride and gone to see Cordelia again, handing her a stack of flyers with a confident hand.

'I know you don't necessarily approve of what we are

doing, but I thought I would bring these just in case any of the other ladies are interested in supporting us,' she said.

'Amelia, I always thoroughly enjoy watching the ballet. The St Petersburg troupe I saw in London was marvellous. Though I am a little concerned by the girls involved in this project, I will of course let everyone know,' Cordelia, always a picture of English composure, agreed. Amelia took refuge in the morbid curiosity of the Shanghai ladies and hoped that their disapproval might draw one or two to the show, just so they could colour their afternoon teas with scandal over the coming months.

The dances had come together beautifully. Though Tamara couldn't match Polina's beauty, her movements were just as smooth and fluid. As Giselle, she far outshone Amelia's Myrtha, but Amelia felt happy just to dance on the same stage as Tamara's stark grace. They had lost no other dancers and everyone, including the occasionally clumsy Ling, had mastered the steps, often staying behind after the morning rehearsal to practise alone or in small groups. Tamara had bought all the girls ballet slippers and was negotiating a price on costumes from a Russian dressmaker, all of which had been funded by a generous donation from Feifei. As January progressed, the dancers arrived each morning filled with hope, the anxious, scowling faces of November gone.

But by mid-January events outside the studio had started to overshadow the girls' fragile optimism. Every morning as they made their way to the studio they had to fight through crowds of angry Chinese holding placards and screaming anti-Japanese slogans, while the heavy-handed and overwhelmed police forces beat them savagely, increasingly desperate to restore control to the city. One morning Lilya arrived, her face bruised and a deep gash on one of her legs.

'I just got carried away by the protesters!' she said, showing off her injuries. 'They swept me clean off the ground!'

'I hope that heals before the show,' Tamara said coolly, with the disinterest of someone who has already lived through social unrest. 'Please take your place at the barre.'

Amelia attempted to emulate the bluster of the other dancers, but really she was terrified by the wild shouts in the streets, the ugly press of human bodies. Will explained to her that it had all started after a Japanese factory was razed to the ground. Hysteria grew on both sides and though Amelia knew the Japanese were the focus of Chinese ire, as a foreigner she noticed more hostile looks on the street. She didn't understand the spidery characters on the protesters' banners but she grew increasingly worried that perhaps the world's most open port would not remain that way for much longer.

'Don't worry about it,' Plum said to her. 'We'll have chased the Japanese devils out of Shanghai before the curtain rises!'

But Amelia did worry, when she did her stretches at night before bed, when she heard Will's pen scratching feverishly in his study, when he woke up with rings under his eyes from all the extra work he was doing.

'You're just a translator,' she said to him one morning when he told her how he had been analysing the Japanese strategy for gaining power in Shanghai, even stretching his language skills to read some texts in Japanese.

'We all have to do our part, Amelia,' he said. She noticed he was possessed by a striking energy these days, and decided it was likely because he, too, was scared. He sought his refuge in words and she in dance. When she was playing the part of Myrtha dancing men to death she liked to picture the contorted faces of the raging protesters and imagined dancing them out of Shanghai before the show.

Will took an odd pleasure in the strange events unfolding in Shanghai. First of all, it showed that his report, which he had proudly presented to Rollo just after New Year, had hit all the right points. The Japanese would try to gain more power in Shanghai, he had correctly predicted, and a high-stakes game of politics would follow, with frequent outbursts of populist violence. Will enjoyed the keyed-up madness of the city, a reflection of his agitated state of mind. He had decided that he and Feifei would leave for Singapore on February

2nd and all he had left to do was to buy the tickets. Between long hours of translating at the consulate and working on his poetry at home, Will allowed himself snatches of daydreams, flickering images of him and Feifei walking together, Singapore a lush backdrop to their romance.

It was a Tuesday morning when Rollo came to see Will. 'Hello, old chap,' he said.

Will received Rollo with an easy smile. 'What can I do for you?' he asked.

'Well, we're all a bit concerned about the 19th Route Army,' Rollo said, dropping his voice so Ralph, who had turned nervous and ghostly as the tide of Chinese anger swelled, wouldn't hear their conversation.

'I imagine so,' Will said. 'The papers say they might pose an even bigger threat to the city than the Japanese.'

'They may be Chinese troops but they've got us surrounded,' Rollo said. Then, looking reflective for a moment, he shook his head. 'How things have changed in just a few short months.'

'That's the way life is, I suppose,' Will said.

'Say, are you all right? You've got high colour.'

'Just exhilarated to be doing such important work,' Will said, trying to sound serious but feeling bubbling giggles catch in his throat. Just two more weeks, and he would be sailing away from Rollo's serious face and the dusty corners of the consulate to live a life these men couldn't even imagine. They thought they had cracked it, with their pompous job titles and political concerns and inexpensive trysts with pretty young things. But Will had broken the world wide open and would drink nectar they could never imagine tasting.

'Right, well, that's good news. We've seen your translations from the local press and they're very good. But we could do with some more *direct* information. We'd like you to go and talk to the army and get an idea of their intentions. Obviously they're under the control of a warlord and we want to make sure the Chinese themselves aren't planning anything on top of all this trouble with the Japanese.'

'Really?' Will looked at Rollo, so earnest in his well-cut suit and important new role. 'They want me to go and talk to the army? Will it not draw a lot of attention, me walking into the middle of the troops for a chat? I'm not sure I understand the strategy. If intelligence were doing their job, we'd have people in there already ...'

'Like Harry MacDonald?' Rollo said spitefully and Will drew back.

'I really enjoyed writing that report, Rollo, but this is not my job. Though I'm flattered I don't want to go treading on toes. There's probably some chap out there just dying to infiltrate them. Someone whose job it is to do just that.'

'Those are the orders,' Rollo said, rising up and looking down his nose at Will. 'You will report back to me what you find.'

Will watched him leave and let a laugh escape. The world had gone mad, sending a translator out to meet and greet a bloodthirsty army. But he might as well go, he thought, no point in rocking the boat before leaving Shanghai. He thought of his uncle in London and felt a twinge of guilt. Shaking it off, he waved goodbye to Ralph and made his way to the outskirts of the city.

Back at the consulate, Will was feeling quite pleased with himself. He had found the army easily, a human wall snaking round the city. Instead of announcing himself as being from the consulate he had instead effected the interest of an innocent passer-by, who happened to speak perfect Chinese. Though some of the troops had been hostile, he had squeezed out the information Rollo wanted. They weren't planning to do anything but protect the city, they said, and they would fight the Japanese bandits 'to the death'. He knocked on the door of Rollo's office.

'Come in.' It was Richard Saunders, the head of the political department. 'Oh, Graves, it's you. I've wanted to speak with you for a little while, actually. Please take a seat.' Will sat, facing Saunders over his desk. 'There seems to be an issue with your press reports. We haven't received any for ... at least two weeks, I would say. I know things are difficult at the moment ... there are a lot of distractions. But it's not like you to slip up on something so important.'

'Sorry?' Will looked at Saunders, officious and cold behind a mahogany desk.

'Those reports really do help us decide where we need to focus our work. You are usually so diligent.'

'I have submitted my reports. I haven't missed a day. And surely you've seen the very long report that I submitted at the beginning of January? I've been working terribly hard for the past few months. It was over twenty thousand words. There must be some mistake.'

'Indeed. There must be. I'll see to it. We've been relying on Rollo for information on the Japanese situation. He's going to go far, that young man.' The cold air in the office whistled by Will's ears.

'Rollo?' he choked. 'Rollo's been telling you about the Japanese situation?'

'Not a thing that man doesn't know about Chinese politics. Outstanding. Anyway, what did you come here for?'

'To see Rollo. I've been to talk to the 19th Route Army as he asked me to and I have some important information for him.'

Saunders laughed at this. 'Well, rather you than me! That's a good one.'

'No, really,' Will said, his voice catching on the injustice. 'Please tell Rollo I came by after completing a task he asked of me. I went all the way to the outskirts of the city to speak with the army. If you would be so kind.' Will left Saunders shaking his head and at a loss for what to do, and walked down to the port to purchase the tickets to Singapore. He would soon be leaving all of this far behind.

Back in the office, he received three knocks on the door in the afternoon from a lifeless official called Grayson. Grayson carried out a number of administrative tasks around the building and the sight of him was enough to send every diplomat running from whatever dull chore he needed completing now.

'Good afternoon, Mr Graves. Could you follow me, please?' Will stood up from his desk, briefly feeling the outline of the tickets in his pocket. Grayson led him to a small meeting room at the end of the corridor, where he gestured for Will to sit down. Heavy with the unreality of the situation, Will sat awkwardly in a chair, looking up at Grayson.

'To start, Mr Graves, I would like to say –'

'Will.'

'Very well, Will. I would like to say how much we appreciate the service you have offered this consulate.' Will felt his mouth go dry. Could they see the tickets tucked away in his pocket? Had someone spotted him at the port? The Lilya incident should have been enough to warn him about the fact that in Shanghai you were never more than two people away from a secret.

'I'm sorry?' he spluttered.

'Mr Graves, it pains me that I am the one charged with the unfortunate task of delivering this news to you. However, in light of recent events the consulate has decided to terminate your employment here.'

'Recent events?' Ugly, hoarse words crowded Will's mouth. He wanted to strangle Grayson, grab his washed-out, skinny neck and twist it in half. But he closed his lips.

'Mr Graves ... Will ... it's because of the reports. That is a large part of your job and you are failing in one of your most important duties.'

'That's not true!' Will felt his voice rise and tried to force it back down his throat. 'There has been a mistake,' he said in a quieter voice. 'I did file the reports, they appear to have gone missing. Rollo knows I've submitted them all. I take my position here very seriously.'

'I'm afraid that's not all, Will. It has come to our attention that you are conducting an ... an improper relationship.' Damn it, Will thought, Shanghai really did have ears everywhere.

'An improper relationship?' he said.

'Whilst we do encourage good relations with the locals,' Grayson said drily, 'there are limits to our understanding. You are a married man.'

Will was silenced by this. He lowered his chin to his chest and gave a small sigh.

'Again, Will, I am very sorry. We do value your service here over the past few months. You may collect your things and leave. You will still receive your salary for this month. Of course we will provide you with passage home. And thank you again ...' But Will didn't hear the end of his speech. He stood up numb, determined to find Rollo.

He pounded on the door, then pulled his fist back. He had to keep his nerves under control for now. Saunders opened it for him.

'Hello. Is Rollo here?'

Saunders shrugged. 'He's at a meeting. But he did tell me to let you know he's awfully upset at the news you're leaving. Many thanks for all your hard work, Will.'

He was fighting a battle after the other side had left the field, he saw, and there was little point.

'Thank you,' Will said and turned to go, shuddering as the door shut behind him. But he remembered something his mother had always said about God closing one door and opening another, and he comforted himself with the thought of Singapore.

Will let himself into the house, finding Amelia sifting through papers in the lounge.

'Oh, hello, dear,' she said distractedly. He was seething, his anger having built to a crescendo on the walk home, but there was little point in worrying her. 'What do you think?' She handed him a flyer so carefully printed in both English and Chinese that it brought a single tear to his eye. 'You don't like it?' she asked, studying his face.

'It's wonderful, dear,' he choked.

'I hope you're coming to the show. Perhaps you could

bring some of your consulate chums.' Her voice was bright and unaffected and he knew then he wouldn't tell her about losing his job.

'Of course. I wouldn't miss it for the world.'

'Darling,' she said, her voice turning down a little. 'What on earth is going on in Shanghai? I'm getting awfully worried.' He moved towards her, placing his arms awkwardly around her frail frame, noticing how much thinner she had grown since she started dancing. But while her bones showed more prominently, so did the blush of life in her face.

'The Japanese are making a racket, that's all. They want to behave as they like and have all the Chinese be nice to them. They'll have to work it out eventually. Just you worry about dancing and leave the politics to me.' She nodded without conviction and went back to her pile of advertisements.

'I'll put the rest of these up tomorrow.'

While many Chinese keenly felt the presence of the Japanese, Feifei was sure none felt it as close as she did. Since the trouble had started, Longwei was often drawn into gloomy moods, coming and going at all hours, shouting at her and Lili and saying unrepeatable things about their fellow Chinese.

'Honestly,' he said one evening, slamming the door behind him. 'Why can't people see what's good for them? The Japanese are the economic engine of this city.' Feifei said nothing, but let him rant on, safe in the knowledge she would soon sail away from all this and find herself on the big screen in America. Charles had sent word that they would take a ship on January 29th, less than two weeks away. She would go to the ballet recital, see Ling one last time, and leave early the next morning.

Ling came round one evening to tell her that Will had dropped into the Paradise, asking her to pass on a message.

'He said something about February 2nd. I suppose you'll be having a poetry reading or an English lesson then?' Ling said, laughing to herself. But Feifei was finding it increasingly difficult to see the mirth in anything and her guilt was growing bigger and more unwieldy. Sometimes she pitied Longwei, understanding that he was just a man, cursed with the greatest weaknesses of his sex. Other times she fretted for Lili and what a future without a mother would look like. Of course she would send for Lili but the poor girl might have to endure months without her mother, while the Japanese tried to turn Shanghai into another miserable colony under the rule of a distant emperor. But mostly she knew her guilt was about Will. He was married, she repeated to herself, a mantra that meant nothing because she was too.

Amelia, Julia and Tamara held an emergency meeting on January 26th. The show was in just two days and the frosty air was thick with tension. The Japanese were threatening to send in their troops and they had already succeeded in closing down one of the city's newspapers. Julia, in the know from her journalism contacts, was afraid the situation would escalate and suggested they postpone the show.

'Nonsense,' Tamara said with a flick of her hand. Her face was pale and tight, exhausted from rehearsals. The three women had met in the studio after a long day practising and without the body heat of the girls, the room was chilly and unfriendly. 'The show must go on. These girls have been working hard for months.'

'We've put flyers everywhere. Polina secured us a venue. Everything's fixed, Julia.' Amelia was scared too, horrors visiting her in nightly visions of surging protesters and the distant sound of eerie gunshots. But she had put so much of herself into the show. Besides, most of foreign Shanghai was still going about its business, blind to the troops bordering the city.

'I'm worried no one will come,' Julia said. 'I hear the Japanese are going to shut down the mills and throw the Chinese workers out. Can you imagine? The streets will be full of protesters.'

'Mill workers are not exactly the spectators we're targeting, Julia, so I think we can tolerate some protests. I don't want to let the girls down.' The discussion was finished. Tamara rose, gathering her coat about her. 'This blasted cold,' she said. 'In Russia we always seemed more prepared for it, somehow.'

The trio walked downstairs and said goodbye to Tamara, who walked back to her shabby lodgings, her mangy fur cutting a lonely figure on the icy street.

'I have to be honest with you,' Julia said suddenly and Amelia felt her stomach lurch. 'There's a party the night of the ballet.'

'So you're not coming?' Amelia said, surprised.

'No, no, I am. But I might have to leave early. Ju Wei is absolutely insisting I go with him. It's at one of the hotels. It's being held by one of the trade associations and someone from his family is being honoured.'

'Surely you don't have to go. I want you to see the whole thing! Me, as Myrtha! I thought you liked that idea.' Amelia squeezed her friend's shoulder but Julia turned away from her.

'I'm his wife now. I have to support him.'

'What nonsense! You're only his second wife,' Amelia said, though she regretted the words as soon as they slipped out. 'I mean, you're still independent.'

'I suppose so,' Julia said stiffly. And with that, she was gone, leaving Amelia alone under the dark sky.

Shanghai was resilient. The whore of the Orient knew how to rouge her lips and put on a good show, no matter what was happening around her. With something tantamount to a war building in the city, the ballet dancers continued to arrive punctually for rehearsals, only glancing out of the window occasionally when there were choruses of fevered shouts or hundreds of angry feet moving in unison. The day before the show they sweated through their warm-ups and practised their pieces, all looking many times more graceful than the cheeky cabaret girls that had first assembled by the barre. They were delighted with the costumes, particularly the ones for Swan Lake, which were unblemished white with spiral-ling tutus. They cooed over the outfits, begging Tamara to let them wear them while practising. Between rehearsals they turned on the radio, their excitement draining as they listened to Japanese threats. But break over, they would pick their limbs back up and follow Tamara's stern instructions.

Amelia bristled with expectations and nerves. For the second time in her life, she was fully focused on a goal. The first had been marrying Will and escaping her parents. That obsession had faded into friendly indifference. But now she felt that familiar drive again. The night before the show, she sat in the lounge with Will and discussed the day's news. The Japanese were still badgering their Chinese counterparts for the dissolution of all anti-Japanese entities, he told her, and they were also agitating for some arrests to be made. Chinese troops had gathered, as had some foreign soldiers.

'It's more than rhetoric,' he said. 'But don't worry, that 19th Route Army out there will fight to the death. No one at the consulate is unduly concerned.'

'I hope they're all still coming tomorrow,' she said.

'Of course,' Will said easily. 'Oh, I translated this poem for you.' He handed her a small piece of paper, tenderly inscribed with his translation and some unintelligible Chinese shapes. It was the latest in a little line of kindnesses he had performed for her – a sweet cake one day, a small brooch the next, a Chinese print to hang above her bed. She unfolded it and read it:

Idling drifting around the country,
Caring only to drink wine,
The Southern beauties had slim waists for you to hold,
And were so light-footed they danced on your palm.

'It was the only one I could find about dancers,' he said, thinking he had been very wise in leaving off the last two lines, which explained that these butterflies were to be found in houses of ill-repute.

'I think it's beautiful,' Amelia said. 'Now I must really get some sleep.' And with a soft kiss to his head, she tiptoed out the room, safe in the knowledge her muscles would remember all they needed to the next day.

The Peking Club was full by nine p.m. The dancers peeked out from behind the stage to admire their audience – elegant Chinese couples, boisterous groups of gossip-hungry Westerners and some sharp gangster-looking types, likely friends of Jimmy Kang. The low-lit club had arranged tables in a semi-circle around the stage where Shanghai's first ballet would soon be performed. Polina was at the front on the edge of the circle of spectators, her body immobile and her face frozen. Looking at her, Amelia knew Polina would be pained watching them dance while she served as beautiful decoration. Jimmy Kang sat at her side, a hat cocked jauntily on his head and a jade-topped walking stick in his hand. Amelia couldn't see Will. Scanning the room for him, she heard Tamara hiss at her to step back.

'Don't you know the first rule? If you can see them, they can see you,' she said. Amelia nodded and retreated, joining the other girls, their giggles bubbling up through the air in anticipation. Julia came backstage and hugged Amelia close.

'You look wonderful,' she said.

'We're dancing Swan Lake first,' Amelia told her, twirling around in her costume.

'Listen, I'll have to leave before the end, I'm afraid. Ju Wei really wants me at that party. You don't mind, do you?'

'It's fine,' Amelia said, though she was a little hurt. Julia hurried away to take a seat next to Polina, flashing encouraging smiles towards the dancers as she left.

Jimmy Kang leapt up on stage to introduce the ballet. Feifei followed him, her walk languid in a white silk dress. Not even the sight of Feifei could dampen Amelia's excitement.

'I'm delighted to present to you the first show of the Shanghai Ballet, here at the Peking Club, soon to be Shanghai's premier entertainment venue. Take it away, girls!' Jimmy gestured at the stage and Feifei, not opening her mouth, clapped softly and stood back, watching as the curtain slowly rose.

Amelia clutched with pride as she joined the other girls fluttering on stage in their perfect rows, their feet gently tapping on the floor as their arms rose in winged arcs. Their costumes glittered under the lights of the nightclub and Amelia saw the sceptical faces of the crowd melt with the magic of the ballet. They were experiencing what she had felt as a child and the realisation brought her close to tears. She was dancing on a cloud by the time they were off-stage.

Jimmy Kang had insisted on a break in the proceedings as many regular club goers liked their entertainment a little more racy. Tamara, agreeing that 'as beggars we cannot be choosers', had allowed him to stage an interlude of dancing girls in skimpy costumes and suggestive singers decked out in sparkles. The dancers gulped down water, with Lilya whining that she wanted an alcoholic drink before the Giselle part of the show, only to be met with a dangerous look from Tamara. Julia rushed backstage, arms flying wildly.

'They *love* you out there! Fantastic!' She flung herself towards Amelia, who embraced her friend tightly. 'You were incredible, Amelia,' Julia whispered in her ear. 'I saw you tonight and I couldn't believe you were that same girl I met at Cordelia's party. Just beautiful.'

Amelia grabbed Julia's hands. 'They really like us?'

'Yes. You're going to be stars! I have to run to the Cathay now, I'm so sorry. Let's meet tomorrow and celebrate your success!' Julia scurried away, almost tripping on her high heels.

The second half of the ballet didn't start until almost eleven, and Amelia noticed the room had emptied out slightly, though Feifei remained by Polina's side, clapping politely as the Wilis filed out onto the stage. This was Amelia's moment as Myrtha. She spotted Will a few tables further back and felt her body flush with new-found affection for her husband, remembering the poem he had placed into her palm the night before. Swallowing nerves, she sprang onto the stage, pouring all her fear and rage into Myrtha, imaging bringing riots to a halt, and dancing Ju Wei, Jimmy Kang and all the men who paid for her friends' bodies to death. The feeling in her limbs was one of total control and freedom, that special ballet dichotomy. But as she moved across the stage, her eye caught on a figure slipping towards the back of the room. It was Feifei in her white dress, looking ghost-like as she made for the exit. Some patron, Amelia thought, trying to drag her thoughts back to the dance. But then she saw another person in pursuit of the first phantom figure. It was Will, no doubt about it, chasing after her. Amelia felt herself wobble on her toes, her body tipping over dangerously. Raised eyebrows and instinctive flinches from the other dancers let her know that the slip-up had not gone unnoticed. There was a communal holding of breath because they knew Amelia was set to embark on a chain of *fouettés*, which when performed correctly elicited the most profound respect for the athleticism of ballet. Pulling her gaze away from the two people at the back of the room, who were locked in a private cage of conversation, Amelia felt the familiar disappointment in her chest and made it surge down to her legs, powering her through the impressive set of *fouettés*, whipping one leg behind her as she twirled on the other foot. When she looked up again, Will and Feifei were gone and the room vibrated with claps and whistles.

'But where are you going?' Will followed Feifei out to the street. 'It's not safe to walk around here.'

'I grew up here, Will. I can look after myself.' A car pulled up by her side and she ducked down to get into it.

'Why won't you talk to me?' When he had seen her trying to leave the Peking Club unnoticed, Will saw no choice but to follow her. It was his chance to tell her that they were to set sail in February. Feifei heaved a sigh.

'Go back and watch your wife. She is a wonderful dancer. I have an engagement. A *private* party at the Cathay,' she said, placing an elegant emphasis on *private*. 'We'll talk soon, Will.'

'We need to discuss Singapore. Dammit, Feifei, if I'm going

to go to another country to live with you we need to make some plans.'

'We will, I promise.' She closed the door and the car drove on. She was gone. There was nothing else for it. He would go to the Cathay too.

There was no sign of her outside the hotel, so he blustered his way through the lobby, asking arrogant directions to the 'party', which led the bellboy to believe he must indeed be invited and tell him where it was. Too anxious to wait for the lift, Will pounded up the stairs to the dining room where he found the party spinning at that special point of the social axis, where it could descend into decadent debauchery or wind up soon, with guests making excuses and collecting their coats. He zigzagged through the room, his eyes searching for Feifei's white gown.

'Will!' Someone grabbed his arm and he turned to see Julia, her smile open as she stood beside her husband. Will nodded at them both and turned, still searching for Feifei. 'Will,' Julia said again. 'Why are you here? Isn't Amelia still dancing?'

'Yes, yes,' he said distractedly. 'I'm looking for someone.' He noticed a knowing look pass between Julia and Ju Wei but ignored it and ploughed through the crowd.

Squeezing past a group of corpulent, self-congratulatory Englishmen, Will found himself in an open space towards the back of the room. There she was, her white dress making her look like an angel descended to the hell of Shanghai in 1932. She was leaning close to a rotund man, seemingly hanging on his every word. Near them stood a group of loud Americans. You could always tell an American by their cheerful expectations of life, Will thought, and this group looked like they thought Shanghai in all its whorish glory had been laid out just for them. Feifei was under a chandelier and the light splashed a halo around her perfectly tended black curls. Will thought she never looked more splendid than at that moment.

'Well, Feifei, I must say I'm just *delighted* to meet you!' one of the Americans was saying earnestly, wearing a suit slightly too big for him. 'Charlie's leading lady, that's what we've all been calling you!' Feifei laughed beautifully. Then he noticed the man, this 'Charlie', snake his hand onto the small of Feifei's heavenly back. Will felt an animal disgust rise in his throat and started towards the group, his voice hoarse as he said: 'I hate to break up a party, gentlemen, but I need a word with Miss Wu.'

Feifei's face, placid and content, contorted at the sight of Will. He took her by the wrist and led her away from the group, while Charles and his consorts watched with amused interest.

'We need to talk,' Will said. 'Let's find somewhere quiet.' She tried to protest, but he silenced her with a firm shake of his head. 'You owe me an explanation, don't you think?' He led her to the corridor, her heels sinking into the plush carpet.

'Will, I'm sorry,' she blurted out as he pulled her into a quiet nook.

'What's going on?' he said in a fierce whisper. Seeing her beauty so dewy and fresh in front of him all he wanted was to possess her, to call her his own.

'I didn't know how to tell you. I have a role in Hollywood.'

'Really?' Will couldn't hide his surprise. He thought that Feifei's dream of being a Hollywood star was like his fantasies of roaming China during the Tang dynasty, befriending poets like Wang Wei and Du Fu. Dreams were a nice way to pass the stationary moments between life, but he never really believed her to be serious. And after he heard Anna May Wong's clear diction, he knew there was no way Feifei could make it.

'Yes, Charles, that man I was talking to, has found a role for me. He works for a film distribution company.'

'There's no role,' Will said decisively. 'You think that reprehensible man can get an unknown Chinese actress a role? Accept it, Feifei, Richard Cable didn't think you had what it takes. He knows better than that–'

'Stop it!' Feifei's eyes flashed a deep red and Will took a shallow breath. 'You don't know him. This is what I've always wanted. Of course I wanted to go with you but I can't turn my back on this opportunity.'

'But with me, Feifei, you have a future. I don't even have a job here anymore. I'm just waiting for you so we can go.'

'What? You don't have a job?' She grimaced and a single round tear dropped from her right eye. She looked concerned, but Will could only think that she was an actress. Maybe she was a cold-blooded plotter, a liar who had used him, a pretender who could be spinning him nonsense right at this moment.

'No.' He gripped her forearm, his fingers leaving red welts on her skin. 'Don't go with him. Do you love him?'

'It's not about love!' she said, her voice rising. 'It's about Hollywood. I'm sorry, Will. I've really enjoyed our lessons. But we're leaving tomorrow.'

'Tomorrow?' Will said, but his surprise was drowned by a low rumble and a loud bang. It felt as though the ceiling above them might cave in. They both looked at each other, shocked, and rushed back to the party, where through the window they saw flames dancing in the sky. The stars were covered in a blanket of orange fire, like every home had set off its New Year firecrackers early.

'Those bastards,' Feifei said, a sob heaving from her chest. 'Those Jap bastards.' Will, who had been staring dumbly through the window at the splashes of hot paint streaking across the sky, turned to face her.

'They're *bombing*?' In response, Feifei gestured at the window and before he could say anything she had scurried to Charles' side, where she was gesticulating wildly.

Will made his way to the window, listening to the rumbles and explosions with the detachment of someone by a warm fire listening to a thunderstorm. The worst part was the pauses in between, when he thought they might have stopped, which were always followed by a louder crash as another building fell. He had his eyes and hands pressed hot against the glass.

Someone moved behind him and he hoped wildly it might be Feifei, moved by the sight of the city on fire to throw herself into his arms and agree to his plans, but it was Julia.

'This is awful. Bombs falling from the sky. This is going to change the world forever,' she said in a low voice. 'But, Will, look where it is. There are some army types over there who tell me it's Zhabei that's under attack.'

'Zhabei? Yes, that's where the Chinese have stationed their troops,' he said. 'But our houses will be fine.'

'Unfortunately that's the attitude everyone here is taking,' Julia said, gesturing at the room of gilded characters, lifting champagne glasses to their lips and pointing at the dancing shapes in the sky as though they were watching a particularly colourful opera. Will's stomach churned. Shanghai was the world's last party before it all fell apart. At least that's how it felt to him. What kind of world allowed Feifei to end up with a man like Charles? Only Shanghai. Julia snapped her fingers in front of his nose. 'Amelia, Will, Amelia! The Peking Club is practically in Zhabei. Jimmy Kang likes a good deal and the place was dirt cheap. You know the International Settlement is always pushing its borders as far as it can go.'

Will felt a sudden attack of dizziness and used the wall to prop him up. Of course, Amelia. Darling Amelia, the one he had betrayed for a woman who turned out to be as conniving as any of the city's glossy professionals, even if she didn't charge by the hour. He had to get to her. He had let their relationship unwind, let their threads go slack. But now he had no Feifei, no job, no Singapore. Perhaps he and Amelia could use the tickets to Singapore, go there and start again. He could dedicate himself to translating poetry ... He saw it all planned in front of him, a path so clear all he had to do was take the first step.

'I'm going,' he said, with a determination that had failed him over the last month, the vision of Amelia the swan suddenly overshadowing with a new intensity the feline outline of Feifei in her white *qipao*.

'I'll come with you. I'm sure the paper would want me

there. They're so sneaky, the Japanese, they got the Chinese to agree to their conditions today ...' The two of them made their way to the exit but just as they crossed the threshold, Ju Wei grabbed Julia's shoulder and yanked her back into the room.

'Where do you think you're going?' he said.

'To report on what's happening out there. I know everyone here just wants to party but people are dying.' She struggled out of his grasp but he reached for her again.

'Are you mad? You must stay here with me until it's safe to go out.' She shook her head, looking desperately at Will to intervene but he turned on his heels, a new objective fixed in his brain.

'You are my *wife*. I can't just let you go,' he heard Ju Wei saying to Julia.

With *Giselle* over, the dancers took to the stage, curtseying proudly as the crowd clapped, some yelling and rising to their feet. Amelia knew they had put on a good show. Even Jimmy Kang was applauding, looking approvingly around the room at the number of customers that had lingered through the ballet, not leaving once the seductive interval had come to an end. For a Thursday night in a new nightclub, it was a large and happy crowd.

Tamara came to the front of the stage and, beaming maternally at all the girls, took a deep curtsey. The crowd whistled and the girls moved off stage, the spectators once again losing themselves in their cocktail glasses and the complex webs of their interpersonal relations. Backstage the dancers were crying, laughing and hugging each other. In the middle of the crowd, Amelia felt finally at home. She was one of them now. Having seen Will leave earlier she thought bitterly that she was more like them than any of the girls realised, a woman left to carve out her destiny without the support of a man. Even Tamara laughed with the girls. She took a step towards Amelia, and face flushed, wrapped her arms around the Englishwoman's waist.

'You were fantastic,' she said softly, and Amelia felt a damp patch of tears forming on the shoulder of her leotard. 'We did it. We really did it.' Amelia found herself crying too, and the pair of them laughed through their salty tears, clutching at one another.

Polina appeared then, three bottles of champagne in her hands.

'Time to celebrate!' she shouted and the girls crowded around her. Ling pulled one bottle out of the crook of Polina's arm and gasped as it dropped to the floor and shattered.

'Don't worry,' Lilya said. 'We're going to be so rich we'll soon be breaking champagne bottles just for fun.' Plum and Lilya got to work uncorking the other bottle and serving glasses to each of the girls. Polina rushed away to get some more and they all clinked glasses, the future sparkling back at them through the wine bubbles.

'To the Shanghai Ballet!' Tamara said proudly and they all took their first sips.

Suddenly the ground shook. Plum lost the grip on her glass.

'What's that?' she said, looking down at the glittering shards of glass. They heard two loud booms.

'Maybe it's a storm,' Amelia suggested, taking a second sip of champagne.

'How odd,' Tamara said. 'Let's go and see.' As she turned to lead the way back out to the front of the club, the walls shook and there was a drawn-out creaking sound. Amelia looked up and saw the roof cracking from the force of one of the walls pushing against it. She screamed as it came crashing down on top of them, shattering their glasses and crushing their bodies.

On the street, all was chaos. People were running, bumping into each other, desperately seeking shelter. Will pushed through the hysterical snakes of people, heading in the opposite direction. He knew Amelia would be petrified. He thought of all the times she had asked him about the Japanese, about the future of Shanghai. Again and again he had reassured her but something bad had been waiting around the corner, a carnivorous disaster in search of prey. He had been wrong about everything, he saw with sudden, uncomfortable clarity. Rollo was no friend to him, he thought, his breath catching in his throat, and Feifei was no love. He had been taken in by both of them, by Lilya, by the night, by Shanghai. He needed to get back to Amelia, to escape, maybe even go back to England and take long walks with his parents under drizzling skies and wrap himself up in thick blankets by the fire.

'Hey, where are you going?' An Englishman grabbed Will's shoulder as he sped past the people running towards the river and away from Zhabei. But Will ignored him. 'Hey, are you blind? The Japs are bombing the Chinese area to hell. Everyone has to leave.' Will's feet pounded against the pavement as he struggled free of the man's grip. His chest heaved and his suit stuck uncomfortably to his skin. He should never have left the show. Feifei's elegant arm dangling by the man's side flashed though his mind, her gentle lips opening into a soft laugh at his crude words, her starry eyes gazing at his greedy jowls. All of it drove him on and soon he found himself on the fringes of Zhabei.

He stopped and looked up at the sky. It was covered in dense smoke that billowed like huge clouds before a storm. He coughed, suddenly aware that the air was thick with the smell of fire and something else. Death. His mind struggled to make sense of the sight he saw in front of him. Neat rows of houses collapsed on top of one another, huge gaping mouths where roofs should have been, piles of rubble where streets once lay. And the sounds. The desperate howls, the quiet mewling. People were choking out their last breaths all around him. A trail of ghosts in his wake, Will pelted down the road towards the Peking Club. He couldn't see the flashing neon that had led him there earlier. He turned the corner, expecting to see the nightclub. What he saw instead was half of it, proud and erect, while the other half lay crumpled on the ground in a heap of brick and metal.

'No, no, no,' he was shouting. He started swinging his arms over his head, waving furiously. 'Amelia! Amelia! I'm here!' There was no one near the club, leaving him with the heavy silence of lives lost. He saw how it had happened, how a domino effect of buildings had toppled into the Peking, crushing the houses next to it and slicing it in half. 'Amelia!' His voice echoed down the street. A staccato burst of gunfire came from behind him and another explosion, lighting the sky again, seeming to show the way to heaven. Staring agape at the sky, Will felt someone approach him. A uniformed European man steered him away from the nightclub.

'Sir, this is the safest route for you. Another building could collapse at any moment.'

X

Feifei paced her bedroom floor, waiting for Longwei to leave the house. She could hear him whistling downstairs, could imagine him smoothing down his shirt in front of the mirror, cocking his hat just so. It seemed an eternity since he had woken. There were two hours until the ship set sail and she was to meet Charles at the port an hour and a half before. Her stomach clutched tightly and her dress felt too restrictive. Lili sat on the bed, her face turned up at her mother expectantly. She hadn't gone to school on account of the bombing the night before, which Longwei had taken in his stride, telling Feifei that the Japanese had been forced into a corner by Chinese ineptitude and imperialist arrogance. But when Feifei had arrived home, she found Lili in Mama's arms, weeping gently and occasionally coughing on the fear caught in her throat.

'Mama! You're alive!' She leapt out of Feifei's mother's arms and grabbed her leg, holding her as though she would never let go. Feifei pushed the image out of her head, smiling gently at Lili. She heard the door close with a masculine confidence. Longwei had gone.

'Mama,' Lili said quietly. 'What are we going to do today? Shall we play a game?'

'I have to go out for a little while, treasure,' Feifei said, picking up Lili, whose chubby legs dangled in the air.

'No! Mama, what if the fire clouds come again?'

'They won't. I promise.'

Lili shook her head.

'Grandmother says they will. She says the Japs are evil bastards.'

'Don't ever say that word again,' Feifei said, but her sternness gave way to a laugh and she pulled her daughter closer. She wondered if she could really do this, if she could really leave Lili here without even telling her where she was going. When she got to Hollywood she would send for her, and her daughter would have the kind of safe, sterile, rich life that one could only dream of in Shanghai. But she couldn't risk saying anything to Lili now, in case Longwei got to her before the ship sailed. Or Mama. She hoped Longwei would look after them. He would be angry, she knew, shamed and furious. But he did love Lili. She set her daughter down on the bed. She was unable to shake Will's expression from the night before from her mind.

'Now, Lili, if you have any problems, you go to Will Graves at the British Consulate, do you understand?' The words tripped off Feifei's tongue without thought.

'Who?'

'He's my English teacher and a very good friend of mine. If you need help one day and I'm not here, you go to him. Get a servant to take you.' She looked deeply into Lili's eyes and noticed the fear reflected back at her.

'Where are you going, Mama?'

'Nowhere.' She grasped her daughter again, holding her tight, tears burning her eyelashes. Without a word, she stood up and picked up the valise she had packed. Charles had promised that America had everything one could ever want, so she had only packed her best dresses to impress the Hollywood directors. She eased a diamond bracelet Longwei had given her years ago off her wrist and handed it to her daughter.

'This is for you. A secret present. Don't tell anyone.'

'Wow!' Lili toyed with the glittering snake, sniffing it, wrapping it around her fingers and running it across her naïve lips. 'So beautiful.'

Feifei replaced the bracelet with the bangle Charles had given her over lunch with Julia.

'Goodbye, Lili.'

'See you soon, Mama.' Lili was so absorbed with the bracelet she didn't notice the valise, or how Feifei struggled down the stairs with it. Her heart beating wildly, Feifei opened the door to her Shanghai house for the last time, ready to set sail for the shinier world of America.

When the doorbell rang after a night without sleep, the last person Will expected to see was a Chinese gangster. He didn't know who Jimmy Kang was, but he knew immediately from the man's gold rings and sinister expression that he operated on the murkier side of the law.

'Good morning,' Jimmy said. 'Can we come in?' Behind him, Julia stepped to the side, revealing herself as though ready for punishment.

'Please.' Will stood back, watching Jimmy, who walked with a slight limp, make his way down the hall, followed by Julia's swinging bob. Once his guests were seated, Will asked Su to make some tea. 'What can I do for you?' Will asked and he saw the way they looked at him, like he was one of those glass people who could shatter at any moment. Perhaps he was. His eyes were ringed with more than tiredness, they were blackened with the certainty of death and the realisation the world was a bad place. He had held an all-night vigil for Amelia and he knew she wasn't coming home.

'Really it's what we can do for you,' Julia said softly, reaching over and taking one of his hands. Will pulled away instinctively.

'I presume you are here to tell me that my wife is dead,' Will said, the words landing cold and flat. Su came in and started pouring tea, her mouth drawn tight, not permitting any of her usual pidgin chit-chat.

'It would seem so,' Jimmy said. 'Polina tells me all the dancers were celebrating, drinking champagne just before the building collapsed. She had gone for another bottle and was out of the area. She is racked with guilt, as you can imagine. She says she should have died.' Jimmy gulped a hot sip of tea while Julia fingered the rim of her cup. 'I found her in the rubble, clutching that bottle of champagne she had gone to get for the girls ...'

'Will, Amelia is almost certainly dead. I'm sure the consulate will help you with everything but we just wanted to offer our help. I went straight to Jimmy's this morning to find out what happened and we decided to come here. Really, if you need help with a funeral–'

'A funeral,' Will said softly, shaking his head.

'We're going to hold a service for the girls,' Julia said. 'I wondered if you would like to read something or if you had any suggestions. And of course I'm writing about this for the paper, if there's anything you'd like to say ...'

'I don't think so, no.'

'That's fine,' Julia said, standing up. 'We'll give you some time alone. This must be a terrible time. But we're here.'

'Thank you,' Will said, his voice weak.

Su cleared the cups.

'Mister, Missy no come home, no? Bomb? Japanese?' Will stood up, flinging one cup to the floor.

'That's right, Su. She's dead.' He stormed out of the front door, letting the cool air soothe his skin. He was as trapped as the bird in Feifei's house. There was nowhere for him to go.

The port was a seething mass of bodies when Feifei arrived. She realised she was perhaps too elegantly dressed for the occasion, her heels hindering her progress through the crowds. People with the ugly faces of longing and need were

217

shoving each other, spitting and cursing. Everyone wanted to leave town.

'I must go to Hong Kong today!' one plump woman was saying, battering men out of the way with her handbag. Guards stood watch over the crowd and Feifei fancied she could see humour in their eyes. She spotted Charles beside them, wearing a brown suit and a large hat. He was scanning the crowd and she raised her hand to wave, her fingertips fluttering excitedly. He had come and it was real. She was going to Hollywood.

'Excuse me, excuse me,' she muttered, making her way through the crowd. People parted a little, the way they always did for a pretty woman, but many shoved hard into her. She felt one curl tumble out of her updo. When she reached the front of the crowd, Charles embraced her. Feifei felt her carriage stiffen. They had never touched before.

'Ready for your new life?' he boomed and looking back at the braying crowd, she nodded.

As they boarded the ship, she noticed a huge number of white faces on board. No doubt the foreign diplomats had secured the most important men of their empires safe passage from Shanghai. But there were Chinese too, rich in silks and gold, who chattered excitedly about the best hotels in Hong Kong and whose house you had to be invited to for mah-jong. Feifei bristled as she followed Charles onto the deck, wondering how all these people, the Shanghailanders and the *shanghairen* equally, could gossip about gambling and unflattering dresses when the night before the city had been a ball of fire. Standing at the edge, looking out at the Bund, her eyes brimmed with tears at the thought of Lili. Lili hidden somewhere behind those safe, majestic buildings.

'You don't seem very excited!' Charles put his arm around her delicate shoulders and Feifei shrank away. 'What's wrong, Anna May Wong?'

'My home,' she said, pointing to the Western façade of Shanghai, the towers and domes and bronze lions of the Bund. 'I am sad to leave.'

'Wait 'til you see California!'

They were due to change ships in Hong Kong. Charles led her away from the port, confident in where he was going, shouting at her to hurry as Feifei took in the unfamiliar surroundings, lost in the cloying smells of the harbour and the colourful shouts in Cantonese. He handed an address to a rickshaw driver who took them to the American consulate, where Feifei was made to sign a marriage certificate.

'You need to do this if you want to get to America, kid,' Charles said, before they rushed back to the harbour. An immigration official questioned them as they went to board and Charles proudly brandished the freshly-signed forms.

'Congratulations,' the British official said, nodding at Feifei.

'Thanks.' Charles stroked her cheek tenderly and Feifei tried to disguise her alarm with a neutral expression. He had never touched her before in this way, like a zookeeper tending to his most exotic creature.

'Bloody rotten lot, the Japs,' the man said, drawing the conversation to a close. 'Safe trip.'

'Right, let's get this adventure started.' Charles took Feifei's hand, enjoying envious looks from other men on board. 'Let's find our cabin.'

'Our cabins are near?' she asked.

'Very,' he said, placing a leading hand on the small of her back. 'So close, in fact, they are actually the same! It's only right that a husband and wife should sleep together.' He chuckled and Feifei felt her heart fall to her stomach as she caught her last glimpse of China over her shoulder.

The air was thick with grief in the Graves household. Will knew he needed to make plans – to return to England or to find another job in Shanghai, to eventually piece together the shattered pieces of his soul and find another woman to lie by his side at night. But for now all he could do was sit in the drawing room, his eyes fixed on the ghostly street outside, his heart beating every time some uniformed soldiers walked past just in case they trailed Amelia behind them. The servants tiptoed around the house. And so he watched, the sombre ticking of the clock his only accompaniment. When he heard a knock on the door he didn't even turn. Su shuffled in, her head hung in mourning, and he turned to her with hope in his eyes and heaviness in his chest.

'Mister, there is visitor.' Will shrugged and she led the unknown person into the room.

There, surrounded in the blackness of death, Rollo's easygoing manner looked almost obscene. That smile always playing at the corners of his mouth was still present, if slightly tempered.

'My condolences,' he said, sombre, and Will wondered that they might not both break into laughter. It was absurd, this pantomime of sorrow parading through his front room. He had never been so popular when his wife was alive and well, nursing sore calves in another room. 'May I?' He sat down in an armchair without a word from Will. 'We're all terribly sorry. We want to know what we can do to help. Cordelia was very fond of Amelia and she's offered her services to help with a memorial service. Of course, perhaps Amelia's family would prefer a funeral in England.'

'She thought my wife was a prostitute.' Will didn't meet Rollo's eyes.

'Listen, old boy, there seems to have been a horrible mix-up about your job and after what's happened I wanted to tell you that we will be able to find you something, somewhere. Back in London if you like, or in Hong Kong. Hong Kong's the Colonial Office of course and there's more to sink your teeth into there. Might be good to get a fresh start.'

'That's very kind of you, Rollo,' Will said, the edge to his words not lost in their politeness. 'I hadn't even thought about a funeral yet.' He shook his head, suddenly feeling an overwhelming sleepiness. Of course a service would be expected, somebody would have to tell her family ... So much administration followed death, the reduction of a person's life into dry details in documents.

'Of course you haven't. It's only been a couple of days. Please think over what I've said.' Rollo rose and Will let him leave, not even calling one of the servants to see him to the door.

Julia had pleaded with Ju Wei to sleep with her every night in the week since Amelia had died. At night, she liked to feel the rising and falling of another's chest, to sense the proximity of someone beside herself. She would reach over and touch him several times in the night, just to confirm she wasn't alone. Ju Wei, used to the Julia who tore down Bubbling Well Road in her motor car, or the Julia who bargained in imperfect and aggressive Shanghainese with the tailor, was alarmed but also charmed by this new woman. She was a wife, a sweetheart broken out of the shell of an independent woman. The two became something like a married couple.

Julia wrote an article about the girls' deaths for the *North China Daily News* and a separate, short article about Amelia. The consulate wives all expressed their grief, but Julia knew they had always thought Amelia a funny bird. The service was held at a Russian church, with much of the proceedings in that language. But Ling's boyfriend read a poem in Chinese, dedicated to his singer lover and Plum. That was the only time Julia witnessed tears from Will, the grief overpowering his tough English exterior.

'That poem,' he said to her softly afterwards. 'That's my favourite. About human life being nothing more than the prints left by geese in snow.' It had all seemed very esoteric to Julia, but she was pleased to see some suffering in Will. Though she had often raged against him for his treatment of Amelia, Julia knew that he was hurting somewhere deep now, and the wound would never heal unless it was allowed to bleed. Julia gave a short Bible reading for Amelia and spoke of their friendship and her pioneering charity. Some of the ladies might have sneered at that, but Julia knew Amelia had done more for the poor of Shanghai than they ever would, their strings of pearls strangling the last of their compassion out of them.

Julia hadn't seen Will since. She simply went through the motions, going to the office every day and writing the latest about the Japanese, then coming home to Ju Wei. The Chinese put up a good fight against the enemy, the 19th Route Army proving loyal to the end. But she wrote about all of this with the professional detachment necessary to absorb the pain of the reality of losing Amelia and Tamara and all of them, the impish girls of the night who had shown themselves to be capable of rigorous training, of creating art amidst horror. She was guilty too, knowing she should have stayed there to the end. More and more she thought of her mother, imagined her reading the news at home and wondered if it was time to return. But then she would feel the heat of Ju Wei's body in the night and she knew she belonged in Shanghai now.

Julia decided to go and see Will again. She read in one of the Chinese newspapers that Wu Feifei had left the country. The actress had been spotted departing for Hong Kong and gossip there said she had boarded a ship to the United States. Julia found it hard to believe that she had really left but knowing that Charles had also skipped town she couldn't help wondering if they had gone together.

She found Will in an industrious mood, ordering the servants as they packed suitcases and piles of books into boxes.

'I hope I'm not interrupting. You're going to England?' She paused at the threshold of his bedroom, where a servant had sent her. Now their master was leaving, the servants had lost all interest in the normal functioning of the household. Two had been eating noodles in the drawing room when Julia entered, which would have been unthinkable two weeks ago.

'Hong Kong. Time for a fresh start.'

'Hong Kong?' Julia had not expected this. 'Don't you want to be with your family at a time like this?'

'Not really. I've been offered a job with the Colonial Office there as a junior official. I certainly can't stand to remain here.'

'No, no, of course not.' Julia watched him hand another book thick with old Chinese script to one of the servants. 'When are you leaving?'

'Tomorrow.'

A little Chinese girl ran into the room then, a long ponytail flying behind her. 'Tomorrow! We're going tomorrow!' Will knelt down and stroked her black hair.

'That's right, darling.'

'Who on earth is this?' Julia said, shock giving her words a rough edge she had hoped to avoid. Grief had driven the man mad, she thought, if he was taking servants and their children with him to Hong Kong. The servants were meant to be even better in Hong Kong, Julia had heard, because they understood they were in a real colony.

'This is Lili. Wu Feifei's daughter.' Julia couldn't hide her surprise, her mouth dropping open.

'No!'

'Yes,' Will said proudly. 'We're going to take her somewhere safe until her mother gets back from holiday, aren't we? And you'll go to a proper British school, none of that French nonsense.' The little girl giggled, jumping up and wrapping her arms around Will's neck.

'Will, may we step outside for a moment?'

Will followed Julia outside and she regarded him for a moment in the hallway, his face younger again, his hair a darker blond after the Shanghai winter.

'Will, you don't have to do this. You know Feifei has left town, and I have reason to believe she went with Charles Rigg, an acquaintance of mine.' She placed a tender hand on his shoulder, which he looked at briefly, and allowed to remain there.

'I know, Julia. I spoke to her before she left. She believes she's going to be a Hollywood star.'

'That's never going to happen,' Julia said gruffly. 'It's madness.'

'Well,' Will said with a sigh. 'No harm in looking after Lili until her mother comes back. Feifei's mother will also be coming with us.' Julia saw it then. He was so in love with Feifei he would lovingly tend to her family across oceans.

'She's not coming back, Will.' Julia looked at him sternly. 'This is huge – you're taking on the responsibility for a young girl for the rest of her life. How on earth did all this happen?'

'Apparently before she left, Feifei told Lili to come to me if she was ever in trouble. Her father's fled Shanghai because of his links to the Japanese and his family threw them out of the house. She came to me and it's my duty to help. God knows I've let enough people down so far.'

'But Feifei left with Charles –'

'That has nothing to do with Lili or Feifei's mother. Now, Julia, if you'll excuse me, I have a tremendous amount of packing to do. Thank you for everything.' He turned on his heels, leaving unsaid words on Julia's tongue. Shrugging, she went down the stairs, hearing Lili singing a nonsense Chinese song in the bedroom with Will.

OCTOBER 1932

望 月 懷 遠 張 九 齡

海 上 生 明 月,

天 涯 共 此 時。

情 人 怨 遙 夜,

竟 夕 起 相 思。

滅 燭 憐 光 滿,

披 衣 覺 露 滋。

不 堪 盈 手 贈,

還 寢 夢 佳 期。

Thoughts afar in moonlight by Zhang Jiu Ling

A bright moon rises over the sea,
You watch this scene at the same time.
My love, I hate this distant night,

The dusk fills my thoughts unexpectedly with you.
In the moonlight I extinguish the candle,
I drape my gown over me and feel the gathering dew.
I cannot bear that I cannot share this light with you,
I return to bed and seek our reunion in dreams.

XI

Will watched Lili as she cautiously marked out notes on the piano, her little lips pursed in tight concentration. This was one of their evening rituals – Lili would perform one of her many flourishing talents for Will. He had even talked to Lili about learning ballet, but was yet to find anywhere in Hong Kong where the young girl could learn. They rubbed along together surprisingly well, the unlikely trio thrust together by circumstance, and something approaching fatherly affection had blossomed inside Will. His new job was easy and undemanding, but he still cut his hours as short as possible to go for walks with Lili and talk to her in English, French and Chinese. She was approaching nine and Will felt he saw changes in her every day. As she plucked out the last few bars of the song she was playing, Will's only servant appeared to announce a visitor.

Hong Kong was not Shanghai. It was a drier, duller version of that city and here the Brits were fully in charge. Will found most of his compatriots insufferable. Their little parties centred around the moral degradation of youth due to the

227

proximity of the Chinese, the best places to eat home-style dishes and whose husband had been whispering a little too often in the diamond-studded ear of someone else's wife. Will had bowed out of their entwining circles early on, realising that as a young bachelor, more or less untainted by the unseemliness of his wife's death, he would serve only as prey for ladies with wrinkled necks searching for suitors for their wooden daughters, who complained of the weather and the standard of servants in the Orient despite never having lived anywhere else. So he left them to their games, finding his solace in Lili, and of course, his poems.

His situation meant visitors were extremely rare, especially in the evening. Will feared an earnest young woman devoted to saving Chinese who were unaware they had fallen into traps laid by the devil might be back – she had visited one morning with a Bible in her sweaty and swollen hand, hoping to recruit someone else to the cause.

But instead the figure of a stout man greeted him from the door frame. The man, whose features were so blandly British so as to be almost indistinguishable, was ringing a distant bell in Will's mind.

'It was a beastly task finding you,' the man said and then Will noticed that he carried a package under his arm. 'Didn't you want to live up on the Peak like everybody else?'

'I prefer somewhere a bit more down-to-earth,' Will said stiffly, standing up to face the man.

'I suppose you might not remember me. I'm Edmund, Julia's friend from the *North China Daily News*. Got a new position down here in Hong Kong. Do you like it much here?'

Will let his eyes slide over the man's butter and milk face, wondering at how he betrayed no emotion at seeing Will after half that merry Christmas party had been wiped out. He knew then that life was not the same for others, the people able to plunge on through the mundane turns of existence without feeling the heavy ache of loss.

'It's not bad. Lili and I enjoy our walks, don't we?' Lili, who had stopped playing, nodded mutely, seemingly awed by this arrival from Shanghai. Like only a child could, she had apparently shed the city like a crusted skin, never mentioning her old life. But Will sometimes heard her weep at night and wished there was something he could say, wished he could make a promise that one day her mother was coming back.

'Right, pleased to hear it.' Edmund, outwardly unperplexed by the presence of a Chinese child in Will's apartment, had clearly been briefed by Julia. 'Well, I brought down a few things they had for you at the consulate. Rollo was adamant you must get this one.' He handed Will a letter. 'And I'm not sure what this is.' He proffered the package but was left holding it to no one until Lili snatched it out of his hands. Will's eyes were fixed on the letter. It was from America. Somewhere in his mind he knew he was meant to offer this man a drink, to talk to him about Hong Kong, his new job, offer to introduce him to the patriarchs of the city with their cloying smell of corrupt success. But instead he stood still, looking at the letter.

'Well, I won't keep you,' Edmund said hastily.

'Oh, right, thank you. How are things in Shanghai?'

'Almost back to normal. The fighting went on all through March but since then we've had a few months of stability, which of course means parties like we're all going to die tomorrow.'

'Of course.'

Edmund left, and Will sat down in a chair, his heart jumping to his throat as he tore the letter open.

It was from her. Lili was preoccupied pulling the packaging off the other delivery brought by Edmund and so he read alone.

My dearest Will,

I have thought about writing this letter for a long time but I haven't known what to say. First of all, I must apologise for disappearing so suddenly, for leading you to believe I was going to go to Singapore with you. I feel wretched about it all.

Perhaps it will make you feel better to know I was tricked. You may have realised by now that I am not the new Anna May Wong, in fact there is no film role for me at all. I am Charles' wife. I suppose I shouldn't complain because he is a kind man and he supports me. There is a big Chinatown here too, and I sometimes make appearances there and they give me money just to talk to people and sign autographs. He also tells me that I might get to be an extra in a film, so I am hopeful about that. The only problem is he doesn't want Lili to join us. If you have any idea how she is, I would be grateful to know. I have been a terrible friend and mother and I only have myself to blame.

Then of course, I am so sad about Amelia and the other women from the ballet. I feel the loss of Ling keenly, even though I am thousands of miles away. I only heard once we had already set sail for America and my fate was sealed.

America is not like Shanghai. I have had to pack away my most beautiful clothes because Charles tells me that is not how they dress here. American women dress so plainly and white people often stare at the two of us on the street. Charles' family are angry that he brought a Chinese home, so it's not unlike being married to Longwei. My English is getting better and I have some Chinese friends, women to reminisce with. There are many things I miss, including, of course, you.

Since coming here I've been reading poems in Chinese, just like you used to do. It was something I never really understood but when I found a book of old poems in Chinatown, I decided to buy it. The words bring me great comfort. And so I shall end this letter with one of my favourites. After all, I was an illiterate child and I think Meng Haoran can more eloquently express what I am trying to say:

The light from the mountains falls suddenly west,
The moon rises gradually from the eastern lake.
I let my hair loose to feel the evening air,

And open my window to rest quietly.
The wind carries the fragrance of lotuses,
And bamboo drips with pure dew.
I wish to take up my lute and play,
But no friend here would appreciate my song.
And so I think of you, old friend,
The one who troubles my midnight dreams !
    Your friend,
    Feifei
    P.S.: Did you ever see Shanghai Dreams? I would love to
know how it turned out.

Will was quiet for a moment, holding the letter to his chest, the words from America seeping through his skin to his heart. Lili had her little face turned up towards him, but said nothing. Will felt a refreshing wave of peace wash over him. He troubled her too, she tossed feverishly in the night, her dreams filled by his form. Perhaps she didn't love him then but she could learn to love him now. He folded the letter and tucked it into his pocket. They might be continents away, but under the same moon they treasured the same desires.

'What's that?' Will asked Lili and she handed a book up to him. He laughed when he read the title: *New Translations of Classical Chinese Poetry*. In the rush of war and the languor of death he had forgotten about his London publishers. He flipped open the book to the first page and saw the dedication there, the recognition that *FF* had made these poems shine truer.

'This is for your mother,' Will said, handing the book back to Lili.

'Mama!' She started to greedily turn the pages, searching for the essence of her lost parent.

Will sat back and watched her, thinking that this was enough. He had a wonderful young girl growing up beside him, his poems had been published and Feifei, in a measured, tempered and chastised letter, had chained their hearts across

231

the seas. Tomorrow they would write, him and Lili, and let Feifei know her daughter was going to be just as safe and beautiful and talented as her mother. And he would tell her that they would be waiting. Waiting for Feifei to return from her midnight dreams.

ACKNOWLEDGEMENTS

Writing *Electric Shadows of Shanghai* would never have been possible without help from a wealth of resources both factual and fictional, as well as the support of a number of teachers and friends.

I found the following reference books immensely helpful for insights into life in old Shanghai: *Shanghai: The Rise And Fall Of A Decadent City* by Stella Dong, *An Amorous History Of The Silver Screen* by Zhang Zhen, *China To Me* by Emily Hahn, *Empire Made Me* by Robert Bickers, *Foreign Devils In The Flowery Kingdom* by Carl Crow and *Shanghai's Dancing World: Cabaret Culture and Urban Politics, 1919–1954* by Andrew David Field. These fictional works inspired and informed my writing: *Shanghai Girls* by Lisa See, *White Shanghai* by Elvira Baryakina, *All The Flowers Of Shanghai* by Duncan Jepson, *The Master Of Rain* by Tom Bradby, *When We Were Orphans* by Kazuo Ishiguro, *The Valley Of Amazement* by Amy Tan, *The Painter Of Shanghai* by Jennifer Cody Epstein and various stories by one of Shanghai's most celebrated authors, Eileen Chang.

The character of Feifei was inspired by real life silent film actress Ruan Lingyu, who tragically committed suicide at the age of twenty-four. Several of her films are available to view online: *The Goddess* and *New Women* offer a glimpse into the golden age of Chinese silent cinema and a cabaret strip scene in *New Women* directly informed the first chapter of *Electric Shadows of Shanghai.*

I am also indebted to my tutors at Oxford University who sparked a lasting interest in Chinese history, particularly Hilde De Weerdt and Laura Newby. Taotao Liu introduced me to Classical Chinese poetry and gave me the tools to make sense of verses from the Tang and Song dynasties.

Despite all this expert input, I have undoubtedly made factual errors, a reflection of my imagination rather than the quality of my sources.

I would like to thank the Madrid Writers' Club for their inspiration, support, editorial input and many pleasant afternoons spent drinking coffee and writing. Julia, Jackie, Sarah, Augusto, Thea and Dad, thank you for reading various drafts and giving me lots of advice. Thanks also to my mother – my biggest fan and fairest critic, the overnight copy editor with the sympathetic ear and flair for language who in another life must have worked in publishing.